One Last Breath
By Kathryn J. Bain

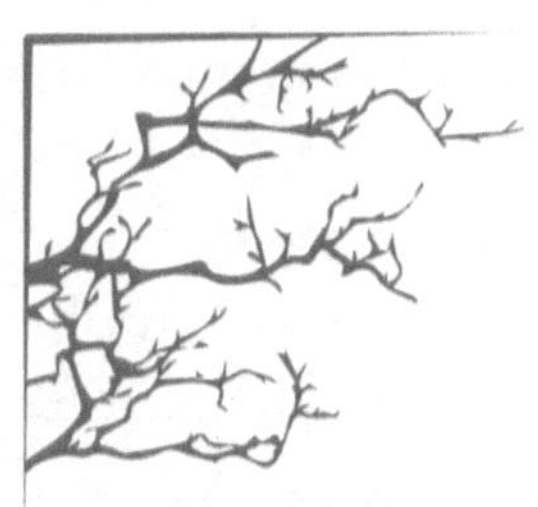

1

BJ Owens rushed into the Catoosa County Sheriff's substation in Lincolnville, Georgia. She didn't bother to stop at the reception desk, instead marching straight back to the sheriff's office. She burst through the door.

"What have you got for me?" She stared down at her nephew, Riley Owens.

He held a manila folder out to her. "By the way, the family's fine."

"I have a few other things on my mind right now." She jerked the file away. "Besides, I just saw them yesterday. I know they're fine." She glared down at him.

"Do you think Lyndsey will listen?"

"I don't know." What BJ did know was she had to get her great-niece away from this creep she'd been dating. The thunderstorm shook the windows as if to shudder its own dislike of the man.

"Sit. I'll get you some coffee." Riley walked around the desk and filled a cup from the pot on a filing cabinet in the corner.

BJ sat down in the wood chair on one side of Riley's desk. He passed her the mug, and she took a sip of coffee. The rich hazelnut flavor did little to ease her mind. She rubbed her eyes, gritty from lack of sleep. After a moment, she opened the file folder.

At the age of nineteen, Cliff Mason was convicted of possession of a controlled substance – cocaine. Currently, twenty-six, the authorities suspected him of getting close to teenagers, both male and female. Mason was on a list of possible child traffickers in the south. He'd been with at least three of four children who had disappeared. But so far, the authorities didn't have enough evidence to arrest him, much less convict.

BJ's stomach jumped with each word she read in the report.

She next stared at his mug shot to memorize his face. With his boy-next-door good looks, it was no wonder these kids fell under his spell. So young to be on the road to hell. BJ's pulse raced as she stared into his emotionless brown eyes.

She shuffled through several pictures of missing children, eventually fixing her gaze upon a photograph of a sixteen-year-old girl who'd disappeared from her home in Miami more than two-and-a-half years ago. The police found Bernadette Lewis' strangled body in a culvert near Orlando almost a year after she went missing. Mason had been her boyfriend at the time she disappeared.

BJ stared at the headshot of Bernadette, a school logo in the upper left corner of the photo. The young girl had been a beautiful thing. Wavy blond hair and green eyes that caught your attention, especially against the dark blue backdrop. She could almost pass for a younger version of Lyndsey, Mason's current girlfriend.

BJ took another sip of coffee to moisten her dry throat.

Thunder blasted again overhead.

BJ stared at Bernadette's picture. "Mason's definitely got a type," she whispered. As long as BJ had a breath in her lungs, this guy would not get hold of Lyndsey. "My body might be a bit slower since retiring, but my mind's still sharp. And I've got plenty of fight left in me."

"No doubt."

She jumped at the sound of Riley's voice, almost forgetting he was there with her.

"As you can see, there's not a lot." Riley leaned back in his chair. "Just enough to want to keep anyone's child away from the guy."

As much as BJ would rather remain home to finish her thousand-piece puzzle than take a seven-hour drive to Jacksonville, she knew she had no choice. Lyndsey's father had asked for her help, and she'd not let him down.

She straightened her shoulders. Rain pelted against the window overlooking the parking lot. It would be slow travelling in this weather. Good thing she'd gotten up early. She shoved the documents back into the file and grabbed her purse.

"I best be going."

"Be careful." Riley stood up and walked her to his office door.

"I always am."

"Not always." He raised his eyebrows.

"By the way, why are you here so early?" She looked over her shoulder at her nephew. "I can't imagine it's just to give me a file."

"Major car accident near Pike's field. Two kids killed." Sadness filled his eyes. "Appears they crossed the center line and ran into a semi."

"Oh, no."

"Yeah. They were heading to Nashville from the University of Georgia, taking the scenic route."

She patted Riley on his chin. How he dealt with this everyday was beyond her. "Well, tell Calley I'll be back as soon as possible to help her with the babe." She missed living with Riley. But the last thing she wanted was to be in the way of his new family. "Here goes nothing."

After Riley kissed her on the cheek, she ran out to her car to avoid getting soaked. BJ paused after starting the engine, bowed her head and folded her hands. "Lord, please hold on to the family of those children killed. And give me the know-how to keep Lyndsey from this man's grip. Or at least forgive me if I end up shooting this piece of garbage. It'd sure be easier if you just took care of him for me. And please God, don't let Lyndsey end up like Bernadette Lewis."

RONALD "RANSOM" MCNEELY glanced at the four small photographs taped to the dashboard. He smiled. While out shopping one day, Bernadette had insisted they take pictures in one of those boxes in the middle of the mall. Mugging for the camera, doing fish lips, smiling, and her kissing him on the cheek. All a reminder of how much fun it had been getting to know her.

His smile vanished in an instant.

She had been too young to die, especially the way she did. How could someone toss her along the side of the road like a bag of garbage? His jaw tightened.

Someone should pay, and if he had any say, that would be Cliff Mason, for selling her to the guy who killed her. There had to be proof Mason trafficked in children. And once Ransom found it, the pimp would spend his life in a jail cell for what he put countless kids through or better yet, get a needle in his arm.

Not a good Christian thought, but Ransom wasn't exactly God's biggest fan right now. Good thing he still had a bit of concern for the afterlife, or he'd have made sure Mason disappeared like the teenagers he sold. And his death wouldn't be by strangulation like Bernadette's. No, Mason deserved a much slower, more agonizing demise. He warranted all the pain Ransom imagined doling out. Something perfected from his days with the CIA. He shook the thoughts from his head, instead focusing on the job at hand.

Getting Mason arrested and convicted would be all the justice Ransom needed. Once Mason was looking at life in prison, hopefully, he'd lead the authorities to the one responsible for Bernadette's death.

Ransom stomach grumbled for lunch. He circled the Jacksonville Publix grocery store parking lot twice before coming across someone backing from a spot in the third row. Once parked, he twisted in a failed attempt to stretch his back. His body screamed for exercise. Sitting in a car playing detective made it hard on the joints of a man his age. Maybe he should do a quick walk around the strip mall. It might alleviate some of the tension in his muscles. Ransom opened the van's door to the stifling afternoon heat. Too hot to walk anywhere today. How could anyone want to put up with this humidity?

On his way to the store's entrance, he grabbed a cart someone had left on the grass median. A blast of cool air hit him when he walked through the sliding glass doors. It felt good coming in from the ninety-two-degree weather. Unseasonably warm for May.

He walked to the far-right aisle, tossing a loaf of whole wheat bread into the cart, then strolled over and grabbed a jar of peanut butter. At the end of another aisle, he picked up several boxes of beef jerky. Next, produce. Apples, oranges, carrots, and celery were best for a stakeout. He'd have preferred bananas, but they browned too quickly in a warm car.

Reaching for a bag of Red Delicious apples on sale, Ransom stopped short. His heart ratcheted up a notch. On the other side of the produce aisle stood Betty Jo Owens. He swore he'd stepped back in time. She hadn't changed much in the last twenty-five years. Though her hair was now silver instead of blond, her gray eyes still held a hint of mischief even while simply examining a tomato.

Memories of his assignment in South Korea washed over him. Cool nights, great food, and getting to know the female army officer who helped him take down a traitor.

"BJ? Betty Jo, is that you?" He rolled his cart toward her. A glimpse at her left hand still showed a wedding ring. Disappointment smashed his initial excitement.

She did a double take. Her hand went to her chest. "Ransom. Is that you? What are you doing here?"

"Buying my veggies." He grabbed a stalk of celery from a nearby bin. "You look wonderful."

She didn't acknowledge the compliment. Instead, she placed a bag of carrots in the green basket she carried on her arm. "I mean what are you doing in Jacksonville? I can't imagine the CIA has a need for a spy here."

Her words came out curt. Could she still be holding a grudge?

"I'm retired," Ransom said. "Decided to move to the sunshine." He stepped toward her. A subtle hint of vanilla floated his way. Ransom couldn't tell if the aroma came from her perfume or the baked goods in her basket. "How about we do dinner and get caught up? You and your husband, of course."

"Perry died a few years back." Sadness filled her eyes.

"I'm sorry to hear that." And he meant it. He knew how much she'd loved her husband.

"Besides, I'm only here for a couple of days visiting family." Her sadness disappeared quickly, and neutrality took over. She tossed some spinach leaves into her basket. "Take care. It was good to see you again." Her icy stare told him she was anything but glad to see him. She turned on her heel and stalked off. Her purse swung in rhythm with her stride.

He couldn't help but grin recalling that same attitude when he knew her in South Korea. She'd been a spitfire then, and it appeared not much had changed since he'd seen her last. He finally tore his gaze away from her.

It was probably a good thing she didn't want to do dinner since he had more important issues to contend with. And he couldn't afford a distraction like BJ with another girl's life on the line.

BJ IDLED THE JEEP IN the grocery store parking lot. After she'd finished her shopping, she had caught sight of Ransom checking out and actually hid until he left the store. Decades later, and her irritation still lingered. She had to let go of the past.

"Ransom." *Of all the people for You to bring back into my life, Lord.* More likely the devil. Nights filled with laughing and falling in love. Inappropriate feelings and actions for a woman who had a wonderful husband back home. She knew it'd been adultery in her mind.

A fleeting reminder of that first kiss rushed in. She was sure Ransom had garnered his nickname because he could hold any woman hostage with his beautiful blue eyes and sharp wit. A shiver drifted in recalling the cold nights in Seoul. The remembered flavor of the food sold by pojangmacha, the street vendors, crossed her tongue. How she missed the good sashimi. She had yet to find a place that compared to the restaurants in South Korea.

Funny. Since Perry died, she'd never given a second glance to another man. So why did her heart want to burst from her chest with one look at Ransom? His hair, while still dark brown, held bits of gray sprinkled throughout. How could anyone who'd lived the life he had still look so good? And she didn't miss the fact that his T-shirt tightened at his biceps.

She recalled those warm, strong arms holding her. Heat flushed through her body.

She mentally shook her head. All wonderful memories, but they had to be selective recollections because not all could have been good. Especially since Ransom had used her to advance his career and hurt her deeply. If that reminder didn't kill any type of emotion within her, nothing would.

Time to shift her attention back to the reason she'd come to Jacksonville. BJ put the blue Jeep in gear and drove east on Beach Boulevard to Hogan Road. Once off the main street, she took a couple of rights and one left turn. A silver Chevrolet van sat near the corner leading into the cul-de-sac. Dark tinted windows kept her from being able to see inside. BJ swung wide to get around it and drove to the white stucco house. Caladiums aligned the yard, and oval beveled glass decorated the front door. She smiled at how well her nephew was doing.

BJ pulled her vehicle into the driveway behind the black Nissan Pathfinder. After another quick prayer, she shoved Mason's file into one of the grocery bags and marched up the stone walkway.

On the second ring of the bell, Phillip greeted her. Worry lines creased his forehead since the last time she'd seen him. Having teenagers would do that to you. Or so BJ had heard. The closest she had to her own child was Riley, the nephew she'd taken in when her brother-in-law and his wife died in an automobile accident. Riley had wanted to be a police officer from the day he moved in at age eleven and stayed true to that conviction. He'd never given her or Perry any trouble. Again she smiled. Those selective memories.

"Miriam's in the back." Phillip helped her unload the groceries then led her to the screened-in patio. Like his cousin Riley, Phillip wasn't much for words.

His wife rose from her padded chair and hugged BJ. After a few pleasantries, Miriam returned to her seat.

BJ looked up at a military plane from the nearby naval base buzzing across the clear sky. The yard looked postcard perfect, from the crisp blue pool to the two date palms in each corner of the backyard near the red wood fence.

"I can't believe you both think this is such a big deal," Miriam said. "It's just a teen infatuated with an older man."

"She'd been drinking when she came home last Friday." Phillip held his hands on his hips. "Something needs to be done before it's too late."

"She promised she wouldn't do it again. And he'll get tired of her like older boys do." Miriam let out a sigh as if remembering something in her past. "Young girls think it's cool to date a guy that old."

"He's *too* old. Someone in his mid-twenties shouldn't want to hang out with a fourteen- year-old. There's only one reason for it." Phillip winced. "And I'm not about to let that happen. You shouldn't want it either."

Miriam's head titled sideways. She looked like she was about to bite his head off.

"He's more than that," BJ said before their argument could get out of hand. She relayed what she'd discovered regarding Cliff Mason.

Neither parent spoke until she finished. When BJ told them about the missing girl who turned up dead, Phillip's eyes widened, and he started pacing. Miriam's face paled. BJ allowed the information to sink in.

"I sure hope this works," Miriam whispered.

"Where is Lyndsey?" BJ sat back on the thick floral cushion on the loveseat.

"Still in bed." Miriam brushed a strand of hair off her forehead. "It's hard to get her up in the morning on the weekends. Getting her to church is like fighting a wild tiger."

"I don't know what we're going to do with her during summer once school's out." Phillip placed his hands on his hips. "She might be too far gone."

"You are definitely your mother's son," BJ shook her head. "Your momma practically said the same thing when you thought drinking was cool. I just had to show you otherwise." BJ hopped up from her seat. "Now, let's go pull her out of bed. It's time to get the show on the road."

A CAR'S BASS DROWNED out the plane flying overhead. Ransom wiped the back of his neck. Jacksonville humidity was a killer, especially when spending the day sitting in a vehicle. He massaged the tight knot at the back of his neck.

He'd still not gotten his bearings since leaving Publix. Just his luck the Jeep Cherokee with the Georgia license plate in the driveway held BJ. Now she sat inside the house he kept surveillance on. His best chance of getting Cliff Mason lived inside that house. But Ransom would now have to go through BJ to get to Lyndsey Chapel. His grip tightened on the steering wheel. How could he justify his plan to anyone, much less her?

A bead of sweat rolled along Ransom's jawline. If this kept up, the police might find him in a puddle on the floorboard. He started the Chevy and turned the A/C to high.

He rolled the windows down, wishing for air. No such luck.

Two boys strolled past, their pants below their backsides. Ransom let loose a harrumph. Why would anyone want to look so ridiculous? Too many moms these days would rather be friends than a parent, and men would rather be sperm donors than fathers.

Like you. Ransom's heart jolted. The words bounced into his mind before he could stop them. While true, he'd like to think he wasn't the same selfish man from years ago. A friend once told him those insults came from the devil who liked to remind him of his past sins. It kept him from feeling the full forgiveness of God's love. Ransom knew the Lord forgave him for all the fornication of his past. Unfortunately, he couldn't say the same for the daughter who'd grown up without a father.

Ransom startled at the ringing cell phone in the console. He pulled it out and glanced at the caller I.D. Too much to ask that it be Darcy. But an absentee dad shouldn't expect instant love when he bounced into his daughter's life.

"Hello, Frazier," Ransom said. "What can I do for you?"

"Ransom, I won't beat around the bush," his former boss said. "The guy you're sniffing around, Cliff Mason, also has the interest of the DEA. They want you to back off."

"Do they know he sells young kids and is basically responsible for my granddaughter's death?"

"There's no proof."

"Not yet," Ransom snapped. "But we both know if they get him for drugs, he'll make a deal for immunity and not serve a minute in jail."

"I'm just relaying the message. Do with it what you want."

"I suggest you let them know to stay out of my way," Ransom growled. His dealings with the DEA in the past had always left a dent in their sides. "I might have aged a bit since leaving the Agency, but I haven't lost my edge."

"You were good when you retired at fifty-six, but all those years of sitting around can make a difference." Hesitation dripped over the line. After a moment, Frazier added, "And these traffickers don't care who they kill."

"You just let the DEA know to stay out of my way." Ransom hung up, not waiting for a reply. Six years wasn't that long. A man couldn't easily forget what had been drilled into his head every day for thirty years.

The DEA stood low on his list of issues right now. Getting past BJ was first. Little doubt she'd never forgive him for knowingly allowing someone she knew close to a predator.

Of course, if Cliff Mason tangled with BJ that would be good news for Ransom's side. In fact, if she was half the determined woman she'd been all those years ago, Ransom almost felt sorry for Cliff Mason.

Almost.

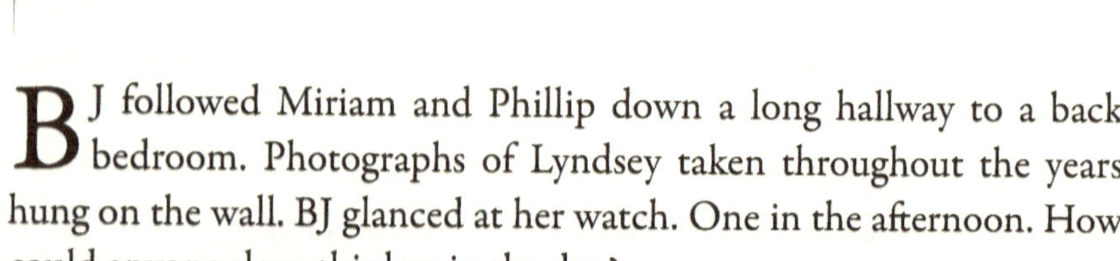

2

BJ followed Miriam and Phillip down a long hallway to a back bedroom. Photographs of Lyndsey taken throughout the years hung on the wall. BJ glanced at her watch. One in the afternoon. How could anyone sleep this late in the day?

Phillip rapped with his knuckle on the door but got no answer. He knocked again, louder. BJ glanced from Miriam to Phillip. Both had furrowed brows. BJ's heart ratcheted up a notch.

"Lyndsey, open up." Miriam pounded with the palm of her hand. "Lyndsey."

"What?" A groggy voice crawled through the closed door. "Leave me alone."

Both her parents let out a sigh of relief, and BJ's pulse returned to normal.

"We need you to get up." Phillip leaned on the wall. His hand clutched his stomach. "We have a surprise for you."

"What?"

BJ twisted the doorknob and popped her head into the room. "It's me."

Lyndsey pushed herself up from her pillow. Her blond hair lay flattened on one side. She squinted. At first a smile floated over her lips, but then she raised an eyebrow.

"What is this?" she asked. "An intervention?"

BJ let loose a laugh. "Of course not. If I wanted to *intervent* you, I'd just take you out to the woodshed." She sauntered further into the bedroom. A musty aroma hung in the air. Dust settled over the dresser and clothes were strewn about the floor. "Now, get your butt up. There's something I need to discuss with you."

Lyndsey plopped back down. "Can't it wait? I didn't get to sleep until late."

"No, it can't. I'll even fix you some of my famous tuna salad for lunch." BJ swatted her great-niece on the backside through her blankets. "Get moving."

"I'm coming. I'm coming."

Lyndsey's lack of enthusiasm didn't do much for BJ's ego. She'd hoped the girl would be happy to see her. After all, they kept in contact on the internet, posting jokes and photos to one another.

BJ walked back to the kitchen while Phillip and Miriam lingered in the dining area. BJ tried to focus on preparing the tuna instead of the impending conversation. The possibility of breaking the young teen's heart made BJ's ache also. She recalled how much it hurt to find out Ransom wasn't what he appeared to be.

"At least I could tell Lyndsey I understood, and it wouldn't be some lame line," she murmured.

She puttered around the kitchen while practicing in her head what she'd say. Thankfully, she'd made this dish so often it took no thought. The aroma of canned tuna filled the kitchen. She added mayonnaise, celery, and carrots. Not one for onions, she chose to leave those out.

Lyndsey finally shuffled in and plopped down on a stool at the island. "So, you got more photos of RJ?"

BJ's pride swelled at the thought of Riley's son. Barely seven-months-old, but she swore he was already the smartest child she'd ever met. "Of course. But we'll look at those later." She patted Lyndsey's back. "Right now, we eat then we talk."

Minutes later, they joined Miriam and Phillip at the dining room table. BJ sat in front of the large plate glass window covered with white shears from the ceiling to the floor. The rest took what she assumed were their usual chairs. A sour look held on Lyndsey's face as if she'd eaten a pail full of lemons.

The meal dragged on. A chill hung in the air from the stern looks on everyone's face.

"How'd you do on your test in math?" Phillip asked.

"Fine." Lyndsey didn't even look at him when she answered.

"Did you finish your science project?"

Lyndsey rolled her eyes. "Yes."

That pretty much ended any conversation until lunch was finished.

Once the plates were cleared, Lyndsey leaned her chin on her hand. "So, what is it we need to talk about?"

BJ grabbed the file near her purse and returned to her seat. "We need to discuss this Cliff Mason you've been seeing."

"I knew it." The teen slapped the tabletop, causing the glasses to jump. "Just because he's a bit older." She scooted her chair back and stood. "I'm going back to bed."

BJ took her by the arm. "It has nothing to do with his age. Sit, please."

Lyndsey's eyes narrowed in her mother's direction. After a moment, she bounced down with a grunt. "Let me guess. Mom told you about him having a record?" Her stare at Miriam should have included daggers. "It was for having pot on him a long time ago. No big deal."

"It was more than that," BJ said. "He got arrested for selling cocaine but pled down to possession." BJ placed her hand on Lyndsey's arm. "But you know I wouldn't have driven seven hours over an old drug offense."

RANSOM STARED AT HIS laptop. He watched and listened in on the conversation from one of the hidden cameras inside the Chapels'

dining room overhead light. He had no authorization to plant the bugs but wanted to make sure if Mason planned to take off with Lyndsey, he was aware of it ahead of time. Some might find it intrusive, but he'd not let another girl be taken and sold by this creep without his knowledge. Besides, if he'd invaded Bernadette's privacy, she'd still be here.

Watching the Chapels the past week, one thing was for sure. BJ had her work cut out with that girl. If his daughter had ever spoken to him the way Lyndsey did her parents, she'd be eating soap for a week.

Not that you helped. That voice again. Yet it was right. Ransom let out a weighted sigh. He couldn't take any credit for Darcy becoming the head of the nursing department in the hospital where she worked. That pat on the back went one hundred percent to her now-deceased mother. Ransom couldn't even take credit for saving his granddaughter. Because he'd failed.

His jaw hurt from clenching it to keep any tears from welling. He needed to focus on getting this Mason creep.

"You said you wanted to talk about Cliff." Lyndsey's voice brought Ransom away from guilty memories.

"Your boyfriend is suspected of selling teenagers." BJ's words were blunt and to the point. The way she'd always been.

"Give me a break." Lyndsey's eyes rolled back.

"It's true," BJ said. "Here." She handed Lyndsey some papers and sat back while the teen rifled through them.

"You made this up." Her voice went low, yet she continued to scan the reports.

"Don't be stupid," Miriam Chapel shouted. "The creep is a pimp. He takes little girls like you, and he sells them."

"I'm not a little girl." The teen matched her mother in anger. "You never had a problem with him before. Why are you doing this to me? You just hate that I like him."

"I want you to see what this guy is." Miriam shoved a hand through her brown hair. "Before it's too late."

Phillip Chapel had yet to say anything. Probably realized it was much smarter to keep his mouth shut than get in between two hysterical females.

Ransom sucked down a gulp of water. It was too warm to quench his hot thirst.

"And what about me?" BJ remained calm, surprising Ransom. He'd be ready to lock Lyndsey in her room until she hit thirty. "Do you think I'm lying, too?"

"It can't be true." Lyndsey's voice shook. Her chair screeched against the tile floor.

"I'm afraid it is," BJ said.

"No. You got the wrong man." Lyndsey trudged over to the doorway. "Maybe the police mixed up the names." She folded against the wall, her finger tracing the doorjamb.

"This is unbelievable." Miriam bolted up. "It's right there in front of you."

"You just don't want me to be happy."

"Of course, we want you to be happy." Miriam's lips formed a tight line.

Phillip got up and placed his right hand on his wife's shoulder. "Let's go in the other room."

"I don't want to go." She shoved his palm off. "I want to knock some sense into my daughter."

"Oh, great. Now you're saying I'm stupid." Lyndsey continued to lean against the wall.

"I-I did not say that." Miriam sputtered. "You're putting words in my mouth."

"Miriam." Phillip kept his tone neutral. "This isn't getting us anywhere. Let BJ talk to her."

BJ had yet to react. Funny how she dealt with this teenager the same way she'd done a traitor accused of passing secrets to the North

Koreans. A smile creased Ransom's lips. Did this kid have any idea who she was dealing with?

Once Phillip and Miriam left them alone, BJ got up and went over to Lyndsey. She tucked her forefinger under the girl's chin and lifted her face. "Do you think I came all the way from Lincolnville just to make you miserable?"

"No. But Mom and Dad could have lied to you." Her eyes pleaded.

"They didn't tell me anything. I had Riley pull up all the information for me."

Ransom wrote the name down along with the town of Lincolnville. He'd do some research later to see if he could figure out who she referred to. Obviously a man with some connections.

"There has to be a mistake." Lyndsey's lip quivered. She smashed her hand against her cheek.

Silence reigned for what seemed like minutes.

"Tell me about Cliff." BJ took Lyndsey's hand and led her back to the table where she sank down in the chair. "How'd you get hooked up with him?"

"Give me something I don't know." Ransom adjusted the knob on the volume.

Lyndsey sighed. "One day I was out having pizza with my friends. He just came straight up to me and said he'd seen me in a magazine. He claimed I reminded him of a model."

"Same thing he said to Bernadette," Ransom grumbled.

"Why'd you go out with him?" BJ asked. "You had to know he was too old for you."

"I don't fit anywhere." Lyndsey lowered her eyes to her clasped hands on the table. "The girls at my school all go crazy for movie stars and singers. I never cared for them. I was always into technology and things like that. Mom used to say I was older than my years." Lyndsey spoke in a soft tone. "Cliff makes me feel real. He treats me like an adult. He doesn't put any pressure on me to do anything I'm not ready for. In fact, he said he thought it best for us to wait to have sex until I was a bit older."

"That's 'cause a virgin goes for a higher price, m'dear." Ransom grimaced.

"The boys my own age, all they ever do is talk about sex and who they've done. Cliff never does that. He says it's no one's business who either of us has been with."

"Unfortunately, in this case it does matter." BJ slid out a photograph from the file. "Look at this girl."

A gasp caught in Ransom's throat upon seeing his granddaughter's smile from the school picture.

"She's pretty." Lyndsey picked up the glossy. "Who is she?"

"Her name *was* Bernadette Lewis," BJ said. "According to her friends, Cliff told her the same things he's telling you. Then one day she disappeared. He claimed they'd broken up a week before, and he hadn't seen her since. They couldn't prove otherwise."

"What happened to her?" Lyndsey's eyes remained fixated on the picture.

BJ pushed another picture across the table. "She ended up looking like this."

Ransom's stomach bounced when he saw the crime scene photograph. His once beautiful granddaughter thrown out like trash. One, two, three. With each number he inhaled to calm himself. He stopped at ten.

Lyndsey hesitated then picked up the picture. "No. He wouldn't." She sniffled. "He loves me."

"He loved Bernadette too, darling. At least that's what he said, according to her friends." BJ pushed Lyndsey's hair behind her ear. "She looked a lot like you. Blond, pretty."

"This can't be happening." Tears rolled down Lyndsey's cheeks. She laid her head in the crook of her elbow and sobbed. BJ pulled Lyndsey against her.

The girl was a lot smarter than Ransom had given her credit for. Lyndsey's hair covered her face, and her shoulders shook.

Ransom gulped a lump in his throat. Earlier he'd hoped to use her to lead him to proof against Cliff Mason. Now, she reminded him of Bernadette. Teen angst. The pain of first love. Adults using her wasn't fair. Bile rose in his throat. How'd he become such a cad?

"Why didn't anyone stop Bernadette from seeing him?" Lyndsey raised her head from BJ's hold.

"Someone might have tried, maybe she didn't listen. Or worse, those around her might have been too busy with their own lives to notice. And some parents just don't care."

Ransom turned down the receiver. He had cared. He'd cared a lot. How badly he wanted Cliff Mason to pay for the pain his family went through. And pay he would.

If it took Ransom the rest of his life.

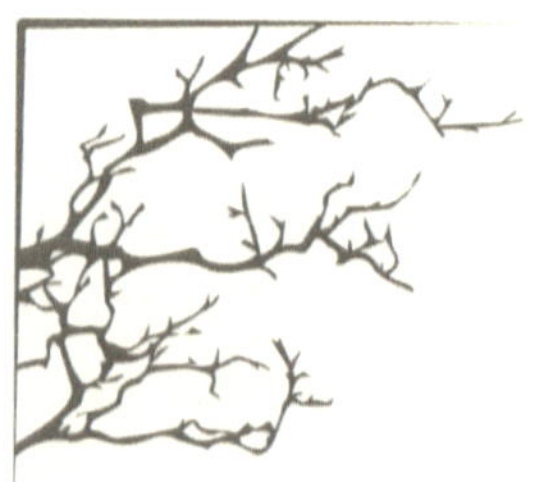

3

Ransom kept the volume down while Lyndsey cried again into her aunt's embrace. She'd apparently realized she'd pinned all her dreams on a demon. His mouth went dry. Too bad no one bothered to warn Bernadette. He'd been too worried she might quit speaking to him like Darcy had done. So instead of looking up any information on this Mason character, he'd let it go. How much he'd rather have Bernadette's silence than the loss he held inside.

Phillip walked into the kitchen, so Ransom swallowed back his pain and turned the volume up.

"Is everything all right?" Phillip placed his hand on Lyndsey's shoulder.

"She'll be fine," BJ said. "But I think we'll go for a walk in the park up the road. I believe she could use a break."

"That sounds like a good idea." He pulled his daughter up into a hug. "I love you with all my heart."

"I know," Lyndsey muttered into her dad's chest.

"Let me go put a brush through this hair of mine, and we'll head out." BJ gave Lyndsey a squeeze on the arm then walked from the room.

Ransom relaxed in the car seat. The hard part was over. BJ had easily gotten through to Lyndsey. But would it last? At least until Cliff Mason called her. With his charm and charisma, could he pull her back in?

A large storm cloud moved in overhead. Common for Jacksonville in the afternoon. Unfortunately, any rain did little to cool things off.

Ransom started the van and let the air get cold before putting the vehicle in gear and pulling from the curb. The park was four blocks

20

over. When he first arrived in the neighborhood, he'd researched the area so he'd be familiar with all the amenities. Best to know where the facilities were in case they were needed.

The park consisted of a hundred and twenty acres. Ransom couldn't be sure where BJ and Lyndsey would end up, but he assumed it wouldn't be by the soccer fields. The best spot would be an empty set of bleachers.

He pulled the van away from the curb and drove the few blocks over. Once at the park, he took a shaded spot in the far corner behind a closed concession stand and pulled out the shotgun microphone. When he'd finished getting the gear ready, he clicked on the laptop and the camera inside the home. The dining area was empty, but he could see a figure in the living room. Miriam had her feet up on the sofa and a book in her hand. Ransom kept the volume low but loud enough to hear as he kept an eye out the window of the van, waiting for BJ to arrive at the park.

Within two minutes, Phillip walked out and patted his wife on the shoulder.

"Do you think this will work?" Miriam's voice held no hint of the enraged mother from earlier.

"It's got to, or we might lose her forever." Phillip sighed. "And if anyone can do it, it's Aunt BJ."

That explained BJ's connection to the family. If Ransom could convince BJ to allow him to use Lyndsey, there might still be a way to get Mason. But no matter what argument Ransom came up with, it was a lame one.

No one in their right mind would hand over a girl to a man they knew wanted to sell her to the highest bidder.

BJ PARKED THE JEEP in a slot at the end of the other cars. Most of the kids were on the soccer field to their right. Three teens sat on a set of bleachers near the road. The two girls had fake black hair and overly done eye makeup. The boy's right arm was covered in tattoos. The teens appeared to be about Lyndsey's age. Probably older siblings of those playing. They passed around what looked like a cigarette.

BJ inwardly laughed. If she'd been caught smoking at that age, her dad would probably have made her smoke a whole pack in one sitting just to get her fill. But then that was the difference between being a parent and being a friend.

Lyndsey had been quiet since leaving the house. Her face was blotchy from crying. BJ would have done anything to keep from hurting the girl, but sometimes short-term pain could avoid more agony in the long run.

"Come on." BJ opened the door and walked to the front of the vehicle, waiting for Lyndsey to join her. The aroma from the kids' cigarette smoke drifted her way. The three sneered at her. She ignored them, instead focusing on Lyndsey. "Feel like talking?"

"Not right now."

As much as she wanted to talk Lyndsey through this, the girl needed time. BJ had given her a lot of information to digest.

"How about we just walk for a while?" BJ kept a slow pace, staying in step with Lyndsey. The baseball cap BJ wore shielded her eyes from the glare of the sun. The aroma of impending rain hung in the air. Children laughed and played nearby.

She scanned the area and became alert to a silver van, similar to the one she'd seen by Lyndsey's house. It seemed odd that the owner would park so far off from the rest of the vehicles. Could be to keep it in the shade.

After circling two soccer fields, sweat coated BJ's arms. Her sciatica caused her left leg to throb. She rubbed her back to try to alleviate the discomfort.

"Can we sit?" Lyndsey finally said.

BJ, grateful for the suggestion, held her hand out for Lyndsey to lead. They sat on bleachers across from the ones the teens had been smoking on earlier. Lyndsey looked like a young child with her pink cheeks and mussed hair.

"Here." BJ handed Lyndsey a Lifesaver mint. "Used to be a commercial years ago that said they made you feel better."

"Do they?" Lyndsey's lip quivered.

"Maybe not in this case." She wrapped her arm around her great-niece. Holding her was the best she could do at the moment.

Kids shrieked and coaches yelled in the field next to them. Every few moments, the sparse audience members clapped.

"I can't believe I fell for everything he said to me." Lyndsey leaned forward with her forearms on her legs. "You must think I'm real stupid."

"No. Almost every girl's fallen for the bad boy with the nice smile and good looks. It's part of life."

"Bet you never fell for some line."

"If I were you, I'd save your money." BJ laughed. "And the worse part, I wasn't even a teenager."

"What do you mean?" Lyndsey looked over at BJ.

"I was in the Army. They'd sent me to Seoul to work as an interpreter. After a while, I realized the government was after my boss who they thought was selling secrets."

Lyndsey sat up straight. "Is that who you fell for? Your boss?"

"No. One of the people spying on him. He worked for the CIA." A lump rose in BJ's throat. Though long ago, the pain still dwelled inside. "He got close to me so he could find out what I knew. I really thought he cared for me. So much so that I started spying for him."

"Was your boss selling secrets?" A whistle blew over on one of the soccer fields. Lyndsey glanced at the game.

"Yeah. I had a lot of respect for the man, so it hurt when I found the proof. It was something I shouldn't have been put in the middle of." BJ nudged Lyndsey with her elbow. "We females do stupid when it comes to men."

"But what I did was real stupid."

"You're smart enough to listen and take all the information in. That's the important part. Most girls would ignore it, and when he called, they'd fall for his charm all over again."

"Well, if I don't talk to him, I can't fall." She gave a stern nod.

As if on cue, Lyndsey's cell rang in her pocket. She pulled it out and stared at the display. "It's him," she whispered.

"If you refuse to answer, he'll come looking for you." BJ placed a hand on the girl's shoulder. "You need to be strong, and just let him know you've been told about his past and what he's been up to."

Lyndsey's breathing intensified. Her eyes remained focused on the screen, but she made no move to answer the call. BJ didn't press her. After five rings, the phone went to voicemail. Lyndsey placed the cell on the bleacher one seat down from where they were sitting. Within seconds, it rang again.

"Best to tell him off now, rather than in person," BJ said. "It'll be harder to do it face-to-face when he's smiling at you."

Lyndsey sucked in a deep breath and nodded. After a brief pause, she slid her finger across the screen. "Hello." Her chin jutted up.

"Hey, pretty lady. What are you doing?" Mason's charm oozed over the phone's speaker. No wonder teens fell for his spiel. After all, calling Lyndsey a lady indicated he saw her as an adult, something teenagers felt they were. Saying she was pretty could only add to his appeal.

"I can't see you anymore." Lyndsey's hands shook.

"What do you mean? Let me guess. Your parents." His tone remained neutral, not hinting at the angst expected from someone during a breakup.

"I heard about you." Lyndsey's face whitened. "What you do."

With the paleness of the teen's face, BJ thought for a moment she might get sick. She took hold of Lyndsey's hand.

"What do you mean?" Mason asked.

"You sell girls," Lyndsey blurted.

A burst of laughter came over the phone. "You're kidding. Stuff like that only happens in the movies." As good a liar as he must be, stiffness still came over his voice. "Your parents are just lying to keep us apart."

"They didn't tell me. My Aunt BJ did, and I trust her more than I do anyone else."

Warmth rushed into BJ at the words. Lyndsey had always been one of her smarter relatives.

"Aunt BJ, huh?" He let loose a laugh. "It's just 'cause she hasn't met me yet. Once she does, she'll see I love you."

Lyndsey wrapped her arms around her legs. "She also told me about Bernadette Lewis."

Silence dripped over the line. BJ stared at the phone, waiting for a response.

Mason's breathing increased. "I didn't tell you about Bernadette because it still hurts. It's terrible to lose someone you care for." A shuffling noise came over the line like he was moving the phone. "I dated Bernadette, then she dumped me for another guy. She ran off with him, and we didn't hear from her again until..." His words trailed off.

The compassion in Lyndsey's eyes said she wanted to believe him. BJ couldn't blame her. The fake sadness would draw in most females. Lyndsey gave BJ a weak smile. At once the teen sat up tall.

"From what I've heard, a lot of your girlfriends end up missing," Lyndsey said.

BJ hadn't told her that, but Lyndsey must have guessed. After all, if he were selling girls, they would have ended up missing also. And when you dealt with a snake, you had to use anything what came to mind.

"I haven't had a good life." Mason spoke under his breath. His anger penetrated the air.

"Yeah, that cocaine arrest didn't help." With each word, Lyndsey's demeanor grew stronger. Her posture improved, her head rose, and her eyes glared at the screen.

"So that's what this is all about." Mason paused. "How about I deal with your mom and dad?" His words came out low, causing Lyndsey to rear back.

"That sounded like a threat to me," BJ hissed. "I suggest you rethink things, young man. Messing with my family would be a step past stupid."

"Let me guess," Mason said. "Aunt BJ."

She wanted to smack off the smug look she just knew he held on his face. "And I can't imagine the people you work with would like to have a bunch of police hanging around asking questions."

"I don't work with anyone else. See, Lyndsey, I told you they just wanted to break us up. They know nothing about me. I love you, Lynds. And if there is someone doing all these terrible things, it's not me."

"Well then you must have a twin because the person the authorities are interested in looks just like you." BJ's fists clenched. "I know quite a few officers, so I'd be careful with the threats."

Mason let out a loud sigh. "I'm not making threats. I know Lyndsey's mom likes me. I've already met her. I just figured I could make it right."

BJ could strangle Miriam for allowing this relationship to get this far. Being a mother wasn't about reliving memories through your daughter.

"I have an idea. Let me buy you dinner." Mason's voice dripped sugar. "I'm sure I can convince you I mean Lyndsey no harm."

"How about we meet at the police station, and you can confess your sins? Might save you some time in purgatory. If not, I suggest you leave Lyndsey alone."

"I love Lyndsey." Mason's tone stiffened. "And no matter what, we'll be together."

Lyndsey pushed the button to shut the cell off. Two large tears spilled down her cheeks. "He said everything right, didn't he?"

"Yes," BJ said.

Lyndsey clutched her hands together. "Then why am I so scared?"

RANSOM COULDN'T HELP but grin at how BJ handled Mason. Better than some agents he knew. She'd remained calm, but her voice held a hint of danger. For some reason Ransom's chest puffed with pride at how she'd called the creep out.

Sweat layered Ransom's face and back. He wiped his neck with the towel he kept on the passenger seat. The urge to get out of the vehicle and tell BJ not to worry nearly overpowered him. However, Cliff Mason's dialing took Ransom's focus away from the two on the bleachers.

Working for the Agency had its advantages when it came to infiltrating things like cell phones. He just failed to mention to the local techs he had retired, and the subpoena wasn't real. Of course, if anyone found out, Ransom could find himself in a federal prison. But if it meant getting the killer of his granddaughter, he'd do anything.

The number Mason had dialed rang twice before someone answered.

"When you going to deliver my package?" A man's voice came onto the line. Static hid the man's tone, but the words were clear enough.

"There's been a hitch," Mason said.

"What type of hitch?"

"Turns out her family's checked into my background. They've convinced her I'm no good."

"Perhaps I may be of some help," the man said. "But don't think for a moment I'll let you off the hook. I hate excuses." A slight accent drifted in, but Ransom couldn't tell what type with the interference over the line. "She's what I want. You've done me good in the past, but there're others I can deal with. So, either get her or give me back my money."

Ransom's jaw clenched tight.

"No need to worry. I haven't lost one yet." Determination sounded in Mason's voice. "I'll get back in her good graces. If not, there're other ways."

"I'll trust you on this one. For now."

"Count on it. As agreed, you'll have your merchandise before the end of June."

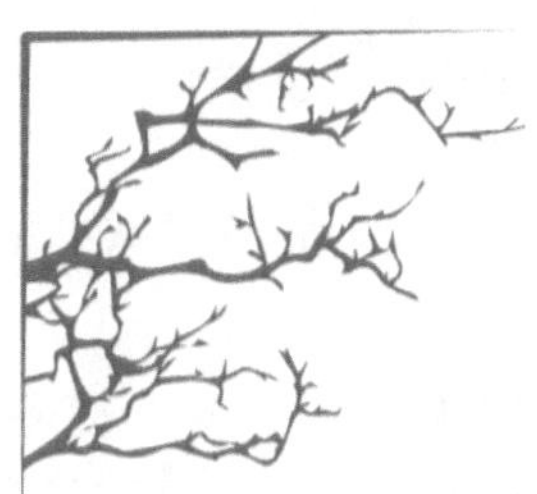

4

Ransom considered telling BJ about Mason's telephone conversation but decided against it. She wouldn't like the fact Ransom was following Lyndsey. But no matter how BJ felt, he planned to stick close to ensure the girl's safety. He'd not let BJ go through the months of anguish he did when Bernadette disappeared. His palms tightened on the steering wheel. *God, how could you let her die?*

He kept focused on BJ and Lyndsey while they ambled back to their vehicle. Five minutes later, Ransom pulled the van out of the lot and returned to his parking spot at the end of the road where the Chapels lived. The Pathfinder no longer rested in the driveway. Ransom turned the volume up on the bug so he could hear any conversation inside the house. Miriam, Lyndsey, and BJ eventually made their way into view of the dining room camera.

"Okay, so I was stupid." Lyndsey flung her arms out at her sides. "You just couldn't wait to say I told you so."

"I didn't say ..." Miriam stopped short when Lyndsey stormed out.

Didn't her mother know that by arguing with her, she'd only drive Lyndsey into Mason's arms?

"I can't seem to get through to her these days." Pain carried in Miriam's tone. "We used to be so close."

"It's just her way of asserting her independence," BJ said. "She wants to be treated like an adult in some respects and a child in others. Don't worry. She'll be all right."

"Are you sure? What if she decides not to listen?" A loud sigh came from Miriam. "Phillip was right. I shouldn't have encouraged that relationship."

29

"But you were reliving something in your past?" BJ raised her eyebrows.

"Wh-what are you talking about?" Miriam lowered herself into a dining room chair. Her face reddened.

"I saw it earlier when you were talking about older men with teenage girls." BJ took a seat next to Miriam. "You had one of those relationships, didn't you?"

She nodded. "I was fifteen, and he was twenty-three. I believed at the time we were in love."

"Understandable. What happened?"

"He said all the right things. We spent the better part of a summer together, hanging out with friends, going to movies and concerts. My heart told me we'd spend the rest of our lives together."

"But he got tired of the relationship" BJ nodded understanding.

"That's an understatement." Miriam blurted a laugh. "He started seeing someone else before he dumped me. But I still have some fond memories of it. Have you ever had one of those relationships that you knew inside was wrong, but the guy just made you feel so special?"

"It's been a while. But I definitely know what you mean." BJ stared directly into the camera as if she knew Ransom watched.

He wondered where he fit into BJ's memories. Her earlier talk with Lyndsey regarding South Korea told him her thoughts of him weren't very pleasant. He couldn't say the same thing. Cool nights, his arm draped over BJ's shoulder. The soft musk of her perfume drifting into him. A passionate kiss here and there. While he could have gone further, he chose not to. Something in him wouldn't allow it. She was too special for him to use like that. Besides, it would have hurt her more when he told her he'd only gotten close to get at her boss.

His gut ached, recalling their last dinner together. The look of betrayal in her eyes. Watching her storm away caused his heart to crash onto the floor. Ransom shook his head. He hadn't been much in the way of a man. Not much in the way of a father.

What good had his life been?

"What's the next step?" Miriam's words brought Ransom back to the conversation. "We've got to keep that creep away from my daughter."

"Don't you worry," BJ reassured her. "We'll come up with something."

"How'd you get so smart about kids, never having any of your own?" Miriam smiled. "I would think it'd come from experience."

BJ leaned forward. "Sometimes it's easier when you can take a step back."

A black Mercedes convertible with dark tinted windows pulled around the corner two blocks down from where Ransom had parked. It drove into the cul-de-sac, circled the loop, and then slowed at the Chapels' home before leaving.

Ransom sucked in a deep breath. No doubt about it. Cliff Mason was checking on his merchandise.

Ransom leaned against the headrest. As much as tangling with BJ would give Mason a headache, in the long run, it could also get *her* killed.

BJ SAT AT THE ISLAND in the kitchen and munched on a carrot. How much better she'd rather have a cookie, but she had to watch her sugar intake. Getting old stunk. She could no longer eat pizza without it upsetting her stomach. Not to mention the weight gain.

The yardman clipped the hedges in the backyard. BJ glanced at her watch. Just shy of five o'clock. The whirr of his clippers drowned out any other sound. Leaves flew in the air with each cut he made along the fence. As loud as his tools were, she wondered how Miriam could be getting any rest laying in the settee in the back room.

The front doorbell buzzed. BJ got up to answer it, but Miriam beat her to it.

"What do you want?" Miriam's voice was harsh.

"Miriam, I just wanted to stop by and clear the air."

BJ recognized Cliff Mason immediately from his mugshot.

"We don't want you around here anymore. Lyndsey is off limits." Miriam started to swing the door closed, but Mason blocked it with his foot.

"But I love her," he said.

"The same way you loved the other girls you manipulated?" BJ stepped through the threshold.

"I don't know what you're talking about." He brushed his bangs aside. His brown eyes were stunning, much more so than his photo indicated.

"That might work with teenage girls, but I'm a bit too old to fall for your gimmicks." BJ joined Miriam at the door. "I suggest you stay away, or we'll be contacting the police."

He glanced at Miriam whose jaw set taut. "You heard her."

"You can't stop the path of true love. Isn't that right, Lyndsey?" He looked behind BJ.

Lyndsey stood staring at him. "You need to leave," she whispered. "And don't come back."

His lips flattened to a line. Within two seconds he pivoted on his heel and stormed down the walkway to his car.

Tears welled in Lyndsey's eyes. BJ's heart ached, watching Lyndsey go through this. She placed her hand on the girl's back and directed her into the kitchen, while Miriam went to her room to call Phillip. Lyndsey cell phone rang as she settled into a chair at the big island. She pulled out her phone but didn't answer it.

"Are you all right?" BJ asked.

"Mom just doesn't understand. I still love him."

"She understands more than you think she does."

"Maybe." Lyndsey lowered one side of her lip. "But now I'm also afraid." Tears welled. "This isn't fair."

"No. No, it's not." BJ gave her shoulder a squeeze. "How about I fix you something to eat? Dinner's still an hour or more off."

"I'm not really hungry."

"Not even for a slice of my strawberry marble cake?"

Lyndsey leaned her head to one side "I can always eat cake."

"That's my girl." BJ pulled the dessert from the fridge. "How big a piece do you want?"

Lyndsey held up her thumb and forefinger about an inch apart. Then the space grew to two inches then three.

BJ laughed. "You'd better be careful, or people might think we're related." She placed a thick slice in front of Lyndsey and cut a smaller piece for herself. A bite wouldn't hurt. After returning the cake to the fridge, she poured them each a glass of milk. "When do you get out of school for summer break?"

"I've got another week. Thursday's my first day off."

"Any major plans?"

"Not really. I thought it'd be fun having a boyfriend with a car so we could go to the beaches and stuff." Lyndsey frowned. "Now I'll get to stay here all day, bored."

"You can always come home with me." BJ put a bite of cake in her mouth. The sweetness made her taste buds come alive.

"To Lincolnville?"

"Have to be. That's where I live." BJ nudged Lyndsey with her elbow.

"Really?"

"Calley's already mentioned she could use some help in the gallery and with the baby." BJ took a sip of her drink. "We can also do some fishing, and I'll ride you on my new Can-Am Spyder motorcycle."

"No way." Lyndsey's face lit up.

"Sure. We'll just have to get you a helmet."

Lyndsey's cell phone rang again. She stared at it. "And it'll get me away from *him*."

"That it would." BJ tightened her grip on her fork. This guy was a bit too persistent as far as she was concerned.

"What's to keep Cliff from following me?" Lyndsey asked.

"Nothing." BJ would keep Lyndsey safe even if it meant sending her to the moon. "But remember, your dad's cousin is the sheriff, so we got the law on our side. And the best thing about a small town, newcomers stick out like a beacon from a lighthouse in the dead of night."

"I doubt Mom and Dad will let me go. If they have it their way, I'll be locked in my bedroom the entire summer."

"You just leave them to me. Besides," BJ looked over her shoulder then whispered loudly with a wink, "I have a feeling they need a break from you as much as you do from them."

RANSOM FOLLOWED TWO car lengths behind Mason, heading down J. Turner Butler Boulevard. At a traffic light, the Mercedes turned west onto Phillips Highway. Four blocks past University Boulevard, Mason pulled into a small hotel. Ransom parked near the corner of the building. He remained in the van while Mason strolled into the main office. Two women, or girls made up to look like women, stood in the doorway of one of the rooms and stared at him. One couldn't have been any older than Bernadette.

The half-day motels announced loud and clear what their true purpose was. The managers knew darn well why customers took advantage of their facilities, but as long as they made a buck, they didn't care. Some owners were just as sleazy as the pimps who walked this area selling their merchandise, whether male or female.

A shiver raked up Ransom's back. Bernadette used to be such a commodity.

The teen continued to watch Ransom. She chewed on her thumb. The older one waved at him while speaking into a cell phone. His heart ached for both. Drugs and death were about their only way out.

Within minutes, a blue Cadillac screeched to a stop behind Ransom's van. Two men hopped out. Their jeans hung low off their hips, and the T-shirts they wore were too big for their builds.

Excitement collided with anxiety. Hopefully Ransom was up for this. He slid the .38 semi-automatic from the sleeve in his door, placing it on his lap. He covered it with a newspaper from the other seat. His pulse raced as he moved his finger over the button to unlock the driver's side door. At the same time, he clicked open the seat belt with his other hand.

One of the men came over and knocked on the side window. The other stood near the rear bumper on the left. Ransom had a good view of him in the side mirror. The guy had two advantages. He had to weigh at least twenty pounds more than Ransom, and he also had youth on his side. Good thing Ransom had the element of surprise.

He shifted in the seat to keep a better view of the brute. He'd be more of a problem then the scrawny man knocking. After a moment Ransom lowered the passenger window. The aroma of car exhaust permeated the air.

"You lookin' for anything spefic?" The guy spoke through gold-colored teeth. His face was oily, and two pimples sat on one side of his nose.

Ransom cringed at the guy's murder of the English language.

Gold-tooth looked at the young girl. The older one had disappeared inside. "She pretty, ain't she?"

"Yep."

"You a cop?" Gold-tooth asked.

"Nope."

"She do you good, old man. Cost ya, though."

Ransom fought the urge to vomit.

Cliff Mason exited the hotel and strolled to his Mercedes. He flipped a salute to Ransom, nothing military about it. Mason then slid into his car and drove off, leaving Ransom to contend with the two goons.

Glancing at the one by his back bumper, there'd be only one way out of this situation. His heart raced.

"What'll it be, old man."

"Was thinking about taking a room," Ransom said.

"I ain't a real fan of liars." The sun bounced off the guy's teeth when he smiled big.

"That's okay. I don't care much for perverts," Ransom said.

Gold-tooth's mouth closed tight. He leaned his arms on the window. "I ain't no pervert. And I don't like you hanging 'round here."

"Girl can't be more than sixteen." He pointed with his head in the direction of the hotel door. "You selling her, you're a pervert."

A terse laugh came from deep in Gold-tooth's throat. "How about you step out so we can discuss it?"

"Wonder what my chances are with two of you." Ransom glanced at the thug in the back. He'd inched up a bit from the bumper.

"What you suggesting, old man? We gonna do ya or something?" Some sort of sweet aroma came off Gold-tooth's slick hair.

"No. But I'm sure you'll be stupid enough to try." His voice remained calm and controlled.

Gold-tooth bound through the window with a Smith & Wesson Model 41, one of the best .22 target pistols. Ransom jerked his door open and bolted out. He swung the .38 into the head of the gorilla coming up the side. The hoodlum dropped out, cold onto the pavement. Gold-tooth rushed around, his weapon in front of him. Once close enough, Ransom gave a side-thrust kick into Gold-tooth's arm. The .22 fell and slid under the van. Ransom slammed the front window of the Chevy into Gold-tooth's face. Blood spattered the driver's side glass. Ransom cracked him over the side of the head. Gold-tooth joined his friend, out cold on the cement parking lot.

Ransom's pulse raced and sweat layered his body. He glanced back and forth for anyone else who might want to be involved. The only person in sight was the young girl still standing in the doorway. Her wide-open eyes stared at the two men on the ground. Ransom loosened his fists at his side.

"Your choice," Ransom said to the teenager. He popped the button to unlock all the doors. "Them or freedom."

She glanced into the room then back at Ransom. Her teeth grabbed hold of her bottom lip, and her breathing quickened. Ransom waited. She again looked over her shoulder then to her left and her right. She darted from the hotel to the passenger side and jumped inside.

Ransom got in and shoved the key into the ignition. The girl huddled against the door. She sucked on her thumb nail, her fingers trembling. Anxiety covered her features. He could almost read her mind. Hopefully, this time she wasn't making a mistake.

"You'll be okay," he assured her. "I know a Christian woman who'll help you."

Large tears spilled down her cheeks, and her lip wobbled with her sobs.

As much as he wanted to pat her on the back for reassurance, he thought better of it. She was scared enough without another man putting his hands on her.

Not able to back up, Ransom drove onto the sidewalk in front of the rooms. He spun his tires, screeching out of the parking lot and back onto Phillips Highway where he headed east. At least he'd be able to save one girl from this living hell.

An ache formed deep in his gut. Too bad someone hadn't done the same for Bernadette.

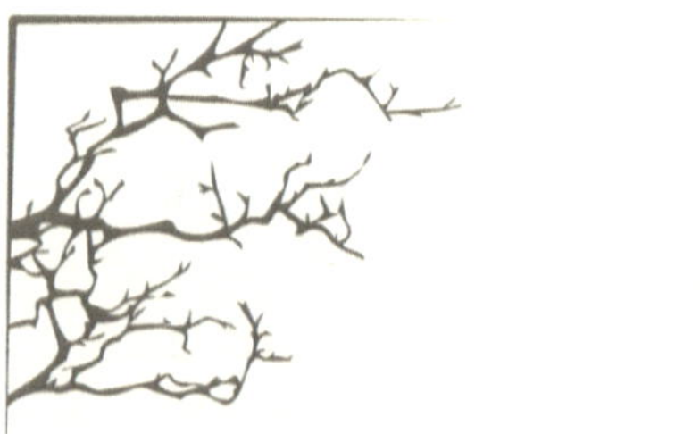

5

It seemed to take forever before the last day of school finally arrived. BJ looked forward to returning home and sleeping in her own bed. She missed Riley and his family, and her three-legged stray cat Stubby.

Mason had tried calling a couple of times, but Lyndsey allowed her mother to get her another phone number. The girl was sure once they left town, he'd not bother her again. However, something inside BJ warned that Mason had yet to move on.

After a quick breakfast snack early Thursday morning, the Jeep was loaded for the ride to Lincolnville. BJ would feel much better when she got Lyndsey under the watchful eye of Riley and the rest of her neighbors.

During the drive home, BJ kept an eye in the rearview mirror for any sign of someone following. Her stomach twisted in knots the entire trip.

Rain tapped against the windshield. The ride from Jacksonville had been a wet one. Lyndsey slept most of the way. BJ thought leaving early would have kept them from hitting heavy traffic, but two automobile accidents on I-75 slowed them once they neared Atlanta. The clock hit three-ten when BJ pulled up behind the building of Forever Art, Calley's shop, just inside the Lincolnville city limits.

"We're here." BJ nudged Lyndsey awake.

She scooted up in the seat and rubbed her eyes but made no move to get out of the vehicle. "Does Calley know?" Her voice was low.

"Know what?"

"About Cliff?"

"Yes." BJ patted Lyndsey's hand. "That's why she insisted I bring you back here. So, she could see for herself you were safe."

"She probably thinks I'm dumb for going out with him."

"There isn't one woman in this town who hasn't made a stupid decision about a man. Calley herself got mixed up with one."

"Is that the married man who died?"

BJ jerked back. She couldn't imagine Calley told Lyndsey about that part of her life.

"I heard people talking about it at her wedding," the teenager explained.

"I won't go into the gossip. I'll leave Calley to tell you the real story. But rest assured, she's not thinking anything bad about you." BJ leaned over and kissed Lyndsey on the head. "Wait until you see how big that baby's gotten."

They rushed through the back door of the store to escape water dripping from the gutters. After wiping their shoes, they proceeded to the front display area. Paintings rested on easels and hung from walls. The artist consignment shop would have its official opening in another week.

"Boy, am I glad to see you." Calley Owens hurried around the counter. "I don't know which has me crazier today, the business or the kid." She drew Lyndsey into a hug. Her hazel eyes shined. "Are you all right?"

"Yeah," Lyndsey mumbled.

"Good." She released Lyndsey and took a step back. "So, are you ready to become a working lady?"

"Can't wait," the teen said. "Where's RJ?"

"He's in his *cage* in back, finally asleep. That boy is as stubborn as Riley." She placed her hands on her hips and let out a loud breath.

"Can I go look at him?" Lyndsey pleaded. "I promise I won't wake him."

"Sure. He's in the first room to the right."

Lyndsey trotted off to the back.

"How's she doing since we last spoke?" Calley's eyes narrowed with concern.

"Pretty well, considering." BJ stepped over to a painting of a cabin in the woods. "Something inside tells me she knew it wasn't a good relationship."

"She has a good head on her shoulders. I'm just glad she's here."

The bell on the front entrance dinged. Calley rushed up to help Sheryl Coufield, who struggled carrying a large package. Her blond hair hung over the shoulders of a long black trench coat.

"Here you go, the last one in the collection." Sheryl closed her blue umbrella decorated with butterflies.

Calley leaned the package against the side wall.

"He's so cute." Lyndsey rejoined them. "He's sucking his thumb while he's sleeping."

"Wait until he tears everything out of your purse and tries to eat it." Calley shook a finger in the air. "You won't think he's so cute then."

"Sheryl," BJ said. "I believe you met my great-niece Lyndsey at the wedding."

"I'm glad to see I've got someone to help me cause trouble. Things were getting pretty dull with all these friends of mine getting married off and having babies."

"Speaking of having babies, how's Lydia doing?" BJ asked.

"She looks like she swallowed a bowling ball."

"I don't think I'd mention that to her." BJ laughed. "I hear pregnant women don't like to discuss their weight."

"I know I didn't." Calley peeled away the brown paper covering the portrait Sheryl had given her. She stared down at the painting of a young girl in a meadow. "Beautiful."

"Yes, it is." BJ leaned over for a better look. The green hues were the perfect color against the white dress the child wore. Cheryl's talent was amazing. BJ could barely draw a crooked line. "Well." She turned to Lyndsey. "I guess we'd better go over to the house. Get you settled." She gave Calley a hug. "Call me when RJ wakes up, and we'll come get him."

"Or you could just leave Lyndsey here." Calley raised her eyebrows up and down. "She can help finish up Sheryl's display for Saturday's show."

"Can I? Ple-e-ease." Lyndsey folded her hands in front of her.

"Are you saying that after eight hours in a car, you're tired of me?" BJ glanced at her watch. "The shop closes at five. How about I come get you then?"

"Thank you. Thank you. Thank you." She hugged her aunt.

BJ strolled out of the shop, relieved. At least Lyndsey would be safe with Calley and Sheryl. And it'd give BJ enough time to stop at the sheriff's station to see if Riley had any more information on Mason.

RANSOM GOT OUT OF HIS Chevy and stretched. When he bent over, his hamstring muscles strained, and his knees popped. He'd been sitting too long these last couple of days. Maybe he'd get a chance to walk around in the nearby woods. That should keep his body from whining.

During the wait for BJ and Lyndsey to drive north, Ransom had sent a note to a friend still with the Agency asking about Lincolnville and someone named Riley. The only person of importance came back to a Riley Owens, the local sheriff. All reports came back positive on the young man. Good for the citizens of Lincolnville. Probably a bad thing for Ransom, prowling around watching BJ and Lyndsey.

He'd also done a check on BJ. She had moved to Georgia to be with her nephew Riley Owens approximately two years before. She'd lived with him for a while before buying a home of her own a couple months earlier.

It had taken two days after Ransom had dropped off the young teen from the motel before Cliff Mason drove past Lyndsey's home again. He'd made a point of acknowledging Ransom with each pass through the cul de sac.

But Mason seemed to have disappeared during the last forty-eight hours. Ransom figured the pimp would follow BJ to Lincolnville, but the Mercedes had been nowhere in sight along the route. Maybe he found another kid and decided against going after Lyndsey. Ransom's chest tightened at the thought.

When BJ left the parking lot of Forever Art, Ransom had been prepared to follow, until he realized Lyndsey remained behind. She was who Mason wanted so Ransom decided to stay put. The large windows made viewing easy. He pulled out his laptop and looked up the owner's name. Calley Owens. How many relatives could BJ have in this town?

After an hour of sitting and watching, a black Mercedes went by and slowed, jolting Ransom's attention.

The vehicle passed the shop then did a U-turn and came back. Cliff Mason stopped in the road and looked in the shop. After a few seconds, he pulled into the parking lot. Using his fingers, he combed his hair back before getting out and strolling into the gallery.

Ransom counted to ten then exited the van and crossed the road. He sneaked to the front corner and leaned forward just enough to get a glimpse inside. Mason stood in the middle of the room talking to two women. Lyndsey tapped her hand against a counter near the back wall. From the frown on her face, she didn't appear very happy to see her ex-boyfriend.

Smart kid.

Ransom crept to the back of the building. A twist of the knob opened the door easily. Typical small town. A snort drew his attention to a room on his left. He glanced inside. A baby slept in a play pen. The aroma of baby powder hung in the air. Ransom stood just out of sight in the hallway and listened.

"I just wanted to talk with my girlfriend," Mason said.

"I'm not your girlfriend anymore." Lyndsey's voice shook. "We broke up."

"Just a misunderstanding. I still love you. I'd never hurt you. Everything your parents said was a lie."

"How'd you find me?" Lyndsey's voice trembled.

"You posted it all over the Internet." His words were smug. "I assumed you wanted me to know where you were."

"I think it's time for you to leave," one of the women said. "Before I call my husband, the sheriff."

"Call him. I haven't done anything illegal."

"You're trespassing."

"By the time he gets here, I won't be." He sneered at her.

"I have a better idea." The blond grabbed a tabletop easel from the counter. "How about you get out of here before I knock you up the side of your head?"

Ransom liked this woman. She had guts.

Mason laughed. "Trust me when I say it'll take a whole lot more than you with a stick."

Ransom stepped into view. "But only one me."

The three females jumped at the sound of his voice.

Mason's face darkened. It took a few seconds before his fake smile returned. "An old guy like you? I'm not worried."

Ransom stood with his legs apart and his hands at his sides.

Mason's lips tightened. He glanced between Lyndsey and Ransom. Finally, Mason stormed out.

"Thank you." The brown-haired lady walked up to Ransom. "I'm Calley Owens. This is Sheryl Coufield and Lyndsey Chapel."

Calley held her hand toward Ransom. He accepted it.

Sheryl glided over and eyed him up and down. She finally reached her hand out to him also. "Your wife must like having a strong man like you to protect her," she cooed.

Ransom shook her hand and grinned. Nice that he could still catch the eye of a younger woman. As much as he enjoyed the attention, he needed to keep focused on Mason and not his libido.

"I would suggest you watch this young lady here." He turned to Lyndsey. "Mason's now followed you all the way from Jacksonville. I get the feeling he won't go quietly."

The girl scooted around the counter and tiptoed behind Sheryl, who narrowed her eyes as if daring Ransom to try something. No way would he take this blond on. With those long manicured red nails, she'd claw him in half.

"What do you want?" Lines formed around Calley's mouth.

Ransom kept his eyes pinned over Sheryl's shoulder on Lyndsey. He had to make sure she understood. "He's not going to stop. His buyer's real anxious to get hold of you." When Lyndsey gasped, he turned his attention to the other two women. "And Mason isn't about to let anyone stop him from getting what he wants. And right now, that's you two." He pointed between Calley and Sheryl.

"Don't worry about us. We can handle what comes our way." Calley's left eyebrow arched. "Now, I suggest you leave before my husband arrives."

Ransom turned to go but stopped just inside the hallway. "I *suggest* you start locking that back door." He marched out leaving the three to mull over his words.

AFTER A FEW ERRANDS, BJ headed into the sheriff's station. The cool A/C formed goose bumps on her skin. An older man leaned over the counter talking to Deputy Green. A citrusy aroma came from his direction. His cologne, BJ assumed. A young girl, about sixteen, stood beside him.

"I barely went over the speed limit. The sign said thirty-five." The man had to be in his upper sixties. "I was only doing thirty-eight."

"During school hours, it's only twenty-five," Green said.

"But I'm new here and would have no way of knowing that."

"There are signs posted."

"I would think you'd give a tourist a break." His face reddened. An English accent filtered through with the man's curt words.

"You'll have to speak to the sheriff, and he's busy at the moment." Deputy Green pulled out a pad of paper. "If you give me your name and number, I'll see to it he contacts you."

"No point in wasting the paper." BJ stepped forward. Just because he came from out of town didn't mean he was above their laws. "My nephew won't let you get out of a ticket. He's a stickler for stuff like that."

"Nephew? Maybe I should be trying to convince you instead of this deputy here." The man jerked his hand forward. "The name's Bernard Ainsworth." He smiled, and his features softened.

When BJ accepted, he gave her a firm shake. She couldn't tell if that flutter in her stomach came from being flattered or not. Maybe her initial conclusion of him as a jerk had been a bit hasty. It'd been a long time since a man looked her way.

"With that accent, you must be popular with all the ladies in town," she said.

The girl rolled her eyes, but Bernard let loose a deep laugh. "Not any woman thus far. I've just arrived." He looked at the teen beside him. "This is my granddaughter, Elaina."

"Nice to meet you, Elaina." BJ gave her a nod. The girl wore a long-sleeve shirt though sweat creased her forehead. "So, Bernard, what brings you to Lincolnville?"

"Someone told me how beautiful north Georgia was so when I decided to retire, I came up here looking. Found a rental on Silver Street this summer to test the area out. I have a beautiful view."

"I'm sure you do." BJ was familiar with the homes on Hitchiti Lake. Most cabins rented out at a high price during the summer.

Bernard held up a slip of paper. "Except for this ticket, it's been a wonderful experience."

"You might as well pay it because talking to Riley will do you no good."

"At least it was well worth the price since I got to meet a lovely lady." He nodded and directed his granddaughter out the door.

He walked to a BMW parked out front. About time Lincolnville got some eye candy for someone her age. He wasn't too muscular, but not overweight like a lot of men her age. Gray hair and wrinkles hung around his eyes and mouth, but the mustache gave him a youthful air.

Deputy Green tapped her on the shoulder. "You can go inside Riley's office if you'd like to wait for him."

"Thank you." BJ's face heated at having been caught staring at the stranger. She rushed into Riley's office and took a seat on one side of the desk.

It was always nice to see a grandfather with one of his grandchildren. Not having children of her own created somewhat of a loss, but she'd been in love with Perry, and when they discovered he couldn't have children, she wasn't about to divorce him over it. God had a reason. Then Riley came to live with them.

BJ leaned back in the chair. She wanted to believe Lyndsey would be out of danger in Lincolnville, but a couple of murders in the last few years proved that not even a small town was safe anymore.

She picked up the family photograph of Riley, Calley, and Riley, Jr. They'd gone through so much in their young lives. What would the future hold for that baby? The door squeaked when it opened, and she replaced the picture on the desk.

"Sorry about that." Riley came in, dropped his black cowboy hat on the credenza under the window, and sat in his chair across from her. He spun the photograph BJ had held moments earlier toward him. A smile came over his lips. "I'm assuming everything went well with Lyndsey?"

"I've dropped her off at Calley's," BJ said. "They're fixing up a display of Sheryl's paintings."

"Calley can use the help. I never realized there was so much work involved for a gallery opening."

"She's received a lot of RSVPs which is good," BJ said. "I was worried with Lincolnville being so small that she might not have a large showing."

"There's a lot of money in the smaller counties around here." He leaned back in the chair. "What brings you by?"

"Checking to see if there's been anything new on this Mason fellow."

"Some speculation on the part of other agencies, but no evidence to arrest him."

"Like what?"

"This Mason isn't actually a big fish in the sex trade world. In fact, he's a newbie. His main source of income is drugs but there're whispers that he might be trying to branch out."

"Talk about a career choice." BJ shook her head.

"Too bad there's a lot of creeps like him out there." Riley inhaled a heavy breath. "Anyway, four kids are missing. All were considered runaways until Bernadette Lewis' body turned up. It was then they made the connection to Mason and the three other kids. One girl and two boys. Someone said he might have a woman helping him."

BJ's throat tightened. How could one human being do this to another? "I'm just glad Lyndsey actually believed me. I can't imagine what any of these parents are going through."

"Thanks to you taking care of the world, her dad won't have to know."

"I don't take care of the world. Only my little piece of it." She chuckled.

The phone rang on his desk. "Excuse me." He pressed down a button. "Yes, Sylvi."

"It's your wife," she said over the speaker.

"Thank you." Riley picked up the telephone from the cradle. "Hello, beautiful."

BJ tried her best not to listen in but when concern came into his voice, she perked up.

"When?" Riley stood up. "I'll be right over."

"What's going on?" BJ jumped out of her chair.

"Seems this Cliff Mason's turned up at the studio."

BJ rushed out of Riley's office, her body trembling. She had to find a way to stop this Mason from getting his paws on Lyndsey.

"Everything's okay," Riley came up behind her, stopping her before she reached the front door. "Some guy came in and scared him away."

"Good."

Riley continued to hold her by the arm. "Calley thinks Mason was just letting Lyndsey know that he could get to her."

"Well." BJ squared her shoulders. "I just might have to show this Mason fellow that I'm still a good shot. Because there's no way he's getting his hands on that girl."

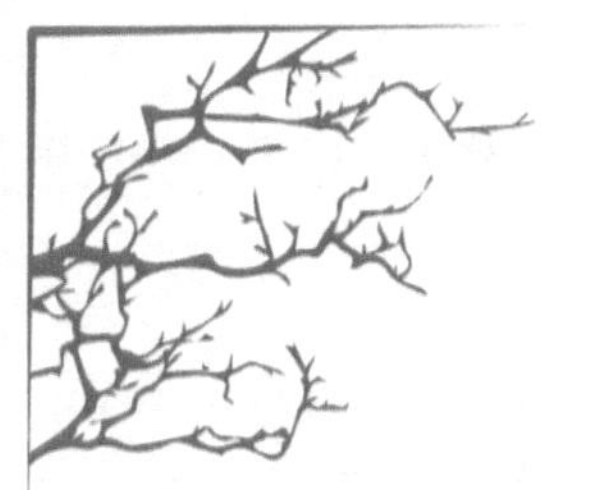

6

The sheriff's cruiser arrived at the art shop, and Ransom took that as his cue to leave. By going into the shop, he'd lost Mason. But in the long run, he wouldn't be too far from Lyndsey. Ransom wasn't up on human traffickers, but he would assume most would have moved on by now for fear of the police. There had to be a reason Mason focused all this time on getting that particular girl.

"Probably had to do with the phone call." If Mason already received payment, he might have spent the money. And desperate men do desperate things. At least Lyndsey was safe for the moment.

After a quick jaunt to a local motel just outside of town, Ransom did a drive through of the small town. Finding no sign of Mason, Ransom pulled into the parking lot of Fred's, a local diner. Writing on the window announced a daily hamburger special with fries and a drink for four dollars and ninety-nine cents.

He strolled up to the front and opened the door. The sizzle of hamburger patties slapping the grill drowned out most of the customers' voices. Red vinyl stools reminded Ransom of his teen years. The aroma of grease only added to those memories. This place could be Alfred's Burger Rama back home in Dallas. The only thing missing was the juke box playing music.

The patrons' talking turned to whispers when Ransom strolled to a red booth in the corner. He gave a nod to those willing to look his way.

Once seated, he glanced outside. A couple of kids played basketball in the park across the street. A woman was being pulled by three large dogs on a leash and another pushed a stroller.

"What can I get you to drink?" A brunette with the name tag Dolly looked down at him. A few strands of hair had come loose from the bun on the back of her head.

"I'll have a soda," Ransom said.

"Our specials are meatloaf with mashed potatoes or fried shrimp with a baked potato. Both come with a drink." She pulled a menu from her pocket. "I'll get your drink right out to you."

His mouth watered at the notion of a square meal. He hoped the food tasted as good as it sounded.

Fred's seemed to do pretty good business. While not full, there were quite a few patrons for mid-afternoon. A couple of teen boys sat at the counter and tapped away on cell phones. The rest of the customers sat in the available booths. Everyone wore shorts, and the women all seemed to have tanned legs.

"Did you see that?" An older man in the booth in front of Ransom's spoke loudly enough to garner the attention of most of the patrons. "That jerk just walked up and passed something to the Willis boy. He's dealing drugs."

"How can you be sure that's what he's doing, James?" a woman said from a booth in the back. "You watch too much TV."

Some of the other patrons laughed.

"It's obvious," James said. "Just watch him."

"I wish these strangers would just leave our town alone." The woman with him shook her head.

Ransom glanced to where the speaker and his female companion stared. Moments earlier the sidewalk had been empty. Now Cliff Mason stood. Ransom's pulse ratcheted up a notch.

A teen came up and talked to Mason. The kid shook his head at something Mason said. They talked for a second, then Mason shoved a small bag into the teen's shirt pocket. It looked like Mason was either dealing drugs or giving away freebies. Give it to them free today; they'll pay for it tomorrow. Ransom's hands curled into fists. This creep needed taking out sooner rather than later. But if Ransom rushed getting Mason arrested, he might lose any chance of finding Bernadette's killer.

"Here's your drink." Dolly placed the full glass on Ransom's table. "Have you decided what you'd like?" Her attention remained on the scene outside while speaking.

"The meatloaf sounds good," Ransom said.

"Aren't those your boys on that basketball court, Dolly?" James used his thumb to point toward the park.

The waitress nodded. The kids continued to play, oblivious to Mason. She glanced out the window again before walking behind the counter where she placed Ransom's ticket in line on a spinning wheel with the others.

Ransom lifted the lid of the dispenser holding red straws in white paper wrappers. Ideas rushed in at how to get Mason off the streets. Putting a bullet in his skull was one such thought, but Ransom brushed it aside quickly. Drug dealing might land Mason in jail but not long enough for him to give up a killer. And the DEA could swoop in on Mason to keep him from other agencies, giving him full immunity from past sins.

"See, he did it again." James' red face was more pronounced due to his white hair. "This time to Duncan's son. I'm not going to put up with this." He scooted out of the booth.

"James, wait." The woman's voice held concern.

"Something's got to be done."

"I'm with you." Another guy, this one about forty, rose from his seat at a booth next to the door.

"Call Riley," James's female companion urged. "Let him handle it."

"By the time he gets here, that jerk will be gone." The expression on James's face reminded Ransom of someone eating lemons. With another look outside, James stormed out the door with the other man following.

They both marched over to Mason standing on the sidewalk. The boys playing basketball stopped to watch. James shoved his finger into Mason's chest. Mason took a step back, raised his palms in the air as if to surrender, and strolled away. James and his friend remained standing on the sidewalk staring after him.

"Melanie, would you like some dessert?" Dolly was speaking to the woman who shared the booth with James.

"You might as well get us some apple pie. I'm sure he'll have to let everyone know what he just did." Melanie shook her head. "You know my husband."

Dolly laughed. "So how are the knitting lessons going?"

"I'm still practicing. One day I'll be able to do more than a row."

The patrons clapped upon James' return. A moment ago he was an idiot; now their hero.

Though Ransom had respect for what the man did, an image of Gold-tooth crossed Ransom's mind. Hopefully Mason won't hold a grudge, because James would be no match for Mason or his goons.

BJ'S HEART RACED AT Mason's boldness. If it wasn't clear to Lyndsey before that Mason was bad news, him stalking her to Lincolnville should cinch it.

Calley fell into Riley's hug with a large smile. "You didn't have to come over. The crisis was averted when the older gentleman showed up."

"Look who's awake." Lyndsey came out carrying RJ. "I changed his diaper for you."

"That is so sweet." Calley took the boy from Lyndsey's arms. "You're such a good worker."

"Thanks." Lyndsey's cheeks turned pink.

"Tell me what happened." Riley escorted Calley to the counter.

"Are you all right?" BJ wrapped an arm around Lyndsey, who smelled of baby lotion.

"Yeah." Lyndsey glanced over her shoulder at Riley's family. "But I'm not sure bringing me here was such a good idea."

"What do you mean?"

"Calley might get hurt because of me."

"Now, don't you worry. Riley will see to it she's safe. You, too." BJ flicked Lyndsey on the chin with her forefinger. "We had a feeling Mason would figure out where you were, so this doesn't come as a total surprise."

"But the other man said that Cliff had a buyer for me."

BJ's throat went dry. "Who was that?"

"The one who scared Cliff off." Lyndsey lowered her head. "I don't think Sheryl and Calley liked him, but I think he was trying to warn me."

BJ walked over to Riley, her arm still across Lyndsey's shoulder. "Did Calley tell you what this other man said?"

Riley nodded, his lips drawn into a straight line.

"This guy obviously knows about Mason and his escapades," BJ said. "I think we need to find him and see if we can't get something on Mason to put him away."

"I agree. Let me look at the security video and see if we can get a clear shot of him."

"I saw it in real time. I'm not in the mood to see it again." Calley kissed RJ on the cheek. "Besides, I think this kid is hungry."

"Can I help?" Lyndsey asked.

"Sounds good to me."

BJ followed Riley to a small room in the back. He sat in a chair behind the bookkeeping desk and clicked on the computer screen, bringing up the security videos. BJ leaned over his shoulder, her heart inching toward her throat with each swoosh of Riley's finger over the touch screen monitor.

Riley finally pressed play, leaned back, and listened. While Mason's words weren't a direct threat, his tone and glibness made it clear he'd have Lyndsey, and no one would get in the way. BJ's nails dug into her palm. "That man needs a crowbar up side of his head."

Riley nodded.

A few moments later, a male voice sounded in the background, too low to hear clearly. And he never came into view of the recording.

"So much for that notion." BJ held her hands on her hips. "Either he was lucky, or he'd made a point of not getting in sight of the cameras."

"We've got one more." Riley pressed a button. "With the rash of burglaries we've had recently, I stuck a hidden camera in the outside wall above the back door."

"You're so smart. Must take after your aunt." She patted him on his shoulders with his hands.

Riley forwarded the screen until a man came into view.

BJ reeled back.

"He doesn't look familiar to me, but I didn't hold out much hope," Riley said. "Maybe someone in one of the other stations will recognize him."

"That won't be necessary." BJ could hardly find her voice. "I know who he is."

Riley looked at her over his shoulder.

"We worked together when I was in the Army." BJ stood there stunned. What could Ransom's connection be to Mason? Didn't he claim to be retired? Not that the man wouldn't lie. Past experience told her he was very capable of deception.

"Who is he?" Riley asked.

"His name's Ronald McNeely." She leaned forward and placed her hands on the desk to catch her balance. "He's smart and was very good at his job with the CIA. That could mean trouble."

"His former profession doesn't concern me," Riley said. "If this is the same Ronald McNeely, he's also Bernadette Lewis's grandfather."

BJ's hand went to her throat. For some reason, the thought of him losing his grandchild raised a welt in her heart. A terrifying thought raced in. What did Ransom plan to do once he found the killer of his granddaughter?

"Do you know how to get hold of this McNeely?" Riley turned in the swivel chair.

"I have no idea," BJ said. "We happened to bump into each other in Jacksonville. Other than that, I haven't seen him in twenty-five years." But would she be able to tell Riley if she knew? She mentally shook the thought out. The man did a number on her years before; she'd not let him do it again.

"Well, if you spot him, let me know." Riley got up from his seat. "The last thing I need is a vigilante on my hands."

"What are you going to do about this Cliff Mason character?" BJ took a step back to allow him to pass.

"I'm hoping a not-so-friendly talk with the local sheriff might convince him to leave town."

"That's my boy." She gave a curt nod.

"Let me say good-bye to my wife and kid before I head out," Riley said. "Maybe I can get some info on this McNeely to see if I can locate him also."

"Good luck on that. Ransom was always very good at his job."

"Ransom?" Riley stopped.

"His name with the Agency." BJ followed Riley to the small kitchen in the far corner of the building where Calley and Lyndsey laughed while feeding the baby.

"Just what I need." Riley kissed Calley's cheek. "A spook running around loose."

"A spook?" His wife looked at Lyndsey who shrugged.

"A CIA agent."

BJ left them to say good-bye. She ambled to the front of the store. Poor Ransom. How had Bernadette's death made an impact on him? Little doubt it ate him up, not being able to save his grandchild. How far would he go to get the person responsible? It was a thought she didn't want to entertain. She rubbed her hands up and down her arms to get a sudden chill out.

"I overheard what you and Riley said." Lyndsey came up behind her. "Is that man really the dead girl's grandfather?"

"Looks that way."

"I can't imagine how bad he wants the guy who killed her."

BJ groaned inwardly. She had no choice but to find Ransom before he discovered the person responsible for the murder. Because once he did, the killer's life wouldn't be worth a dollar. And the notion of Riley putting Ransom in jail for the rest of his life caused an ache in BJ's already tumultuous stomach.

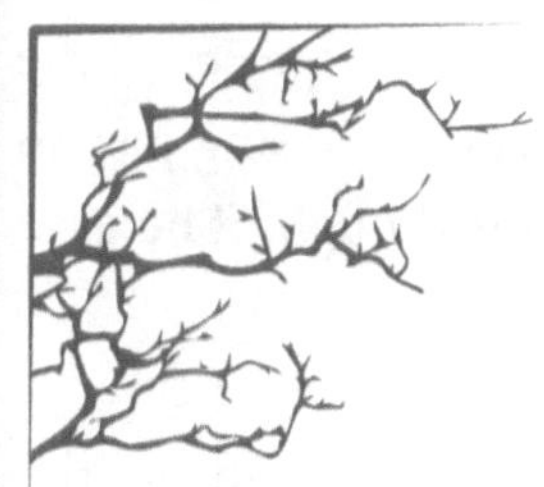

7

BJ hadn't caught sight of Ransom since discovering he was in Lincolnville the day before. But her gut said her spook was nearby. She grinned at Riley's use of the word.

Lyndsey hadn't slept well the night before, so to keep her mind off Mason, they stayed busy organizing the spare bedroom. Boxes from when BJ had moved from Riley's still sat in the closet. Dust covered the lid of a cardboard box Lyndsey carried over to the chair in the corner. BJ rubbed her nose to keep from sneezing. Inside were old knickknacks from her home with Perry. Would she ever display her Willow Tree Promise Musical Figurine again? She clasped it in her hand. This was the time she and Perry should be traveling and seeing the world. Never in her dreams, or nightmares, would he get cancer and leave her. She placed the hand-carved couple back in the box and let loose a low breath. Time to move on.

Her wedding ring sparkled from the overhead light. BJ stared at the diamonds. She just wasn't ready to remove them just yet.

BJ scooped up a bin of trophies and placed them by the doorway to take it into her room later.

"What are those for?" Lyndsey pushed open the flap.

"Shooting."

"Wow. Most of them are for first place." She pulled a small award out. "Except this one. But still, second isn't bad."

"That's what happens when you want to stroke a boy's ego."

Lyndsey's forehead creased.

"Should have been first," BJ said. "But I liked one of the boys competing, so I allowed him to win." She took the award from Lyndsey

57

and held it up. "Later that night he invited the corn queen to the fall dance instead of me. I was so angry for purposely losing just so he wouldn't hate me. The next year I showed him though." She gave Lyndsey a wink. "Beat him real bad."

"How'd you learn to shoot?"

"My daddy taught me. We used to go out target practicing all the time." She smiled. "It was our thing. None of my brothers really cared for it. Came in handy when I was in the Army."

"Did you ever have to shoot anyone?" Lyndsey spun the trophy in her hand.

"Last year. Not one of my better days, but it had to be done."

"I'm sorry. I didn't mean to upset you."

BJ set the trophy back in the box. "Wasn't you who upset me. It was the man who forced my hand." She swallowed hard, recalling the loud blast inside Riley's house barely a year ago.

"Look at all these old pictures." Lyndsey had moved on to a floral cardboard container on the bed filled with old photographs. Funny how easy she could be distracted.

BJ plopped down beside her. "Back then we didn't have computers or cell phones to keep photographs on so we just shoved them in albums or whatever we could find to keep them in."

Lyndsey held up a picture of a young woman dressed in a green Army uniform. "Is this you?"

"When I was much younger." BJ nudged Lyndsey with her shoulder.

"You have a lot of pictures from back then." She shuffled through the box. "Is this Uncle Perry?"

BJ nodded. She placed her hand over her heart. Why did his loss still hurt after all these years?

"I remember him taking us cousins to Disney World," Lyndsey said.

"I think he had more fun than you kids."

"And who's this? He looks familiar." Lyndsey stared at a picture before giving it to BJ. "He was hot looking."

BJ's heart leapt to her throat. Ransom. Hot looking was the best way to describe him then with his blue jeans and buttoned down shirt opened just enough to show some chest hair. "He was a man I used to work with."

"Did you ever go out with him?"

BJ's stomach lurched recalling how close she'd come to falling for Ransom's lines. It would have been so easy to cheat.

"Are you all right?" Lyndsey put the photograph back in the box. "I didn't mean to make you sad."

"You didn't." She patted Lyndsey on the leg. "It's just that I still miss your uncle."

"We'll just have to find you someone else who gives you those jolts." Lyndsey raised her eyebrows up and down.

"Jolts?"

"You know when your heart jumps every time you see them." A frown appeared on Lyndsey's face. "Like what I had with Cliff."

BJ hopped off the bed. "Aren't we the two saddest sacks you ever did see?" She placed her hands on her hips. "I say we take these to my room then head out to dinner. I don't know about you, but I'm starved."

"Me too." Lyndsey patted her stomach.

"Besides," BJ said, "if we keep going on like this, we'll both end up in a puddle."

Within thirty minutes, they'd changed and walked out the front door. BJ pulled the Jeep into Fred's lot. The diner filled up fast on a Friday due to the rib eye steak special so BJ ended up driving around back before she found a parking space.

On the steps to the front door, Lyndsey tugged on BJ's sleeve. "There he is." Lyndsey pointed at Cliff Mason standing across the street. He gave a nod in her direction when she caught his eye.

"Let's get seated then I'll call Riley." BJ held the door open for Lyndsey to enter first.

Inside, there were no empty booths. And all the swivel stools at the counter were filled. BJ's stomach growled when the smell of searing steak hit her nostrils. Before entering, she'd been prepared to go somewhere else if they couldn't find a seat. But the aroma had now settled in her system. Nothing else would do.

People murmured to each other while waiting for their food. Two teen boys glanced up at Lyndsey and nudged each other grinning. Just what BJ needed, a bunch of adolescent testosterone hanging around this summer. She might want to make sure her pistols were ready for firing.

James Newman and his wife Melanie stood to leave. They ate at Fred's every night except Sunday when it was closed. On more than one occasion, Melanie had said she knitted worse than she cooked.

BJ strolled over to them. "Can we steal your spot?" she asked.

"Of course," Melanie said. Their used dishes still covered the table.

"You forgot these." BJ bent down and picked up two gold knitting needles left behind.

"Thanks." Melanie stuffed them back in a yellow and green bag. "I keep misplacing them. We're going to go broke having to replace silly needles." She smiled, but it didn't reach her eyes.

James focused out the window. "I can't believe that creep is back."

BJ realized he spoke about Mason who had just stuffed something into a teenager's front jean pocket. "He won't be there long," she said. "I'm calling Riley to get rid of him."

Melanie swung her bag over her shoulder. The needles stuck out of the top. She glared out the window. "The last thing we need is more kids getting hooked on drugs." A tear formed in her left eye.

BJ patted her arm.

"I'm sorry," Melanie said. "Jimmy's birthday is coming up, and I'm an emotional wreck right now."

"I fully understand." BJ continued to hold Miriam's arm. "How about I call you, and we'll make plans to go to lunch soon?"

"I'd appreciate it."

James pulled his focus from Mason to BJ. "Tell that nephew of yours to run that guy out of this town, or I'll see to it he's out of a job."

BJ dropped down onto the booth bench. Only the town council could fire Riley, and they liked her nephew far more than James. She watched Melanie walk toward her car. Her shoulders slumped with each step. It wasn't fair for any child to die before their parents.

James paused at his car door, turned, and glared over at Mason. Melanie said something to him. After a few seconds, he got in the Lincoln Town Car, and screeched out of the lot.

"Hello, ladies." Dolly tugged a pad from her apron pocket. "What can I get you to drink?"

After placing their orders, BJ retrieved her cell phone from her purse and called Riley. "That Cliff Mason is standing in the center of Pineview Park. I think you'd better get over there to see what it is he's handing off to the kids and to give him that talk you mentioned yesterday."

"I'm on my way."

Lyndsey had yet to take her eyes off Mason. "He's letting me know he's here, isn't he?"

"Looks more like he's selling drugs. But Riley's on his way."

"Boy, do I know how to pick them." Lyndsey sighed.

BJ reached over and patted Lyndsey's hand. "Too bad creeps like Mason can't be taken out and tarred and feathered like in the old days." She paused. "Did he ever give you drugs?"

"No. He claimed he no longer did them."

Bernard Ainsworth and his granddaughter, Elaina, pulled their blue BMW into the empty spot James and Melanie had vacated. When they got out of the car, they looked toward Mason who smiled in their direction.

BJ's heart lurched. Elaina was blond and blue-eyed. If Mason couldn't get to Lyndsey, would he settle for someone with similar features?

Before she could finish the thought, the sheriff's cruiser skidded to a halt across the street, and Riley jumped out of the car. Deputy Green came from the opposite direction. No one made a sound in Fred's Diner. All too busy staring out the window.

Riley confronted Mason, who carried an arrogant look on his face. He must have said something Riley didn't like, because he shoved Mason onto the hood of the cruiser and searched him. Riley yanked out a plastic bag from the guy's front pocket.

"Well that should take care of him for a while," a man said from the counter. Others echoed the sentiment.

BJ agreed. Time to start enjoying her time with Lyndsey.

Bernard and his granddaughter strolled by. "Looks like we'll have to go elsewhere," Bernard said. "Unless you want to wait?"

BJ scooted from her side of the booth and stood. "Why don't you two join us, Mr. Ainsworth? You could be waiting a while for a seat." She shoved Lyndsey over.

"If you're sure we're not intruding." He stood to the side of her, his cologne smelling of harsh musk and vanilla. "And if you call me Bernard."

BJ introduced Lyndsey to the two. "It probably wouldn't hurt for this one to get to know another closer to her own age. I'm sure she'll be tired of me in a matter of days."

"It'll be good for Elaina also," he said.

Elaina stared down at the table with sad eyes. She wore a long-sleeve blouse over a spaghetti string shirt. Her collar bones jutted out. To say she was thin was an understatement. If BJ had her way, she'd feed the girl cake and ice cream throughout the summer.

Bernard glanced out the window at the goings on across the street. Deputy Green placed a handcuffed Mason in the backseat of his cruiser. "I thought a small town would be a safer place. Guess nowhere is."

"At least he's taken care of now," BJ said.

Soon another dealer would start selling in their town. But at least Lyndsey was safe from Mason's grasp.

They spent the next hour talking and eating their steak dinners. Bernard explained how he'd come from England a couple years ago so he'd be closer to Elaina. The girl hardly spoke and only picked at her food. Probably why she remained so thin.

When BJ first met Elaina in the sheriff's station, she thought the girl was sixteen, but on closer inspection, she appeared closer to nineteen or twenty. Her frailty made her look younger.

"Can I get some ice cream?" Lyndsey asked once she'd devoured her meal.

"You think you have room?" BJ asked.

"There's always room for ice cream." She nudged BJ's shoulder.

"True." BJ rose from the booth to allow Lyndsey to exit.

"You want some, Elaina?" Lyndsey stopped at the other side of the table. "Looks like they have chocolate," she sang.

Amazing how much her mood improved with Mason out of the way.

Elaina looked over at her grandfather who gave his head a nod. Once at the soft serve machine, Lyndsey actually got Elaina to smile.

"Your granddaughter's pretty quiet." BJ moved into the spot Lyndsey had occupied seconds earlier. "Good thing Lyndsey's not."

"I'm glad she's got a friend. It's hard when you're new." His accent wasn't as harsh as at the sheriff's station. "She's too old to be taking care of me like she does. Tomorrow I'm going to Chattanooga for a couple hours. She hates traveling because I don't do shopping like women do, but she'll not complain. At least not too much." He grinned.

"You're not attending the opening at Forever Art tomorrow night? It's the big event of the year for Lincolnville."

"I hope to be back before then. And it'll give Elaina something to do as a reward for being good."

"How about you leave her with me tomorrow morning while you go to Tennessee?" BJ checked on the girls in the corner. "She and Lyndsey seem to be getting along pretty well."

"I can't impose on you like that."

"It's not an imposition. In fact, have her bring the dress she'll be wearing, and we can meet you at the gallery after dinner. Then you won't have to hurry."

The girls returned to the table with chocolate soft serve ice cream in a bowl. Lyndsey had covered hers with chocolate syrup and gummy bears while Elaina ate hers plain. They discussed Elaina coming over the next day.

All agreed she would arrive at eight in the morning.

Once in the Jeep, BJ debated sharing her concerns with Lyndsey about Mason possibly chasing after Elaina instead. In the end, BJ decided it best to discuss her thoughts so Lyndsey wouldn't let down her guard.

"I'm worried about the look Mason gave Elaina when they arrived," she said. "He might decide that taking you is too much trouble and go after her instead."

"But he's in jail. He can't get anyone now."

"Even so, he probably works with others. I'm not very familiar with this whole sex trade business, but these creeps make good money or they wouldn't be doing it." An ache developed in her chest. *God, help these children.*

"We can't let him have Elaina." Tight lines formed around Lyndsey's mouth.

"I agree," BJ said. "That's why, tomorrow, we need to find a way to warn her."

BJ SPENT THE RIDE HOME discussing with Lyndsey how to bring up her relationship with Mason. They both decided the best approach was to be straightforward and honest.

Back at the house, they lit a cinnamon candle to try to get rid of some of the musty odor from the closet and finished cleaning. At a little past nine, BJ brushed her teeth twice trying to get the bell pepper flavor from her taste buds.

Once in bed, she pulled out her netbook and scanned the internet for information on human trafficking.

Could this be real? People stealing children?

Her blood ran cold glancing through the statistics. The average age of teens in the sex trade business were between twelve and fourteen. Mostly runaways. Los Angeles, San Francisco, and San Diego had the biggest trade. Except for drugs and weapons, human trafficking was the next largest crime industry.

How can people be so sick? Selling people to others. Of course, if people wouldn't buy, they wouldn't sell. "Need to take a dull knife to a certain portion of their anatomy. That'd solve the issue." She closed the computer, set in on the nightstand, and then folded her hands on her lap. "Please God, protect these children. Do away with these urges these men have."

She shook her head. It amazed her how cruel humans could be to one another. Killing in the Middle East like they're snuffing out ants. Teenagers right here in this country killing for the thrill of it. When would it all end?

"I think it's time for you to send Jesus back down here." She spoke to the ceiling. "I can't imagine it can get any worse down here."

She pulled out her Bible hoping for some comfort. Plenty of Psalms to sooth her aching soul. She paused to meditate on Psalm 37:1-3, *Do not fret because of those who are evil or be envious of those who do wrong; for like the grass they will soon wither, like green plants they will soon die away. Trust in the Lord and do good; dwell in the land and enjoy safe pasture.* After a few moments, she let loose a yawn and rubbed her eyes. Always happens. She recalled the minister stating that the devil hated when someone read their Bible, so he'd make them sleepy. That's all right. She'd put in a good days work. Tomorrow she'd look up some verses for Lyndsey to help her through all this.

Within seconds of turning out the light, her cell phone rang.

Her heart bounced upon seeing Riley's number. *Please God, let everyone be okay.* "You're up late," she said upon answering the phone.

"Heading home now. But I've got some information on this spook McNeely," he said. "He's driving a silver Chevrolet cargo van."

BJ recalled the same type of vehicle at the end of the cul-de-sac leading to Lyndsey's home. A similar one had driven past when they arrived back from dinner. She hadn't thought anything of it at the time. Too relaxed from all the food she'd eaten.

"He was spotted at Fred's yesterday," Riley continued. "I've got Green out looking for him." Riley paused. "We've also got a problem with this Mason character."

"What kind of problem?" BJ's stiffened.

"He's a government informant for the DEA. They're using him to get to a large drug dealer."

"So, what's that got to do with anything?"

"The last place they want him is in jail." Riley let out an exacerbated breath. "We had to turn him over, and I have little doubt they plan to let him go."

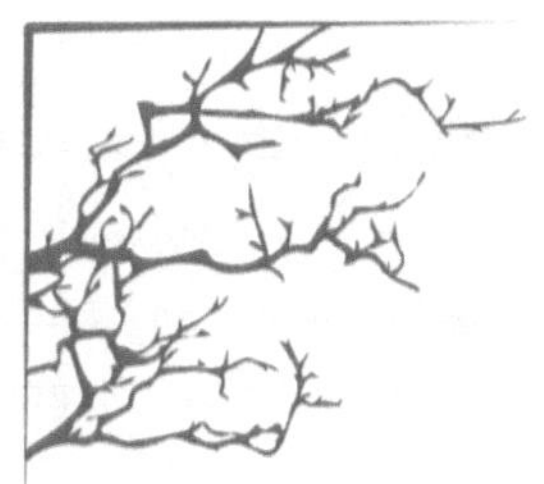

8

Earlier in the evening Ransom had followed BJ's blue Jeep to a white brick single-family home. He stayed far enough behind so BJ wouldn't catch him trailing her. Mason should be out of commission at least for the night. If he posted bail, he'd eventually show up wherever Lyndsey happened to be. And based on the incident at the Jacksonville motel, Mason definitely had help. If so, Lyndsey could be taken tonight, leaving Mason with the perfect alibi.

Ransom parked in a vacant lot kitty-corner across the street from BJ's. Trees gave him a hiding place and a good view of her house.

Within seconds of getting on his laptop he knew the layout of BJ's newly constructed three bedroom, two bathroom home. Twelve hundred square feet in total. She'd bought the property a couple months ago and got a permit to add a deck on the back shortly after. She also owned the two-and-a-half acres the building sat on. What looked like pecan and magnolia trees dotted the landscape. Right now BJ had the only house in the area.

Ransom slid his window open a couple inches and did the same for the one across. A breeze carried in from the east. Mosquitoes buzzed somewhere behind him. The clock on the dash read nine fifty-three. Exhaustion felt like it'd taken up residence in his muscles and his mind. How long had it been since he'd gotten a good night's sleep? Days? Weeks? Months? His eyelids drifted closed.

A bump on top of the van jolted Ransom awake. A nearby street light cast a halo on the area. Shuffling overhead drew his attention. Paws. Could be a possum. Or maybe a squirrel, but squirrels were usually bedded down by dark.

67

"Meow."

Ransom smiled. Another thump. This time the yellow three-legged cat jumped onto the hood. The feline shot a look back at Ransom, its eyes reflecting in the moon. Ransom tore off a piece of beef jerky and opened the door. The day he got the van, he'd removed the overhead bulb so no light came on.

"Here you go, boy." Ransom rested the food on the hood.

The animal stared at him. It sniffed the air before limping over to pick up the piece of meat.

"Definitely a cat. A dog would have pounced on it." Ransom rubbed the soft fur, receiving a loud purr in the quiet night.

Once the tabby finished with the snack, Ransom gave it the remainder of the meat. This time, the cat put the piece between its teeth and jumped down, rushing across the road. A car came into view. Ransom got back in the driver's seat. A police cruiser slowed at BJ's driveway. The deputy turned on his interior light and waved to the shadowy female shape in the window.

The cruiser blinked its headlights then disappeared into the night.

Within minutes of the officer disappearing, a silhouette crossed the street about a half-block down. Ransoms' pulse quickened. It'd been years since he'd felt that rush of adrenaline kick in.

With the gun at his side, Ransom got out of his van and crept through the trees. Once away from the street light, he crossed to the side where BJ's house sat. Footsteps shuffled to his right. A male figure appeared. Ransom stalked him in the dark. His movements became natural as the past crawled back into his soul.

On the job, he'd never taken foolish chances without back-up. But this time was different. There'd be no one to ensure his safety.

The stranger came into full view of the lit back porch light. Ransom's heart jolted at the sight of the man sneaking through the woods.

Cliff Mason.

How was he free from jail? He must have good connections. Good enough to get away with selling Bernadette. Ransom's fingers tightened on the gun. He snuck closer. It all came down to this piece of garbage. The person who sold his granddaughter.

It would be so easy to deal with him right now. Ransom paused behind a tree. He raised his pistol. One bullet would be all it took, and no one would ever know. He put Mason in his sights, and cocked the hammer back. Ransom's hand was steady. He hesitated.

Was this the man he'd become? He inhaled a deep breath and lowered his weapon.

A twig snapped to Ransom left. Someone or something else was in the area.

Mason, himself, stopped and glanced around. He darted around the side of the house. Ransom followed. A hundred feet from the house, the blip of a key fob and red lights came from a car parked down the road from the van. Within seconds, the engine started, and the black Mercedes sped off in the opposite direction. Ransom returned to the home and searched for the other intruder.

"Hiss. Mrrr."

He glanced behind him at the cat. "Good job."

He took his finger off the trigger of the gun and stared in the direction the car disappeared.

No. Killing Mason would be too quick a punishment. Besides, Ransom knew other ways to get information. And they didn't include a bullet.

SCANNING THE AREA, BJ became alert to a sedan leaving. Her fists tightened at her sides. How could the government allow an animal like Mason to run lose? She glanced at her clock. Ten fifty-one. Too late to call Riley, and if she contacted the station, they'd certainly get hold of him themselves, waking Calley or the baby. She went to the gun cabinet in the corner of the living room and pulled out her Browning 725 Citori 12 gauge shotgun. Great for shooting birds and anyone who decided to come in uninvited. Depending on where she aimed, she might not kill the intruder, but she'd definitely leave a mark. She slid a bullet into the chamber.

BJ hadn't seen the vehicle arrive. However, in the glow of the streetlight, she did notice the outline of a van parked in the woods across the street. Though it was too dark to see the color or anyone inside, she had no doubt who kept watch. Ransom. She assumed he came to town following Mason. If so, why was he keeping watch over *her* house?

Something scratched at the back screen. BJ startled. After getting her bearings, she went over and glanced out the window. The light was kept on all night to keep unwanted critters away from the back porch. BJ hesitated, and then reached over and slid a knife from the butcher block set on the counter. After disarming the alarm, she opened the door.

Within seconds, Stubby, her three legged cat, pranced inside. BJ shoved the deadbolt back in place. "What have you been up to?" She folded the cat into her arms.

"Mew."

His breath smelled of meat. More particularly, beef jerky. Ransom's meal of choice when on a stakeout in Korea. She'd almost bet a fresh package of celery sat on the passenger seat of that van.

She paced the living room. All the lights were out but the one in the hallway. As BJ wore a tread in her carpet, thoughts and questions raced through her mind. Should she confront Ransom? Maybe warn him about Riley looking for him. She plopped down on the sofa only to bounce right back up.

"He had to know what Mason was up to before Lyndsey got mixed up with him," she muttered. Her jaw tightened. "How could he?" She stormed to the kitchen and poured herself a glass of water, gulping it down in one swallow. "Why would anyone allow a girl to get involved with such a monster?"

Her pulse raced. Using BJ was one thing, endangering her niece another.

And he wouldn't get away with it this time.

RANSOM HAD BEEN TEMPTED to look for the Mercedes. But in an unfamiliar town, that wouldn't be smart. If he got lost, that gave Mason the advantage. Besides, the creep wanted Lyndsey. He'd be back. Ransom had hoped he'd at least have one night's peace before Mason could see a judge. He was a viper who could slither out of any situation.

An isolated subdivision was good for Mason if he tried to grab Lyndsey. Even better for Ransom. He scooted back down. He shook his head and stretched his neck to keep from dozing off, but his body ached for rest. It used to be he could go days but as he'd aged, he needed sleep more and more. Creeping around only added to his tiredness. It'd been a while since he tried to keep up with someone else. The tension wrung the energy out of him.

In minutes, thoughts turned to that of Bernadette, as seemed to be the norm when he had nothing to do. Of course, an hour didn't go by when she wasn't on his mind. He and Bernadette had gotten to know each other well in the months before her disappearance. She never held it against him that he'd been a terrible father to Darcy. Bernadette had found a friend in her grandfather. He'd listen to her complain about her parents, never offering her any advice. After all, what did he know about being a parent? It worked better that he lent an ear so she could vent to him instead of taking her anger out on her mother. They'd also go to movies, most of which he didn't care for, but it made her happy. He smiled, recalling how she'd introduce her grandpa, the spy, to all her friends. Unlike Darcy, Bernadette seemed proud of him, and he of her, with the straight A's she'd garnered in school.

Amusement parks had been a favorite place for her. She'd wanted to go to Wild Adventures in Georgia to see a favorite band. When her mother found out Ransom bought them all tickets, she made an excuse not to allow her daughter or anyone else to go. Darcy wanted nothing to do with him or his gifts. Tears had rolled down Bernadette's cheeks. She and her mother got into an argument, and the next day she disappeared, leaving a hole in Ransom's heart.

He scrubbed a hand down his face wanting to erase the memory from his mind. If he'd asked Darcy privately about the tickets, then maybe ... The thought hung suspended. Too many "what ifs" lately.

He opened the laptop and clicked on a site for news, hoping for a distraction. After a few moments, he yawned.

"Grandpa. Grandpa. Help me," Bernadette called out to him.

Ransom ran down the hallway checking the closed doors. All locked. He'd kick them in one at a time but each room remained empty. The more he pushed on, the longer the dim corridor became. Bernadette's cries increased with each step he took.

At once the vision bounced. Ransom stood in the center of a two lane road. Bernadette ran toward him, never getting any nearer. Fear penetrated her eyes. She would glance over her shoulder, running from some dark figure. Ransom's legs wouldn't work. No matter how hard he tried, he couldn't move. Bernadette finally got within feet of him. Before he could pull her to him, a ligature snapped around her neck.

Ransom jerked awake. His dream always ended the same. The gray skin. The red marks around her throat. His beautiful granddaughter gone. *God, how could you allow her to be taken away?* He punched the console.

Maybe he shouldn't have been the one to identify her body, but he couldn't allow Darcy to do it and Bernadette's father had yet to get over his daughter's death. He worked himself day and night trying to forget.

Ransom pressed his fingers to his temples, trying to force the vision out. A crunch of dried grass sounded behind the van. He glanced into the rearview mirror but didn't see anyone. No one at the side either. He waited and listened. Maybe the cat had come back for more food.

He rubbed his eyes. Was he seeing things? No. Someone was coming around the back of BJ's house. Ransom opened the door.

"Going somewhere, old man?" Gold-tooth, the guy from Jacksonville, walked from the back of the van, holding a Sig .22 pistol.

ILLUMINATED BY ONLY the moon and street light, BJ, flashlight and rifle in hand, tiptoed across the road. The black night kept her from seeing well, but a male voice sounded from where the van was parked. Reflections of two silhouettes stood near the vehicle. She crouched down behind a tree twenty feet away and listened.

"We got us some unfinished business," a man said. He smacked the other figure in the side of the skull, sending him to the ground. The thug stood over him and kicked him in the ribs. "You not so tough now, is ya?"

"I'm not the one who had the friend helping me out in Jacksonville."

BJ recognized that man's voice. Ransom.

"Ain't nobody here but you and me." The assailant shoved his foot into Ransom's stomach.

He grunted.

"How's that feel, old man? You gonna pay for taking off with my property."

"She isn't property." Ransom's words came out in angry spurts. "She's a kid."

BJ flicked the flashlight on and aimed it at the guy standing over Ransom. The man spun around, raising his arm in front of his face. His beige pants hung low on his hips, and a large T-shirt covered a thin body.

"I suggest you drop that gun before I call the police." She remained hidden behind a tree, the rifle pointed at the man's belly. "We don't care much for strangers starting trouble in these parts."

The man raised his weapon. BJ shot at the dirt inches away from his feet. "Next time I go higher."

The pistol slid from his hand. He jerked around and disappeared in the dark.

Ransom grabbed the gun and climbed up the side of the Chevrolet, one hand on his stomach. "Thanks."

BJ walked over to him, her finger still on the trigger of the rifle. Once close enough, she could smell the sweat from both men. "Looks like you're still making friends the hard way."

He grunted a laugh then winced. A drop of blood from a cut on his forehead trickled down his jaw line.

"I suppose the least I can do is get you cleaned up." BJ put the safety back on the weapon. Once she had Ransom cornered inside, she'd give him a good piece of her mind.

The bass from loud music faded in the distance. BJ assumed it came from the attacker's vehicle which he might have parked on the other side of the woods.

"You shouldn't have left Lyndsey alone," Ransom said.

If she hadn't come out, Ransom might have found himself seriously hurt. BJ swallowed back a snide remark. Instead, she passed him the flashlight and placed his arm over her shoulder. He leaned on her, limping. His smoky wood scent infiltrated her system as it draped around her. Memories of walking around Seoul flooded in.

ONE LAST BREATH

Ransom stopped in the middle of the street. It took a moment for BJ to realize the ringing in her ears came from the house alarm.

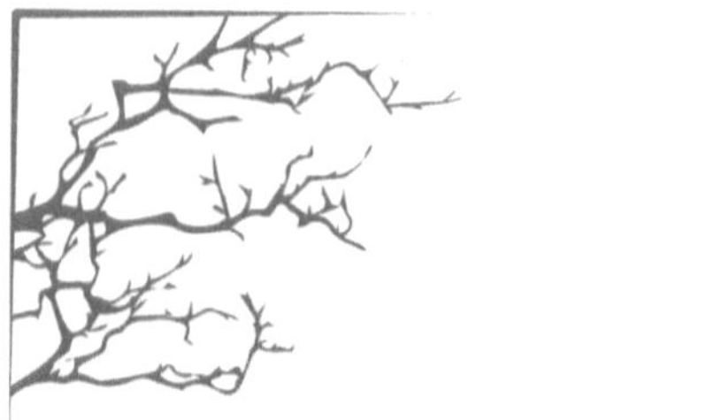

9

With his arm over BJ's shoulder, Ransom had forgotten the dull ache in his ribs. He'd over-exaggerated the pain to lean closer to her. However, when the alarm blared, all pretenses disappeared. He ran after BJ to the side of the house where she raised her rifle. The back door swung open, and Lyndsey stuck her head out.

"Aunt BJ," she spoke in a harsh whisper. "Aunt BJ."

BJ's facial expression relaxed, and she lowered the weapon. "I'm right here. What are you doing sneaking around?"

"I got up and couldn't find you." She glanced over BJ's shoulder to Ransom. A look of anxiety filled her eyes.

"Well, let's get that alarm off before Riley has the SWAT team out here." BJ hurried to a key pad inside the foyer and input some numbers. The alarm finally silenced.

The cat Ransom had met earlier looked up from the arm of the sofa in the living room. Once he caught a glimpse of Ransom, he yawned then returned to his rest.

The living area was spacious even with the large couch, two recliners, and entertainment center that held what Ransom guessed was a forty-two inch high definition television and a stereo with CD player. The aroma of wax hung in the air.

Lyndsey kept an eye on Ransom while BJ led him to a chair in the eat-in kitchen. The teen's right brow cocked up on one side. "Are you really Bernadette's grandfather?" she blurted.

He nodded. His side hurt enough without bringing his heart into it.

"I'm sorry for your loss." Her bare toe scrapped against the white tile floor.

"Thanks." He swallowed back burning tears.

The look on her face told him she didn't know what else to say. She'd probably overheard her parents offer the same condolences to friends. Not that it mattered much. No words could fix the pain in his soul.

He mentally kicked himself for ever considering using the teen to get at Cliff Mason. He never saw her as much more than a prop for revenge. Here she was trying to give comfort the best way she knew, yet weeks ago he had hoped she'd fall into the hands of a predator. Ransom's stomach churned thinking about it.

What type of a man had he become?

Lyndsey turned to BJ. "He's the one in the picture, isn't he?"

BJ nodded, and her face reddened. "Why don't you try to go back to sleep?" she said. "Everything's going to be all right."

"Okay." Lyndsey crept to the hallway. She continued to watch BJ and Ransom over her shoulder until she was out of sight.

There was no sound of a bedroom door closing. Ransom figured the girl kept it open to make sure he didn't make any untoward advances on her aunt. A smile came over him at the notion, and some of his gloomy tension lifted.

"So you still have a photo of me?" he asked with a grin.

BJ remained silent. She stared down the hallway Lyndsey had just entered. BJ's lips tightened and lines formed on her forehead.

Ransom's better mood instantly disappeared as fast as it came. He took BJ's soft, warm hand in his. "Don't worry. She'll be okay."

"She's not been sleeping well." The edges of BJ's mouth curved downward.

"It's to be expected." He gave her palm a squeeze.

She shook off his hand and moved to the kitchen sink. "Let's see about getting you fixed up." She turned on the water and soaked a washcloth. "So who was your friend out there?"

"More like a friend of Cliff Mason's."

BJ spun to face him, her eyes wide.

"You didn't think he'd be out there on his own, did you?" Ransom tried to keep his tone from being too blunt.

"I guess I was just hoping he'd move on." She winced once the words left her mouth.

"To what? Another kid?"

BJ swallowed hard. "I never really gave it much thought. I just want him to leave Lyndsey alone."

Ransom stood and walked to BJ. "He will. Eventually."

She reached up and patted the washcloth on his temple. He flinched from the pain.

"Sorry." BJ's eyes were still the light blue-gray he'd remembered.

Ransom held her fist, clutching the wet cloth. "It's been a long time."

"Yes, it has." Her voice came out unsure.

"Time's been good to you. Nothing has changed."

"Except a lot more wrinkles."

"You're still the prettiest woman in town." He caressed her cheek with his knuckle.

BJ let loose a laugh. "And you're still the biggest bag of baloney I've ever met." She turned away and rinsed off the cloth.

Ransom placed his hands on each of her arms. "I'm sorry I hurt you."

"It was just your job."

"Not all of it." He stared at her reflection in the window.

She raised her chin and glared at him in the glass. Her soft demeanor disappeared in a flash. "So tell me, why have you been watching Lyndsey?"

BJ'S BODY HEATED AT Ransom's touch. She scooted over to a chair for fear her legs would no longer hold her. Ransom sat next to her. As hard as she tried to remain mad, her anger all but dissolved because of the brief sadness on his face with Lyndsey's earlier mention of Bernadette. His pain ran deep. Yet she couldn't allow herself to fall again. It would only mean a broken heart.

She glanced toward the front window when car lights shined through the crack in the curtain. BJ walked over, moved the curtain aside and gave a wave, letting the deputy know he could move on. Would he have stopped if she didn't come to the window? She hoped he didn't expect her to get up every hour just to confirm they were safe. She waited until his taillights disappeared before returning to her chair.

She walked back to the seat at the table. "Why are you watching Lyndsey?"

"I figured I'd use her to get Mason." He stared at his steepled fingers.

BJ bolted up from the chair. "Get out." She pointed to the front door. "How could you accuse me of wanting Mason to move on to another kid when you were —" BJ stopped talking. Her breath backed up. She couldn't even bring herself to say the words.

"I no longer want that." He held his hands up in a surrender motion. "Let me explain." When she didn't move, he added, "Please."

She lowered herself back down. Her glare should have burned a hole through him.

"I knew Bernadette was seeing an older man. But I'd retired and wanted to be her grandfather, not some spy checking up on the girl." He played with the salt shaker on the table. "It wasn't until she disappeared that I found out about Mason."

BJ let loose a stuck breath. Seeing his vulnerability made it hard for her to stay angry. *God, why can't you make life easy?*

"By then it was too late," he continued. "The best I could do was find her and bring her home." He swallowed hard. "Instead..." His bottom lip wobbled. He clamped his jaw tight.

"I'm sorry," BJ said. "This must be hard, especially for a man like you." She fought the urge to take him in her arms to comfort him, but she didn't dare get too close emotionally or physically.

"Hard on her mother, too." Ransom swiped a hand across his cheek.

BJ got up, pulled a glass from the cupboard, and filled it with water. She placed it in front of Ransom. He took a sip then sat staring at the liquid.

"Darcy." He paused and cleared his throat. "My daughter and I don't get along well. Being an absentee father will do that."

"I imagine." BJ prayed her tone wasn't condescending. That would be the last thing he needed right now.

"But no matter how bad a father I've been, I still would have done anything to stop her from going through this."

"I'm sure of it." BJ meant the words. She never considered Ransom being particularly cruel to anyone but her.

"I promised her I'd find out who killed Bernadette. A promise I plan to keep."

"And you will. You were always determined to use any means necessary to get the job done." Her stomach soured thinking about how he'd planned to involve Lyndsey.

"It took me almost a year after the funeral to find Mason. By then, he'd moved up to Jacksonville. Within a month he'd gotten close to Lyndsey." Ransom leaned back in the chair and exhaled a loud breath. "I just hoped if I could follow him once he absconded with her, then I'd find the guy who killed Bernadette."

BJ clasped her hands together to avoid throttling him. "Quite a long shot, wasn't it?" She was surprised any words came through her clenched lips.

"Yeah. But then I realized Lyndsey was a lot like my granddaughter. Young and naïve. Just wanting to belong." He leaned his forehead on the palm of his hands. "And she's related to you. No matter what, I'd never let you go through what I did."

When BJ finally looked him in the eye, her nerves were steadier. "I understand how bad you want to get the guy who killed Bernadette, but I wouldn't allow you to use Lyndsey. No matter the circumstances."

"But what if I want to help?" The teen stood in the entryway to the hallway, her arms crossed over her chest. "Cliff should pay for what he did."

"It's too dangerous." BJ's voice rose.

"But not if all of you are watching out for me." Lyndsey stepped toward them.

"No." Ransom stood. "BJ's right. And I don't know how large this operation is. You could get lost, and we might never be able to find you."

Lyndsey reared back. Her eyes opened wide as if shocked from a slap.

Ransom walked over and placed a hand on her shoulder. "I thank you for wanting to help. But Mason's my problem. Trust me when I say I'll deal with him."

The tone in Ransom's voice sent a chill racing through BJ's body.

THANKFULLY, DAYLIGHT came quick. Ransom hadn't dared sleep with Gold-tooth now in the mix. After staying for an hour inside the house, Ransom had returned to the van. BJ's yawning told him how tired she was, but he knew she wouldn't rest until he left.

A deputy cruised by and slowed at the driveway. He had stopped by every thirty to forty minutes during the night. BJ stood in the window and waved, sending him on his way. She glanced over in Ransom's direction and nodded her head. His teeth clenched together. They shouldn't have this type of worry. Someone needed to put Mason out of commission soon.

He rolled his window down to let in some cool morning air. Everything smelled so fresh and clean. Crickets sounded in the field across the way. Not a cloud rolled in the sky, and so far the humidity level had remained low.

A car's engine broke the quiet. Ransom sat up straighter. A dark blue BMW rolled past him and pulled up in front of BJ's home. Ransom wrote down the tag number in his notebook. A man got out of the driver's side and escorted a girl up to the doorway. They entered when BJ answered.

Ransom's heart ratcheted up a notch. Could this guy be someone BJ was dating? After being so close to her for just those few moments, Ransom's feelings for her had resurfaced. Deep inside, he'd never stopped loving her. She'd always been the one he compared other women to. And none measured up.

Not too long after entering the home, the stranger returned to his car and left. Ransom tossed the notebook onto the passenger's seat. The teen he left behind must be a friend of Lyndsey's. A quick glance of his watch told Ransom it was just after eight. He dialed the number BJ had given him the night before.

"Hello." She sounded alert considering the late night she'd had.

"It's me." He cleared his throat. "Ransom."

"Still playing guard?"

"Yeah. But I need to head out for a little while. I doubt Mason will try anything with a house full of people and the deputies driving by." He put the key in the ignition. "Make sure you keep an eye out."

"We're not going anywhere, and I've got my gun loaded. We've got an art gallery event tonight. The same place Mason showed up the other day. The girls will probably want to get ready early." BJ laughed. "Nothing a female likes better than getting dressed up."

"Does that include you?"

"Sometimes." Her voice sounded light and airy. He imagined she held a smile on her face.

"I'll call you when I return so you can get some down-time." He started the vehicle. "Let me know if anything happens."

Within twenty minutes, he pulled into his parking spot in front of Room 312 at the hotel between Lincolnville and Ringgold, Georgia. Nothing fancy, just two double beds and a television.

Normally he wouldn't have rented a room, but with BJ having the attention of the sheriff, that gave Ransom some back-up. Even if they didn't know it.

He placed his laptop on the nightstand and reclined on the bed. He needed sleep, or he wouldn't be any good to anyone.

His phone alarm woke him two hours later. He got up and turned on the shower. The hot water soothed his sore ribs. Age was getting the best of him. He'd never have let someone sneak up on him in the past. But he'd not let getting older be an excuse to lose.

After drying off, Ransom shaved and put on a clean pair of jeans and a T-shirt. He then walked over to his closet and pulled out the nice suit he kept handy. Hopefully the gallery showing didn't require formal wear.

He hung the suit on a hook in the van, and then crossed the street to a nearby fast-food restaurant for a quick bite. The clock hit eleven forty-three when he finally drove back out onto I-75 before turning onto the main road to BJ's.

In the rearview mirror, the blue Cadillac came out of nowhere and raced up on him. Ransom accelerated, but the vehicle closed in. Gold-tooth flashed a smile from behind the windshield of the car.

The caddy smacked the van's bumper. Ransom lurched forward. The seatbelt tightened across his chest. Gold-tooth got up beside the Chevy then swerved his car over. Ransom pulled the steering wheel to the right to avoid a direct hit. He then jerked the van left into the side of Gold-tooth's car. The Cadillac skidded onto gravel and went a couple feet up a side hill. Dust flew in the air. Ransom pushed the van's pedal to the floor, but Gold-tooth caught up within seconds. The two vehicles rounded a corner side-by-side.

A semi sped sped toward them. The trucker blared his horn. Ransom gripped the steering wheel. Gold-tooth slammed on his brakes. Smoke from burnt rubber blew into the air. The semi-driver locked eyes with Ransom. His heart rate increased. The large truck toppled and skidded onto its side sending the rig into Ransom's lane.

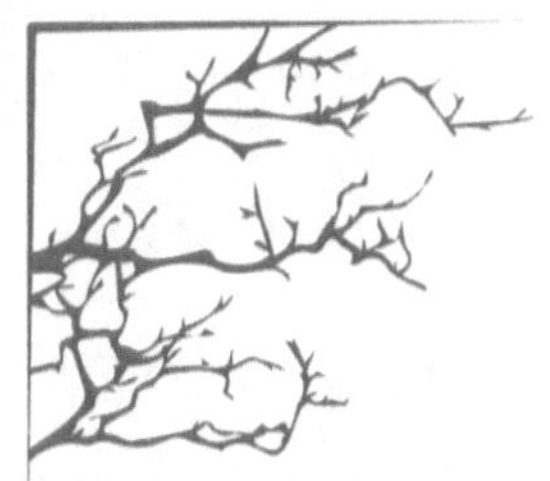

<h1 style="text-align:center">10</h1>

BJ tried to read the paper, but her mind couldn't comprehend the words she skimmed over. All she could think about was Ransom, and the excitement his nearness created. He still got to her without even trying. Watching over them. Protecting them. Who did he think he was? Some kind of superhero? Didn't the man know he was too old to fly?

She glanced through the newspaper until she found an ad for a department store in Chattanooga. Not that she intended to buy anything, but it might help her focus on something other than the warmth of Ransom's hand on hers. That magnetic pull of his eyes. Or that tight shirt he wore across his still muscular chest. Sweat formed on her brow. Obviously, the ads weren't doing their job.

"Ugh." She tossed down the paper.

"What's wrong?" Lyndsey glanced from the computer screen where she and Elaina played a game.

"Nothing good in the paper. That's all." BJ got up and strolled over to them. "Elaina, I never thought to ask, but is there any food you're allergic to? I'd hate to feed you something that makes you blow up like a puffer fish." The closer BJ got to Elaina the more she could smell baby lotion coming from her skin. BJ only recognized it because of Riley, Jr.

"No. I don't have any allergies." Elaina's voice was soft and low.

"Are you just staying with your grandfather for the summer?"

She shrugged.

Lyndsey looked over her shoulder at BJ. "I'm supposed to stay until school, but my mom's been calling me almost every day trying to get me to come home." Lyndsey rolled her eyes. "And I haven't even been gone a week."

"That's 'cause she misses you." BJ shuffled her hand through Lyndsey's hair, messing it up.

"Does your mom call you all the time, too?" Lyndsey asked Elaina.

"Uh-uh." She shook her head. Her eyes focused on the clasped hands on her lap. "My mom doesn't want me around."

"I can't imagine that's true." BJ placed her hand on the back of Elaina's neck. "You're so polite and nice. I know I'd be missing you."

She shrugged again.

BJ's heart ached for the girl. How could parents be so cruel? The woman probably had some guy she'd rather focus on. Too often the case these days. "Well, you're welcome to stay here as long as you'd like."

"Thanks." Tears dotted Elaina's lashes. "Excuse me." She got up and walked to the back. The bathroom door locked behind her.

"Her mom is so mean," Lyndsey said.

"I agree. If I have anything to say about it, she'll be a constant staple around here this summer." BJ kept her focus on the bathroom door. "Have you had a chance to speak with her yet about Mason?"

"No." Lyndsey frowned. "I wonder what she'll say about me once she finds out."

"A person who thinks no one loves her isn't going to believe anything bad about someone else." BJ patted Lyndsey on the shoulder. "If you don't feel up to it, I'll find a way."

"I'll do it." Lyndsey lifted her chin. "After all, I'm the reason Mason came to this town."

RANSOM STARED AT THE van he'd driven into the ditch to avoid a direct hit from the semi. Everyone had fared well in the accident with only a couple bruises and scrapes. The truck carried paper products so damage was minimal.

After a quick check, Ransom realized there wasn't much harm to the Chevy. Hopefully it'd still be in running order once he got it back on the road. He tried to reach BJ, but there were no bars on his phone.

"I can't believe that guy, trying to pass on a curve," the semi-driver said to the deputy at the scene. The trucker appeared to be in his forties, and his belly hung over his belt. His truck lay toppled onto its side, blocking both directions on the two lane road.

Gold-tooth had done a U-turn and disappeared when the semi went over.

Except for checking on any injuries and Ransom's cell phone to ensure he wasn't talking at the time of the accident, the police had yet to speak to Ransom. He paced, trying to get the deputies attention, but it did no good. Ransom needed to go or at least call BJ and warn her.

Finally finished with the truck driver, the deputy strolled over to Ransom. The nametag on his shirt read Green. "I've got a tow truck coming to pull you out." His breath smelled of coffee. "There's a good shop in —"

"I assume you work for Riley Owens?" Ransom interrupted.

"He's the sheriff 'round here."

"My name's Ronald McNeely."

"I know." Green barely looked up from the notes he was taking. "Sheriff's been looking to talk with you. That's him pulling up now." He used his head to point to a cruiser coming up on their left.

"Well I suggest you have him get over to his aunt's house instead. I've been keeping an eye to make sure no one comes after Lyndsey Chapel. And the guy who caused this wreck wanted me out of the way real bad."

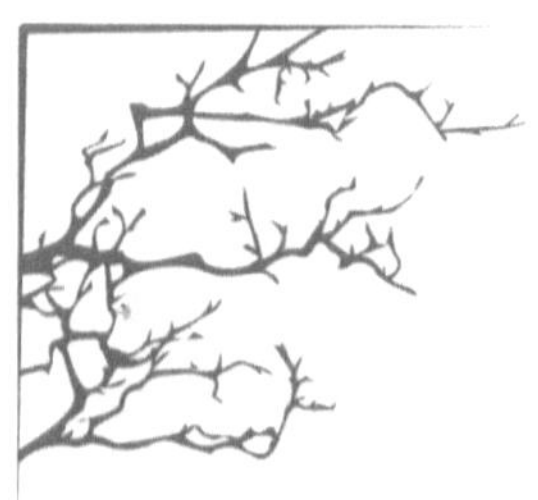

11

BJ stepped back to allow Riley in. After she introduced him to Elaina, the girls went into the back room. BJ fixed her nephew a glass of sweet tea. They leaned against the kitchen counter and looked out over the backyard.

"So what brings you over, other than to visit?" The sugar from the tea filled BJ's taste buds. "You're usually in the office or out writing tickets, looking for a wife." She teased.

"I already got one that way." Even with the humor, he remained serious. "There was an accident on Desmond involving your friend McNeely." He raised his eyebrows. "Someone ran him off the road."

"Is he all right?" BJ's hand went to her throat.

"Yeah. He seems to believe someone wanted him out of the way." Riley gulped half his drink. "I thought I'd come check on you."

"Was it Mason?"

"No. He said it was some guy from Jacksonville he'd had a tussle with. Your spook claimed the other driver works with Mason though."

"He's not my spook," she growled. "But this other man could be the thug who knocked Ransom around last night."

Riley straightened. "What are you talking about?"

"While playing guard across the street, someone came after him." After a second of silence, she added, "Don't you worry about it. I chased him away. I'm not going to let anyone get to Lyndsey long as I've got a gun and a breath in my body."

"You should've called me," he grumbled.

Since Perry's death, Riley had done nothing but want to take care of her. What did he think she was? A weak, foolish female? BJ choked

88

down her agitation. "It was late," she said. "And I didn't want to wake the babe."

"You'd better watch your back or these guys might see to it you breathe your last." Riley reached over and gave her a hug. "And the idea of only being able to tell my son about you doesn't sit well with me. I'd rather he see it firsthand."

"I'll be fine. The girls and I are staying inside, and both the rifle and Beretta are loaded." She patted his clean shaven jaw. Nice to see Calley's had such a good influence on him. "We'll be heading to the gallery later this evening unless Calley needs us sooner."

He released her and finished his tea. "She's got everything ready and is planning on taking it easy until five. Then she'll head up to deal with the appetizers."

"I believe in the art world, they're called hors d'oeuvres." She elbowed him.

"That might be, but I do want you to be careful. I'll continue to have someone ride by every so often to check on you." He turned to leave and then hesitated. "What's your deal with the spook?"

"Just old friends."

"As worried as you were when I told you about the accident, I gather it's more." He grinned and rushed out.

BJ balled her hands into fists at her sides. She could only imagine what others in town would say if they knew Ransom had visited her house in the middle of the night. She sauntered to the large picture window and watched her nephew drive away. The spot where Ransom had parked his van earlier was now empty. He'd taken quite a few good kicks last night. Could he really be all right after a car accident?

There she went again, caring. "Ugh." BJ shook her head. The word was becoming her favorite one for the week.

"What's wrong?" Lyndsey walked in from the hallway.

"Ransom's had an accident." She bit down on her cheek to keep from showing her concern.

"Is he okay?" Lyndsey asked. Amazing how Ransom got females hooked so easily.

"I think so. But I'll call to check." She got the number from her caller I.D. and dialed. After two rings, the cell went to voicemail. Maybe he was hurt. No. Riley wasn't one to sugar coat these things.

She shoved her finger across the screen to turn it off. How could a man she hadn't seen in years cause her such distress?

THE SQUEALING WINCH from the tow truck pulled the van out of the ditch. A bit scraped, and a dent here and there, but not too bad. The accident threw Ransom's suit to the floorboard, but there didn't appear to be any wrinkles. If need be, he could always find a dry cleaner to press it before evening. That was, if he were even allowed into the gallery opening without an invitation.

He stood under the trees on the opposite side of the road to get relief from the sun blaring down. The aroma of diesel from the tow truck had replaced the rubber odor that had lingered after the accident. Burn out marks decorated the road where Gold-tooth had skidded.

The day seemed to drag on between getting the Chevrolet out of the ditch and dealing with his insurance company. Ransom was glad the sheriff had taken his word about the danger BJ and Lyndsey might be in. Though he'd only spent about two minutes with the man, Riley Owens appeared as competent as people said.

After speaking with his claims adjuster, Ransom checked his phone. Thankfully he was finally able to reach BJ.

"I heard what happened," she said. "Are you all right?"

"Yeah. Van's just banged up a bit." He ran a hand over his chin. "Everything quiet with you?"

"They've got patrol cars checking on us every few minutes, or so it feels," BJ said. "Riley even has someone following Mason in case he comes across that Cadillac who went after you."

"Guy's probably on his way back to Jacksonville. Be stupid for him to stick around." Ransom figured if Gold-tooth were still in town, he and Mason would have made a move by now.

"We'll be heading to the gallery in a little bit," BJ said. "The girls are putting on their makeup as we speak. We should be safe with Riley there."

"Can anyone go or is it a private affair?"

"By invitation."

So much for bringing his suit. "No other way in?"

"No."

"Guess Mason won't show. I'll keep an eye from outside."

"Unless you'd like to attend. My ticket says I can bring a guest. Good thing you know someone with connections." She chuckled.

"Sounds good."

"How about I meet you in the parking lot?"

"You got it." Ransom hung up. A smile crossed his lips. While she didn't say it was a date, he planned to make the most of the evening ahead.

BJ'S HEART FLIPPED. What was she thinking? She must be out of her mind. With a trembling hand, she replaced the receiver to the phone on her nightstand.

"Stop that," she scolded. "You're not a school girl."

"What's wrong?" Lyndsey asked.

"Nothing. I just can't figure out what to wear." BJ walked over and scanned the racks in her closet.

Lyndsey and Elaina remained in the doorway of BJ's bedroom. Lyndsey's blue dress with the bubble hem went to mid-thigh, showing off tanned legs. Her white heels added two inches to her height. Elaina wore a black jumper over a thin, long-sleeve red blouse with a pair of flats. One of the girls had on sweet perfume, but BJ couldn't tell which. Probably both since most young girls liked to share.

"Last night you took out the black one," Lyndsey said.

"Thinking of changing my mind." She stared at her closet.

"He's coming, isn't he?" Lyndsey bounded in and plopped down on the bed, a large smile on her face.

Elaina glanced between the two.

"Who's coming?" BJ tried to control the hysteria in her voice.

"You know, Mr. McNeely. The guy you call Ransom."

"Ransom?" Elaina asked.

"Yeah. He's real good looking. He and Aunt BJ knew each other years ago."

BJ rolled her eyes. How ridiculous could she be? It wasn't like she wanted to impress the man. She tugged the black tank dress off the hanger.

"No. You should wear," Lyndsey bolted up and dug through the closet, "This." She handed BJ a red dress with a slimming band around the waist and a slit that went mid-thigh.

"That's a bit fancy, don't you think?" BJ held it against her and stared at herself in the mirror. She caressed the lace fabric with the back of her hand.

"It's perfect." Lyndsey put a finger against her cheek. "And Elaina will do your makeup. She's real good at it." She waved with her hand for Elaina to come in.

"If you'd like," Elaina spoke in a soft voice.

The apprehensive look on Elaina's face told BJ if she turned her down, it might crush her. "Like?" She pulled Elaina into a one armed hug. "Darling, I need all the help I can get."

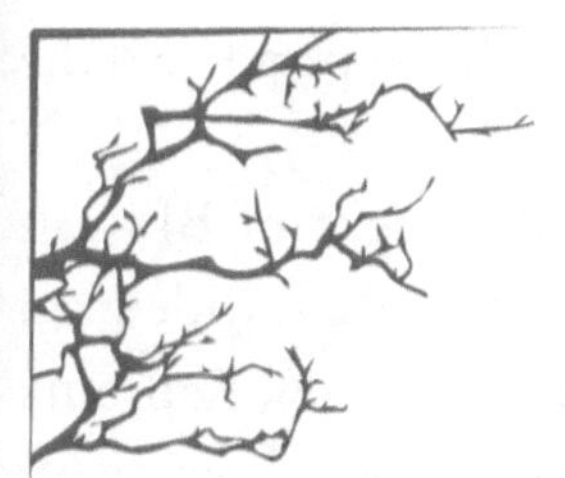

12

Ransom's pulse raced at the idea of seeing BJ again. Her tone earlier on the phone told him the anger toward him for going after her boss years ago had disappeared. After twenty-some years, he sure hoped so. Even though, at the time, he'd put her in a bad predicament. Thankfully those days were over.

He arrived at the gallery at five minutes to seven. People gathered out front waiting to get inside. All the men were dressed in suits and ties so Ransom fit right in. The sun sunk into the horizon, casting an orange glow in the sky. With no clouds in sight, it looked like it'd be a nice evening.

Within two minutes, BJ pulled up in the space behind him. Ransom waited until she removed the key from the ignition before he stepped from the van.

Lyndsey opened her car door and trotted over to him. Her blond hair hung in ringlets at her shoulders.

"Hello, Mr. McNeely. I understand you'll be watching over me tonight." Her smile said she didn't mind. "This is my friend, Elaina." She pointed to the girl behind her.

"Please call me Ransom." He shook Elaina's hand. The girl was beautiful with straight golden hair that swept past her shoulders. It surprised him there weren't several teenage boys tagging along.

"Ransom? That's a funny nickname." Lyndsey asked.

"One day maybe I'll explain to you where it came from."

He fixed his gaze on the vehicle where BJ fidgeted with her hair in the rearview mirror. After what felt like minutes, she finally looked at the three people waiting for her.

93

"Come on, Aunt BJ." Lyndsey hurried back to the Jeep and held the door open for her.

Beneath the driver's side door Ransom caught sight of BJ's calf muscles that led to a thin ankle into a pair of black sandals. A wide strap went over the top of BJ's foot. When she came into full view, Ransom's breath left him. BJ's dark red dress tightened at her waist, showing off a very nice figure. A comb held her hair up on one side. Her perfume floated over him. Sophisticated yet extremely feminine with a hint of gardenia and cedarwood. He cocked his elbow for her to take, and she accepted.

She glanced at the Chevrolet. "Your ride looks a little beat up for sure."

"As long as it runs." He worked to hold back a smile, but a grin came through anyway. He felt good, having her on his arm again. If things went well tonight, maybe he could find a way to get back into her good graces.

BJ COULDN'T BELIEVE all the patrons attending the official grand opening. And the food. Champagne, stuffed mushrooms, and shrimp were laid out on a long buffet and white roses decorated the small serving tables. BJ would almost bet nothing this fancy had ever occurred in Lincolnville. Riley had silenced the bell on the front door so it wouldn't go off every time a guest entered. A woman in the back oohed and aahed at almost every display.

And the way Sheryl fluttered from patron to patron, working the crowd helped even more. While the citizens in Lincolnville already knew her, those from out of town, as far away as Atlanta, were truly impressed with the artist.

Sheryl rushed over to welcome BJ and the others. "Well, well, well. What have we here? BJ didn't take any time getting hold of you." She flicked her fingers over Ransom's bicep.

Great. BJ shook her head. Tomorrow the phone would probably ring off the hook from friends wanting to gossip. "He's a former colleague who just happened to be in town," BJ said.

"Well, from the way the other single women in the room are looking at him," Sheryl spoke with a glance over her shoulder, "I suggest you hold on tight."

What did BJ care if others wanted Ransom? It wasn't like he was hers. She caught a blue-haired lady giving Ransom a smile. BJ scooted closer and tightened her grip on his arm.

Within minutes, Lyndsey and Elaina wandered off. BJ was sure they'd be all right as long as they stayed inside the gallery.

Pastor Matthew Winters and his wife, Lydia, entered seconds later, followed by Allison Regan, Calley's sister. Once BJ introduced them to Ransom, Sheryl escorted them around the three rooms of displays. She had by far the largest exhibit, with two artists from Chattanooga taking up space in the smaller rooms. She introduced the group to the other painters who appeared more stoic than excited about being there. One held his nose so high BJ thought he might drown if a rainstorm came through.

Once back at the front area, BJ went to the buffet table and filled a dish with caviar, blueberries, and strawberries stuffed with cream cheese.

"I'm so glad to see the place full," Allison said to Sheryl. "I was worried with it being so far away from Atlanta."

"Art lovers will drive for hours for an event," Sheryl said. "They like to think they're in the know."

"Thankfully the evening wasn't ruined by Mom." Allison frowned. "She couldn't wait to tell my uncle about the official opening. Hopefully he won't put in a surprise appearance."

"Without a ticket, he can't get in." Matthew placed his hand on Lydia's back. His broad shoulders and massive chest stretched the fabric in his suit jacket.

His wife's protruding belly did the same to the silk fabric of the purple dress she wore. "I can't believe how wonderful everything looks. I don't know who I'm more proud of, Calley or Sheryl."

"Calley did do a magnificent job." Matthew added. He kissed Sheryl on the side of the head. "So how's my child's future godmother doing?"

"Couldn't be better," Sheryl sang. "You know how much I love all this attention." She spun but stopped mid-turn. "There goes the party." She placed her hands on her hips and scowled at James and Melanie strolling in.

"Cut that out." Lydia smacked her friend's shoulder. "You know he enjoys the limelight as much as you do."

"Yeah, but I hate to share." Sheryl gave them a large toothy grin before strolling over to the couple.

"So how are you holding up?" BJ leaned over to Lydia.

"Glad I work from home." Lydia kept her attention focused on Melanie when she walked into the room, her shoulders slumped. "She's not doing too well this year. Jimmy's dying has been rough on her." Tears entered Lydia's eyes. "Such a shame. Melanie used to be a social butterfly. Now she hardly goes out." Lydia spoke in a soft voice.

While talking with Lydia about the upcoming birth of her daughter, Ransom made small-talk with Matthew about Lincolnville. BJ noticed that Melanie did a quick tour of the rooms before taking a seat on a bench in the corner. Her eyes wondered but she didn't really seem to be looking at anything.

Sadness filled BJ at the pain Melanie must be enduring.

"Excuse me." Lydia rubbed her pregnant stomach. "Carrying around this ball makes me tired. I think I'll sit for a moment." She shuffled over and lowered herself next to Melanie.

"She's a good one." BJ told Matthew.

"Yes she is. She'll make a wonderful mother, too."

"You *both* will be good parents."

"Pictures?" Rayleen Davenport, the photographer for the evening lifted her camera.

BJ felt small standing between Ransom and Matthew. When Rayleen clicked the button, the flash momentarily blinded.

"I believe I'll go check on my wife." Matthew headed to the corner where Lydia and Melanie sat.

"Why do I get the feeling he'll also be giving some comfort to Melanie as well?" BJ said.

"Why's that?" Ransom asked.

"Matthew's the minister of the local church. And this is Rayleen. She's married to a friend who works for the DEA."

Ransom's Adam's apple bounced. "Nice to meet you."

His words were kind, but the look of apprehension said he was anything but happy to meet someone associated with the DEA. BJ smiled. Probably has to do with competition between the government entities.

"Rayleen, how is Ty these days?" BJ asked. "I haven't seen him here tonight."

A dark shadow cast over her features. "Ty and I are separated." She flinched. "It's hard to work on a marriage when you're never together." There was a catch in her throat.

"I'm sorry to hear that. You're both such good people."

Clapping and cheering came from the room holding Sheryl's exhibit.

"Must be a sale. Guess I'd better get to work." Rayleen waved the camera in her hand. "See you soon."

BJ hated the ache in the woman's eyes. Rayleen was still obviously in love with Ty. BJ and Perry had had their problems, but they were at least able to work through them. *God, if there's a way, please help them find it.*

She and Ransom circled the gallery again then lingered into the main area where the snack tables were. BJ grabbed a champagne flute glass holding water. The door opened, and a rush of warm air drifted in. Bernard Ainsworth walked in, wearing a black suit, crisp white shirt, and black tie. Over his arm hung the sweater Elaina had worn at the diner the day before. He looked good for a man who'd spent the day at a meeting.

"BJ." He kissed her cheek, and then held his hand out to Ransom. "Bernard Ainsworth."

"This is Elaina's grandfather," BJ added.

"Ronald McNeely." While shaking Bernard's hand, Ransom placed his other on BJ's back.

"How did Elaina behave?" Bernard glanced around. "No trouble, I hope."

"She's such an angel." BJ sipped her water.

"I'll assure you she has her moments when her horns come out."

Bernard let loose a chuckle under his breath sending chills over BJ's shoulders. She couldn't quite put her finger on it, but something about his words set her on edge.

Ransom appeared to feel the same way. His jaw tightened the moment Bernard arrived.

"I brought Elaina's jumper in case she felt a chill. I never know how cold these places might be." He stared at a painting of an elk over the dessert table. "What do you think of the exhibit so far?"

BJ smiled at how proud she was of Calley. "It's very —"

"What is he doing here?" James Newman yelled. His thin finger pointed to the large plate-glass window.

All the patrons went quiet. Everyone stared at Cliff Mason, who strutted from his Mercedes toward the gallery.

RANSOM'S MUSCLES TIGHTENED the second Ainsworth touched BJ. The man was pretentious with his gray mustache sitting on top of his tiny lips. He needed a shave in Ransom's opinion. His perfectly tailored suit only made Ransom dislike Bernard more. And using the English term jumper. With what little accent the guy had, little doubt he'd been here long enough to know Americans called it a sweater.

And it hadn't gone past Ransom that BJ's posture straightened when Bernard arrived. She seemed to be enjoying every second of the attention he was giving her.

However, James's announcement about Mason in the parking lot changed BJ's demeanor from one of contentment to anxiousness in a matter of seconds. Ransom kept his focus on Mason as he strolled up to the door like a peacock in full plume. Riley Owens met him at the entrance.

Lyndsey snuck up beside BJ who took hold of the teen's hand. Elaina stared anxiously at her grandfather whose jaw appeared locked.

"May I see your invitation?" Riley asked Mason.

"I'm sorry. I wasn't aware I needed one." He stared at Lyndsey. "You really don't want to make a scene, do you?"

"He might not, but I sure will." James marched up to the doorway. He put his hand on Mason's chest and drove him from the doorway to the stoop. "The last thing we need is a drug dealer among us decent folks. Now get."

Mason shoved James's hand away. James again pushed Mason back a couple more feet. Riley stepped between the two before it got too physical.

BJ shot Ransom a worried glance.

"Excuse me." After depositing his glass of soda on a nearby table, Ransom walked outside. When Mason caught Ransom's eye, he glared. Ransom glanced at the parking lot and up then down the street. No sign of Gold-tooth.

"Get out of here," James hollered. "And get out of this town."

Melanie rushed out to her husband's side. "James, stop."

"Yeah, James." Mason stepped forward. "Stop." His eyes narrowed to slits. "I'd hate for anything to happen to you."

"Are you threatening me?" James's hands balled into fists at his side.

"You need to leave," Riley said to Mason. "If not, I'll arrest you for trespassing."

"We all know how well that'll work." Mason grinned. "I'll be out in an hour, just like before."

A stern look held on Riley's face. "Except I'm so busy, I might not get to the paperwork tonight."

Ransom liked this sheriff. Little doubt he'd keep Mason in a holding cell until morning. DEA informant or not.

"I'm going. But you'd better watch it, James." Mason's voice remained controlled. "You've got a real pretty wife here. Wouldn't take much for a man like me to take her away from you." He leaned close to Melanie. "Give her what she's been missing all these years." He placed his hand over his crotch.

Slap.

Everyone stood in stunned silence. Melanie had given the guy a good shot across the cheek. Mason rubbed the side of his jaw and stomped back to his car. He paused, turned, and rested a glare on the Newmans that should have left a mark redder than the handprint on Mason's cheek. James wrapped a protective arm around his trembling wife.

The ding from Mason's open car door made the only sound in the night. "You'll pay for that, lady. Trust me."

"I think maybe a night in jail would do you good." Riley stepped forward.

"Then I suggest you arrest your lady friend for the slap." Mason sneered. "Last time I looked, assault was against the law."

Mason had the upper hand in this situation. Riley would have no choice but to take Melanie in also. Ransom marched to Mason's open car door and leaned toward the man. "This town's off limits and so is anyone in it." Ransom lowered his voice so only Mason could hear. "Trust me when I say I know how to bury a body where it's never found."

The two glared at each other for a few seconds before Mason dropped down in the car seat and skidded out of the lot.

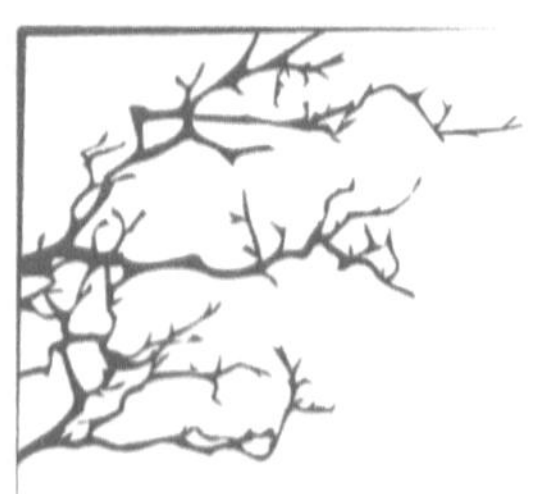

13

BJ had yet to take her eyes off Lyndsey who continually glanced out the front window of the gallery. Mason had her scared. The girl's trembling fingers told BJ that much. But between Ransom and Riley hovering over her, if Mason was watching, he'd have to be aware they had Lyndsey well-guarded.

"I'm not sure Lincolnville is the type of place for me," Bernard said. "Seems everywhere I go there's crime. Might have to head back to England."

Elaina's face paled. Lyndsey grabbed her friend's hand.

"You can't get away from crime, even in your merry old England." Ransom's tone sounded a touch snide. He swigged the remainder of his soda.

BJ enjoyed the two men's attention. It'd been a while since any man other than her husband gave her much notice. "Lincolnville is probably one of the safest towns in the United States," BJ said. "We just have junk that flows in every once in a while."

"It concerns me when it comes to Elaina." The Englishman touched his granddaughter's cheek.

"She'll be fine." Lyndsey swung her arm over Elaina's shoulder. "I'll see to it."

Ransom laughed. "And who's gonna protect you?"

"You will." She batted her eyelashes. The levity released some of the tension from her face she'd exhibited moments earlier.

"Excuse us." Matthew strolled up beside them. "We wanted to say good-night. I need to get this wife of mine home to bed. She's dead on her feet."

Lydia slouched against him. "Yes, she is."

"I'll see you in church?" He kissed BJ on the cheek.

"Of course. Would you like to join us, Bernard?"

"I've got another meeting tomorrow." He looked over at Elaina. "Maybe I'll drop her off on my way if she'd like. Then she can walk home."

"Or stay with us for lunch," BJ said.

"She could even spend the night." Lyndsey raised her eyebrows in hopeful anticipation. "Then you don't have to worry about her?"

"Unfortunately tonight's not good. She's got some chores to do. Maybe next time." He finished his wine in one gulp. "In fact, we need to be going ourselves." Bernard gave BJ a kiss on the cheek. His lips were wet from his drink. "We'll see you soon."

Elaina clung to Lyndsey's arm.

"Come along, Elaina." Bernard's stern voice surprised BJ.

"See ya." Elaina gave a slight wave of her hand.

"Bye." Lyndsey kept watch on Elaina until she disappeared.

Ransom leaned over to BJ. "I noticed you didn't invite me to church," he whispered.

"I figured if you were watching Lyndsey, you'd be there." BJ enjoyed watching Ransom squirm when Bernard was nearby. Elation sat in her stomach, even after Mason's rude appearance.

They milled about for another half hour before Ransom escorted BJ and Lyndsey to the Jeep. He held the door open for BJ. When she climbed into the seat, the slit in her dress opened. Ransom gazed at her toned legs. She let loose a cough to draw his attention back up.

"See you tomorrow." He slid his finger down the side of her face.

"See you." Her voice choked.

He chuckled and walked away.

How could she let him get to her like that? Touching her gently. Creating feelings she continually fought. "Ugh." He made her so angry she could chomp through nails.

"What's wrong?" Lyndsey asked.

"Nothing. Just tired."

"Oh. I thought maybe you were thinking about Elaina." Lyndsey's voice lowered. "I'm worried about her."

"You mean with Mason out there?"

"Not really." Lyndsey stared out the passenger side window. "She's just very emotional. When I told her about Cliff, she said people hurt each other too much in this world."

"Unfortunately that's true. And from what Elaina said about her mother, she knows better than most."

"She told me she ended up with her grandfather because her mom didn't care about her, and she never knew her dad." Lyndsey slapped her lap with her palms. "How could her mother hate her?"

"Beats me." BJ inhaled deep. "Elaina seems to be a nice girl."

"I don't think she eats right." Lyndsey's voice came out like a whisper in the wind.

"What do you mean?" BJ asked.

"Did you see how thin she is? I think she's... What's that word? Anorexic?"

BJ pondered the thought. Granted Elaina had the look of a frail fairy with her thin arms and legs, but she didn't appear malnourished or gaunt.

"Maybe I'm being dumb," Lyndsey continued. "But her hands are shaky all the time. Something's definitely wrong with her."

"Maybe we need to keep an eye on her and put her in our prayers." BJ took Lyndsey's hand from over the console. BJ made a decision to keep a watch on the girl the next time she came close. If Elaina was sick, BJ would have to find a way to help the girl through it. *Please, God, if she is ill, don't let it be anything serious.*

THE NEXT MORNING, RANSOM sat in his van in the Lincolnville Church parking lot. His mind blurred with fatigue after spending another night in the van. But something nagged at him about Mason. Why'd he try to get in that event the evening before? He had to know Riley wouldn't allow it. Ransom pulled out his notebook and wrote three reasons off the top of his head:

Mason had a drug deal going on inside;

He was staking out the place to find a way to get to Lyndsey;

He was letting Lyndsey know he had no intention of going away.

Could be one, all three, or a number of other things Ransom had yet to consider. And Mason wouldn't likely have a chat with Ransom to let him know his plans. A bead of sweat tickled his spine. He let out a heavy sigh. How much more he'd rather be spending time with BJ then dealing with this. While last night had been fun, he wouldn't let Darcy down. Not again.

People wandered past Ransom's vehicle. Many wore jeans, which made him feel more comfortable. The only suit he had he'd worn to the gallery. Today he'd put on a pair of tan slacks and a black polo shirt.

He regarded the building before him. Vast white pillars stood at attention to greet guests as they climbed the stairs to the entryway. It had been a while since he'd gone to a service, especially in an old-fashioned building like this, complete with bell tower. He wasn't sure about going inside. God hadn't been there for Bernadette, why should Ransom be there for Him?

Bernard's BMW pulled up to the side of the road just past the entrance leading to the parking spaces. His eyes were wild and his hands animated. Elaina shrunk down in the seat. After a moment, she got out and meandered through the lot, glancing back to the street where her grandfather had taken off. Elaina hesitated at the bottom of the steps leading to the entrance and looked around. She chewed on a fingernail, turned, and stared at the church, then looked back to the road. If Ransom didn't know any better, he'd say the girl was about to bolt.

Elaina jumped when Lyndsey rushed out of the church and ran to greet her. Elaina painted a smile on, but it failed to soften her expression. What was the teenager up to? Meeting a boyfriend her grandfather disapproved of? Not surprising. There had to be a boy out there interested in such a lovely young lady. Ransom couldn't imagine much had changed with regard to a boy's interests since his days as a kid.

Once both girls were inside, Ransom forced himself out of the car and followed a young couple with a baby. When he entered the sanctuary, he glanced around. BJ sat in a pew in the center aisle. Next to her were Lyndsey and Elaina, heads together, whispering to one another. Lyndsey appeared to be doing most of the talking. Ransom chose to stay in the back row off to the right. The entire room had an understated elegance with large chandeliers dangling from wrought iron chains and a large wooden cross over the chancel.

He spotted Sheryl in the front row with some of the other women he'd met the night before. James and his wife were in the next aisle over. Melanie seemed to have aged considerably overnight. Her pale face glanced around the room as she ran a trembling hand through her hair.

Ransom returned his gaze to where BJ sat. When he caught Lyndsey's eye, he gave a head nod. She nudged her great-aunt with her shoulder. BJ glimpsed his way but gave no reaction. How much he'd rather be next to her than in the back. To ease some of his disappointment, he convinced himself that being in the last row was the best place in case Mason showed up.

The upbeat praise and worship music surprised Ransom. From the historic look of the building, he'd expected more of a gospel service complete with a choir. Instead there were electric guitars and two drum sets. After the singing, James went to the stage to give the announcements and accept the offering. Finally, Matthew Winters came to the podium. He spoke on Bible verse Psalm 22:1-2, *My God, my God, why have you forsaken me? Why are you so far from saving me, so far from my cries of anguish? My God, I cry out by day, but you do not answer, by night, but I find no rest.*

He preached that man's will was not always God's. Ransom swore Matthew was speaking right to him. A lump formed in Ransom's throat and lodged there the entire sermon. His vision blurred on more than once, thinking about how much he blamed God for Bernadette's death.

The service ended with prayer about God's love and grace to forgive anything. Ransom needed that prayer some days more than others. He waited until BJ passed before stepping from his aisle. She wore the same perfume as the night before. He inhaled deep to take it in.

"Good service." He meant it.

Ransom trailed after BJ who continually glanced around, concern on her face. Once at their vehicle, he took her by the elbow and led her a couple feet from the Jeep. The two girls leaned against the side panel, murmuring to each other.

"What's the matter?" Ransom asked.

"Calley said Riley received a call early this morning. Usually means something bad's happened." Her lips tightened. "I just hope it's nothing too serious."

"I haven't seen Mason either this morning," Ransom said. "Little doubt he's around though, watching. If we get lucky, maybe Riley actually did lock him up and throw away the key."

Sheryl caught his eye. She grinned big and gave him a wave of her fingers. While she came on too strong for his tastes, probably for most men, Sheryl did seem like a nice lady.

He returned his attention to BJ. "I'll follow you home to make sure everything's all right."

She nodded. "I guess since you're keeping an eye on us, I can offer to feed ya." She beeped her key fob.

"I appreciate that." He held the door open for her.

"Funny," BJ said. "I half expected Mason to show up in church this morning. Not that it wouldn't do him some good."

Before Ransom could respond, BJ shot a worried glance behind him. He turned. James Newman guided his frail wife to their car.

"I'll be right back." BJ walked over to Melanie and James. She said a few words then pulled Melanie into a hug.

"Her friend doesn't look too good," Ransom spoke more to himself than anyone in particular.

"Her son was murdered a couple years ago about the same time some guy stalked Lydia," Lyndsey said. "Today would have been his birthday."

"How do you know so much about the goings on in this small town?"

"I hear people talk." She shrugged her left shoulder.

BJ had enough to worry about without a friend being in need also. But then BJ was the type to care for others. She'd been adamant years ago that her boss couldn't be the person selling secrets in their unit. It almost killed her when the truth came out. Yet, she helped support the man's wife through the entire trial and court martial.

BJ started back toward them, giving a quick glance to the car Melanie left in.

Lyndsey raised her hand to block the sun from her eyes. "Do you really think God forgives all our sins?"

BJ leaned on the Jeep staring at Ransom as if anticipating his response.

"I sure do," he replied. "He's a loving God who wants us to learn from our mistakes."

"Some sins shouldn't be forgiven." Elaina shuffled a pebble between her feet.

"But if someone wants to change bad enough, don't you think God should forgive them?" BJ wrapped an arm around the girl. "All of us sin, and God doesn't see a difference between a liar and a murderer."

"I can't believe it's that easy." Elaina stared toward the street.

BJ took the girl by the shoulders and forced Elaina to look at her. "That's because forgiveness is hard for us to dole out, so we assume it's just as hard for God to give. Like Matthew said, even if it's Him you're mad at, He understands you need someone to blame and sometimes He's your easiest target." She paused. "Do you understand?"

Elaina nodded.

Ransom took a step back. It was almost like BJ had been reading his mind. He turned away and inhaled some fresh air to get his bearings. But how could he forgive a God who took his lovely Bernadette?

Before getting in the Jeep, the sheriff's cruiser pulled into the parking lot. Riley stopped behind BJ's vehicle and got out.

His face held a grim look. "Mr. McNeely, I need to ask you to accompany me to the station."

"Why's that?" Ransom asked.

"I have some questions to ask you." Riley stepped closer and lowered his voice. "I'd appreciate you doing it voluntarily."

"Riley, what's going on?" BJ asked.

Her nephew let out a weighted breath. "A body was found in Saunders Woods this morning."

"Oh my word." BJ's hand went to her mouth. "But what's that got to do with Ransom?"

Lyndsey and Elaina's eyes widened more with intrigue than concern.

Riley looked at the ground, then at Ransom. "It was Cliff Mason."

14

BJ couldn't take her eyes off the cruiser pulling out of the lot with Ransom in the front seat. Every nerve in her body quivered. Could he have killed Mason?

"What's going on?" Sheryl rushed up.

"Cliff Mason's been murdered." BJ shook her head to refocus her attention. Ransom needed help. "Excuse me, I need to take Elaina home."

BJ hopped into the Jeep followed by the two girls. She ignored all the church-goers' stares as she sped out of the parking lot.

"Aunt BJ, are we going to help Ransom?" Lyndsey asked.

"We sure are." She glanced over at her great-niece and then at Elaina in the rearview mirror. "But I assume your grandfather wouldn't care much for you being involved."

"It's okay." Elaina gave a shrug. She stared out the window, a frown on her face.

"No, I think I'd better take you home."

Elaina wiped at her eye. Was she upset by the murder or the fact they were taking her home?

Within ten minutes, BJ came up on the houses by the lake. One more beautiful than the next. Each had a boat ramp, most with a large vessel floating on the water.

"Which one are you staying in?" BJ asked.

"The gray one." Elaina pointed to the end of the road.

The large home had a wraparound balcony on the second floor. It also had its own private beach. A blue bicycle leaned against the side of the house and two jet skis rested on the water. BJ had never thought to

110

ask Bernard what he did for a living. Whatever it was, he'd done well. She drove down the driveway and pulled in behind the blue BMW. BJ was sure he'd said he had a meeting so he couldn't attend church. Doesn't matter what excuses were used, God will have you found out.

"Something must have happened to keep Grandpa from his meeting." Elaina responded as if reading BJ's mind.

"Well, don't you worry about it." She reached over and patted Elaina's knee. "And even if your grandfather doesn't want to go to church, if you do, just let me know." She gave the girl a wink. "I'll come get you any time you like."

"Thanks." The fresh smell of the lake spilled into the vehicle when Elaina opened the door. She trudged up the front porch steps, hesitating with her hand on the doorknob. She gave a quick wave before disappearing inside.

"It's strange, but she seems to not want to go home," Lyndsey said.

"Maybe she hates to leave you, her friend." BJ had other concerns at that moment. She didn't have time to think about a young girl's strange moods. She put the Jeep in reverse and sped toward the sheriff's station. Her thumb beat out a drum solo against the steering wheel. What had Ransom gotten himself into?

"Do you believe he did it?" Lyndsey stared out the passenger window.

"What? Who?"

"Ransom. Do you think he killed Cliff?" Lyndsey's voice faded. Her bottom lip trembled and a tear slid down her cheek.

BJ slowed and pulled the vehicle to the side of the road. "I don't know." She took Lyndsey's hand in hers. "I'm sorry. This can't be easy for you. I know how you felt about Mason."

"I'm all right." The girl raised her chin in defiance of her tears.

"At one point, you cared deeply for him. I'm sure something inside hoped we'd all be wrong about him. And that's okay."

"Is it?" Her voice diminished to a murmur.

"Of course. You can't turn your feelings off just because people ask you to. Or you know you should."

"But what he does ... did to Ransom's granddaughter."

"Nothing's ever been proven, which made it even easier for you to hope."

"No matter what, we both know he was a drug dealer. So that makes him no good. Made him..." Lyndsey let out a loud breath and shoved her hands through her hair. "I wish I could stop thinking about him."

"You will. In time." BJ leaned over and kissed Lyndsey on the side of the head. "I guess we'd better get over there to help Ransom before Riley's beaten a confession out of him." She maneuvered the Jeep back onto the road.

Lyndsey let loose a laugh. "Uncle Riley wouldn't do that."

"Not usually. But Ransom can wear on a person's nerves."

"Aunt BJ, why is he called Ransom?"

"I really don't know. Ransom was his name when he worked for the CIA. He never really told me where it came from. Maybe he's so good at getting hold of a woman's heart he keeps it for ransom until they do whatever he wants." BJ stared out the windshield.

"Is that what's happened to you?"

"What?"

"He's got hold of your heart?"

"Not yet." BJ kept focused on the street in front of her. She'd help the man, but then keep her distance. The last couple of days she'd been playing with fire. Within this short period of time, Ransom had been able to get hold of her head. All she could think about were his fingers in her cheek and how nice he looked this morning at church. The attraction she felt for him unnerved her.

If she didn't stop, it was only a matter of time until Ransom had her heart as well.

THE A/C INSIDE THE building wasn't cool like most places during the summer. Sweat gathered under Ransom's armpits. Every once in a while he'd hear a loud buzzing noise. He had enough familiarity with the sound to know it was jail cells opening and closing.

Ransom perused the small station. Other than the restrooms, from where he sat, he could see two offices behind glass windows and a set of doors leading to rooms in the back. One office was empty. In the other Riley stood speaking with a man who appeared to be in his mid-fifties. The sheriff's face was red, and he pointed his finger at the stranger's nose.

Ransom sat in the main space where several deputies clicked away on the keyboards of their laptop computers. The only female, with a nametag that said Sylvi, answered the phone when it rang. After a few moments, Riley's door opened, and both men walked out. Ransom stood.

"Family's important to me. Just let Calley know that." The man's mumbled voice held a slight Southern accent.

Riley ignored the man's words. "Mr. McNeely. This way." He pointed for Ransom to go to his office.

The stranger bumped Ransom on his way out, not bothering to apologize. His frame didn't have the build for such a large suit jacket. From Ransom's experience, guys who wore larger clothing were either trying to appear bigger or were hiding something underneath.

Riley scowled at the guy leaving. When BJ and Lyndsey rushed in, BJ paused and gave the departing figure a scorching glare before rushing to her nephew.

"Wasn't that Joe Mercer?" she asked.

"Yeah." Riley nodded. Ransom imagined it had to be tough for Riley to speak through those clenched teeth.

"What's he doing here?" Concern layered BJ's expression.

Ransom made a mental note to check this Mercer out. Always wise to know all the players.

"I'll talk to you about it later." Riley pointed to a chair. "Mr. McNeely, have a seat."

BJ remained standing with one foot inside the office, a stern look on her face.

"You need to wait outside," Riley told his aunt.

"I'd like to know how this Mason fellow was killed." She blocked her nephew from closing his door.

"His body was found in the woods on Crossroad Forest Road. According to the M.E., he'd been stabbed," Riley said. "Now if you don't mind, I have an interview to do." He walked to the other side of his desk. "Alone."

BJ shot her nephew the same look she'd given Ransom when he mentioned using Lyndsey to get Mason. It would have been enough to send warning bells off in any man, but the sheriff seemed unfazed.

Lyndsey wrung her hands as she stood on the outside of the door. Her stare directed on Ransom. On her face, she wore a frown. Mascara stains smudged beneath her lower lashes, and she appeared close to bursting into tears. Could her concern be for him or Mason, some guy she honestly thought she loved?

"By the way, Lyndsey, where were you this morning around five?" Riley asked.

"In bed." She stared up at her aunt.

"Of course she was in bed." BJ placed her hands on her hips. "You don't for one second believe she'd be out traipsing around this town looking for trouble, do you?"

"I needed to ask." Riley held up his hands.

"And do you need to ask me where I was?" The look in BJ's eye said if he did, she'd jump over and smack him.

Riley lowered himself into his chair. Ransom remained silent while these two verbally sparred. From the exasperated look the sheriff gave her, this wasn't the first time BJ had intervened in one of his cases.

"BJ, it's going to be a long day." Riley's voice came out heavy and tired. "I'd like to see my family sometime during it. Would you mind closing the door behind you?"

Her nostrils flared. She leaned over Riley's desk. "Well before you start, ask yourself something. If Mason was only stabbed, would Ransom have done it? After all, it'd get him no closer to finding the killer of his granddaughter." She placed her hand on Ransom's shoulder "So unless Mason was beaten to death, I'd almost guarantee Ransom didn't do it." Her chin jutted out.

While the hand on his arm comforted, along with BJ's vote of confidence, Ransom wasn't sure she'd made a good argument for his innocence. And her pointing out he was now at a dead end on Bernadette's case didn't make him feel any better.

"Are you finished defending his honor?" Riley said. When BJ remained still, he added, "I'm trying to keep this informal, but I can always move to an interrogation room in the back."

She huffed, swung her purse strap over her shoulder, and stormed out. The windows vibrated from the force of her slam.

Riley shook his head then looked Ransom in the eye. "Before you get involved with my aunt, ask yourself one question Mr. McNeely, are you strong enough to do it?" He glanced through the glass at the woman glaring at him from the other side. "Otherwise you'll be in for a long ride."

Ransom nodded. "Something to consider."

"Anyway, like I said, Mason was stabbed. According to the coroner, it looks like death occurred between the hours of three and six this morning. I need to know your whereabouts."

"Parked in a van outside BJ's house. And no, I have no one who can corroborate. Not even the officer who drove by at four fifty-two this morning."

"The fact you know that helps." Riley shrugged. "Of course, you could have killed Mason before or after. And you had a strong motive for wanting him dead."

"I had a greater reason for wanting him alive. Dead he can't answer my questions."

The phone on the desk rang.

"Excuse me," Riley said, picking it up. "Yeah."

Through the back window, Ransom watched two squirrels in a large oak tree.

"Get the Newmans in here," Riley's voice had a touch of anger to it. He hung up the phone and directed his attention to BJ who paced in the outer office. Riley ran a hand over his chin. A triangle formed between his eyes, causing the hairs on the back of Ransom's neck to jump to attention.

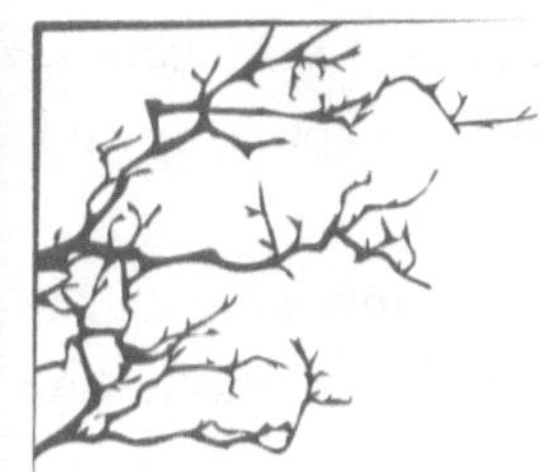

15

BJ stormed back and forth, glancing into Riley's office every few seconds. She glimpsed her watch again. Nineteen minutes. It shouldn't be taking so long to discuss Ransom's whereabouts. The glance Riley gave BJ after receiving a phone call sent a shiver over her back. Could there be proof Ransom killed Mason?

"Ugh," she murmured. If she didn't stop this, she'd start caring for him all over again.

James Newman rushed through the front door taking BJ's mind off Ransom for a moment. "What is this about?" he grumbled. "Calling me down to the police station on a Sunday."

"Cliff Mason's been killed," BJ said.

"Who's Cliff Mason, and what's that got to do with me?"

"He was the guy selling drugs in the park." BJ then whispered, "the one you argued with last night."

Riley and Ransom walked from the office.

"I need to talk to you for a minute." Riley took hold of BJ's elbow.

His low tone formed goose pimples on her arms. He led her to his office, closing the door behind them. Unsure if she really wanted to have this discussion, BJ remained standing in case she needed to make a quick escape.

"What's the matter?" she asked. "You're pale as the siding on my house."

"Mason was killed with a knitting needle. According to the store, it's one of Melanie Newman's."

"You can't believe she did it." BJ leaned on the desk with the palm of her left hand. "Everyone knows she's always losing those things."

117

"Two sets of prints were found. We're assuming one is Melanie's." He rested a hip on the desk. After a jump in his Adam's apple, he said, "How did your fingerprints come to be the other?"

His words hit her like ice water to the face. Her prints were on the murder weapon? No wonder Riley appeared sick to his stomach. She racked her brain trying to recall, and then it finally hit her. "I picked one up at Fred's the other night when I was taking over the booth the Newman's had just been in. You can ask James."

Riley's expression softened, and he released a relieved breath.

BJ placed a hand on her hip. "You couldn't for a second think I'd kill someone in cold blood."

"I didn't want to." He looked out at James marching back and forth. "I don't want to consider anyone in this town, but I have to go where the evidence takes me." Riley walked BJ to where Ransom and Lyndsey sat in black chairs. He turned his attention to James. "Where's Melanie?"

"I'm not going to bring my wife down here." James shoved a finger in the sheriff's chest. "You know today is Jimmy's birthday. And she's not feeling well. I won't allow you to put her through this. It'd only make things worse."

"I need to speak with her. Today." Riley stood tall. BJ felt proud to call him one of her own.

"I'll call you later if she's up to it," James said.

"We'll need her fingerprints." Riley leaned an elbow on the front counter. "But we can do that at the house."

James's eyes wide opened. "You can't believe she had anything to do with this."

"Calm down." BJ took hold of the man's soft, pinstripe jacket sleeve. "It was one of her needles used to kill the man." She gave a quick glance to Lyndsey who flinched at her words. "They need to have her prints for elimination purposes."

Ransom placed an arm across the back of Lyndsey's chair and whispered something in her ear. She shook her head.

"I'll try to make it as gentle as I can with Melanie, but I need them today." Riley stared at the floor. "In the meantime, where were you this morning between the hours of three and six?"

"What? Me?" James sputtered. "You can't imagine I had anything to do with this, this murder."

"You had a shoving match with the guy the night before. I need to ask."

"I say we have a parade to celebrate the death of a drug dealer and get on with our lives." James waved his hands in the air.

Lyndsey got up and rushed to the ladies room in the corner. BJ was tempted to follow but decided to allow the teen the time alone she needed.

After a moment, James finally said, "I was at home. In bed. With my wife." He turned to go, stopping with the door open. "And call before you come so I can make sure Melanie's up to a visit, or I'll not allow you in."

Everyone seemed to give a collective sigh upon James's exit.

BJ recalled Melanie's paleness at that morning's church service. An ache set in her own stomach. *Please God, let Melanie feel your loving arms around her.* "He's right," BJ said to Riley. "Melanie was pretty upset this morning. She told me she was going home to take something to help her rest. She's apparently not been sleeping much."

"I need to know where she last saw that needle." Riley stared out the window.

"I agree." BJ nodded.

Lyndsey walked out and over to BJ.

She put her arm around the girl's shoulder then looked at Riley. "So are you done with us for now?"

"Currently. But I might have to ask you and Mr. McNeely some more questions later."

The door swung open. Ty Davenport and his partner, who BJ only knew as Howard, stormed into the sheriff's station. Howard's face carried the same stern look she recalled when he'd questioned Calley about a murder the year before. BJ almost swore he wore the same suit and tie also.

Funny, Ty was his polar opposite. His massive shoulders and whiskered face made it seem impossible to believe a government agency employed him. Unless you considered he worked undercover for the DEA.

"Owens, we need to talk." Howard's eyes were cold. He marched passed them all without a single word.

Ty kept his head down, not acknowledging anyone's presence as he followed Riley back to his office.

A shudder raced through BJ. She had a feeling Cliff Mason's murder brought with it a whole new set of nightmares.

16

"Who are they?" Ransom raised his head in the direction of the sheriff's office. Ransom imagined the large men sucked most of the oxygen available.

"Ty Davenport and Detective Howard. DEA," BJ said. "You met Ty's wife last night. The photographer."

A phone rang on the desk next to them. Sylvi reached over and answered it. She gave information to another deputy about a shed fire on Lilliput Street, and he rushed out.

Ransom wished he'd insisted on driving his own vehicle to the station. But with it a couple blocks away, his shotgun microphone was of little use to overhear the goings on in Riley's office. "I'd love to stick around to find out what they're talking about," Ransom said. "Something tells me it has to do with Mason."

"Considering he was their informant, I'd say that's a good bet." BJ nodded. "However, Riley won't tell you anything. He's not one to share office gossip. But give it an hour, and we'll know everything. That's the good and the bad about a small town." She placed her hands on her hips. "How about we take you to your van, then you can come over for that meal I promised earlier?" BJ headed into the heat with Ransom and Lyndsey following.

"Truth be told, food does sound good. I'm starved." Ransom placed his arm over Lyndsey's shoulder. "This way I get to eat and protect you at the same time."

"Protect me?" Lyndsey stopped and looked up at him. "Why? Cliff can't get at me now."

"I'm sure he still has others out there."

She looked at him with eyes wide.

"Don't worry. They won't get you." He needed to learn to be a bit more tactful. The girl had been through a lot. He leaned toward her and whispered, "Besides, it gives me an excuse to be near your aunt."

"I heard that." BJ stopped at the driver's side door of her Jeep. "What makes you think I want you hanging around?"

"Give me a break." Lyndsey giggled, alleviating some of the girl's sadness.

"I guess Lyndsey's reaction does."

Gray smoke floated to the sky in the west but no harsh aroma hung in the air. Ransom assumed the plume came from the shed fire on Lilliput. Without wind, the smell didn't have much of a chance to coat the area.

He climbed into the back of the Jeep so Lyndsey wouldn't have to get out once they got to the van. It would have been almost faster to walk with the church being so close. Earlier the lot had been full. Now his cargo van and a red Ford Escort were the only two vehicles in sight.

BJ slowed, passing the four-door sedan. Her lips all but disappeared when she saw the man seated inside.

"Isn't that the same guy who was at the sheriff's office earlier?" Ransom used his chin to point in the direction of the Ford.

"Joe Mercer." BJ's bitter tone said the guy was no good. She took out her cell and dialed a number. "Calley, how are you today? Good. I called to thank you for the invite last night. I had a wonderful time." A pause. "Yes, I believe he did also." She glanced in the rearview mirror at Ransom and rolled her eyes.

As much as he enjoyed her friends asking about him, Ransom had questions about the guy in the red car.

"I thought maybe you'd like to come over for dinner." BJ laughed at something Calley must have said. "You know me well. Right now, he's sitting in front of the church. Okay. If you need me, call."

Ransom got out and paused at BJ's window. Once she opened it, he asked, "What's up with this Mercer guy?"

"He's Calley's uncle and a convicted rapist."

RANSOM REARED BACK at BJ's words.

"Mercer claims he's a redeemed Christian, but we still don't want him near Calley or the baby," BJ said.

"Can't say I blame you."

BJ glared at Mercer one last time, and then turned back to Ransom. "My place in a few moments?"

"See you there." Ransom hit the key fob to unlock the van door. As he climbed in, he noticed a figure lurking behind the church. If he didn't check it out and the church was vandalized, BJ would probably shoot him. Ransom sneaked around the side of the building. He immediately recognized the woman sliding down onto a bench on the patio.

"Excuse me," Ransom said. "Mrs. Newman?"

She glanced up. Though she smiled, it did nothing to ease the pain in her eyes. "You're BJ's friend. I didn't get a chance to talk with you at the opening last evening. And please, call me Melanie."

"Melanie, I'm Ronald McNeely." He held his hand out to her. Though she sat in the warm sunshine, her hands were cold. "Are you all right?"

"This is the only place I used to find peace. Now I'm not sure God's listening anymore." A tear drop crawled over her lashes. "My son was killed almost two years ago. This time of year is hard for me."

"I heard. I'm sorry. It's not easy to outlive your children."

"No, it's not." She cocked her head at him. "You sound like you know that from experience."

"My granddaughter." He turned his face away so she wouldn't see the deep swallow he took to keep tears at bay.

"I'm sorry." She shook her head. "Too young and innocent. Too many, many young ones."

He couldn't be sure if she was actually talking to him or herself. For a moment, he considered telling her about Riley wanting her fingerprints, but she had enough on her mind without finding out Mason had been murdered not too far away.

"I used to be able to rely on God for anything," she said. "But I'm having a hard time with this. Maybe my sins."

"I'm sure it had nothing to do with you." Ransom's heart broke looking at this poor woman as she wilted before him. "God and I haven't been on speaking terms in a while, but I'm sure he didn't take my granddaughter because of anything I did. Same with your son."

"Thank you." She smiled. "And why are you angry with God?" She motioned for him to sit on the cement bench beside her.

He sat, leaning forward with his forearms on his legs. "I guess for not saving my Bernadette." Ransom stared off. "She didn't deserve to die, especially the way she did." He kicked a rock. "It's not fair to outlive her. And to make matters worse, the only man who knew who killed her is dead also."

"And you wanted to beat it out of him?"

"Took all my power not to."

"The same way you wished you'd saved your grandchild?" She sat silently looking at him, her eyebrows raised. "Could be it's not God you're mad at. Maybe it's the man you shave with every morning."

Ransom lowered his head. "Maybe."

"And just maybe God took out this other person to show you it's time to move on." She patted his shoulder.

He shrugged "Could be why God put me here today. To tell you the same thing."

She smiled, causing her eyes to shine. Color rushed to her face. "Could be. Could be."

"Can I offer you a ride home?"

"No. I think I'll just sit here a while longer. But thank you for checking on me."

Ransom gave her hand a squeeze before leaving. As he rounded the corner of the building, James Newman got out of a blue Lincoln parked in the lot next to the van.

"Mr. Newman, I'm Ronald McNeely." Ransom shook the man's hand. "Your wife's around back. She's one nice woman."

"Yes she is." James raised his chin. "She's going through a rough time right now."

"So she said." Ransom glanced over his shoulder to the corner he'd just come around. "Take care of her. She needs it."

James nodded and marched to the back of the building.

Ransom climbed into his van and sat there thinking over Melanie's words. She might be right, maybe it was more himself he was mad at then God. Funny how a stranger can point things out about ourselves that we can't see, or aren't willing to consider.

He put the key in the ignition and started the engine. BJ had dropped him off over ten minutes ago. The Ford hadn't moved from its parking space. Ransom slowed going past, making sure this Mercer character knew Ransom got a good look at him. Not that Mercer planned the Newmans harm, but why take chances. Crooks were less likely to commit a crime if someone could identify them.

At the exit, Ransom paused and scribbled down Mercer's tag number. A convicted rapist and Mason in the same town. Seemed like a very large coincidence.

BJ KEPT AN EYE ON THE rearview mirror for anyone who might be following. Like Ransom said, there could be some of Mason's minions nearby. She gave a quick glance over to Lyndsey who stared out the passenger window. She hadn't said a lot since they left the station.

"How are you holding up?" BJ pulled into the driveway and put the Jeep into park.

"I'm doing okay. I just wish this was over."

"It could be. Better to be overly cautious."

Lyndsey nodded with a frown.

"Maybe next weekend we can head up to Chattanooga and get some shopping in. You probably could use some new clothes for summer."

"Really?" Lyndsey's face brightened.

"Sure. Might even take out the motorcycle later today if the weather holds up."

"That would be fun." Lyndsey opened her car door but didn't get out. "I just hope once Mom finds out Mason is dead, she won't make me go back home." She glanced at BJ out of the corner of her eye.

"I know she misses you. But I'm not ready to let you go yet." She nudged Lyndsey with the knuckle of her index finger. "And I know for a fact Calley's still in need of help." BJ pulled the keys from the ignition. "Now, let's get some food in us. I have a feeling Ransom needs it."

"Me, too." Lyndsey licked her lips. She had a spring in her step walking into the house.

Funny how quick a teenager's thoughts could shift. BJ should let her know how much she enjoyed her company. It'd gotten a bit too quiet since leaving Riley's place after he and Calley married.

Once on the front porch, BJ glanced around. The smoke from the fire stung her throat a bit. Lilliput was just on the other side of the woods. If the fire caught on, it could mean her home might be in danger.

BJ gave one more look up and down the street for any sign of Ransom but saw none. Hopefully he was all right. She clenched her teeth. So much for not getting her heart involved. Could be something as innocent as he's late because he stopped for gas.

In her bedroom, she deposited her purse, pulled out her cell, and dialed Sylvi at the sheriff's station.

"Sylvi, what's going on with this fire? It seems pretty close to my place."

"Don't worry," Sylvi said. "It's contained. Whoever took off with Cliff Mason's car put it in Carl Regan's abandoned shed. They must have come back later and set it on fire."

BJ finished her call and joined Lyndsey out in the kitchen. The girl had taken out the leftover roast, lettuce, tomatoes, mayonnaise, and mustard.

At the sound of a car door shutting in the distance, Lyndsey rushed to the window. "He's here," she announced. "Why doesn't he park in the driveway instead of over in the woods?"

"Probably plans to stay there tonight."

"He really thinks someone might still be after me?" Her forehead wrinkled.

"Probably just making sure." BJ placed the pitcher of sweet tea in the center of the table. "I have a feeling he's come to like you a little bit."

"Me?" Lyndsey laughed. "It's more you he wants to see."

As much as BJ tried to fight it, she'd come to enjoy seeing him also.

SMOKE HUNG HEAVIER on this side of town. The sky was blue and a tiny white cloud drifted overhead.

Ransom paused before getting out of the van. He typed in Mercer's details on the password protected site. Within seconds, the information came up. Except for one rape conviction, everything came up clean on the man.

Ransom waited for a truck to pass before he crossed the road to BJ's house. He'd taken a step onto the driveway when his cell phone rang.

"Hello, Frazier." Ransom's voice was glib toward his former boss.

"I heard about this Mason chap," he said.

"Apparently someone stabbed him with a knitting needle."

"Knitting needle. That's different. Sounds like a weapon of convenience." After a second he said, "You didn't by chance..." He left the words hang over the line.

"No. I wanted the creep alive." Ransom paused at the bottom of the porch steps.

"I thought as much. Besides, murder's not quite your style." Frazier hesitated. "What's the status of your investigation?"

"I've got some threads out there, but nothing concrete. Mason's death puts a kink in everything."

"Well, after I heard about the killing, I did some checking."

It always amazed Ransom how Frazier kept tabs on his current and retired agents.

"Seems this Mason was believed to be supplying children." Frazier cleared his throat. "He was giving them to a select group of clients. The feds are keeping an eye on them but haven't got anything concrete."

"What do you mean select group of clients?"

"There's about twelve of them. They have parties with these kids. Pass them around. That kind of sick stuff." He let out a low breath over the line. Ransom imagined Frazier's eyes turned to slits. After all, the man's own daughter should be close to ten or eleven. "A fed I know has some photos he's going to forward of the men they've spotted so far. They can't seem to get pictures of the victims, but the authorities are fairly sure it's a sex club."

"They should kill the lot of them." Ransom picked up a rock from the grass and lobbed it across the street.

"Yeah. These sleazebags apparently think they're better than your average pervert because they don't take in anyone younger than twelve."

"Why haven't the feds picked them up?"

"Can't prove it. These creeps are good. They meet at different locations and don't leave any cigarettes or garbage so no DNA to find out who they are. And somehow the kids are sneaked in. Can't prove it if you can't locate the victims."

"How do you know they aren't just a bunch of old guys buying drugs from Mason? After all, he was a dealer."

"One of the pervs got caught in a store bathroom with a teen boy. He's trying to make a deal."

A disquieting thought rushed through Ransom. These creeps might have used Bernadette in this club. Being passed from man to man. His hand tightened on the cell.

"As soon as I get the pictures, I'll send them on. You might have seen one or two with Mason these last few months. Help the feds find a way to nail 'em."

"I'll see what I can do." Ransom slid his phone into his pocket and stood in the heat, wanting nothing more than to kill someone. Kidnapping and using children for their own sick enjoyment. Too bad it was illegal to put a bullet in each member of this group. It took a moment and three deep breaths before he was able to walk up to the front door.

When he went to knock, Ransom's hands were shaking.

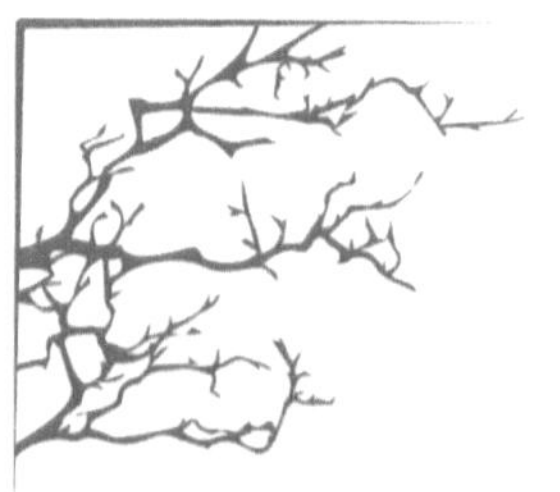

17

When BJ ushered Ransom through the door, a frown marred his face. "Has something else happened?" Her heart pounded against her ribcage.

"No." His eyes focused on something behind her. "Just need some lunch."

His furrowed brow said otherwise, but BJ didn't press him. When she turned, Lyndsey stood within a few feet.

The smile hadn't left her face since BJ told her she could stay the summer. And BJ was positive whatever caused Ransom's sour disposition would interfere with that happiness. Best to wait until the girl left the room to get into it.

During lunch, Lyndsey did most of the talking, animated about her plans for the next month. She appeared oblivious to Ransom's bad mood. BJ hadn't felt very hungry until she smelled the roast. Now it was all she could do to keep from gulping down her food.

"When can I get a ride on your motorcycle?" she asked BJ.

"Weather's supposed to hold up. How about later this evening once it cools down a bit?" BJ crunched on a cheese flavored potato chip.

"Motorcycle?" Ransom grinned.

"Yeah. A Can-Am Spyder." BJ held up her chin. Why shouldn't she have a bike?

"Can I get a ride also?" He raised his eyebrows up and down.

"We'll have to see." Her heart rate increased thinking of Ransom's arms around her waist. She took a sip of her sweet tea to cool herself off.

"Good lunch." Lyndsey finished her last bite of roast beef then bounced up from the table. "I'm going to call Mom and let her know what's happened. Okay?"

"Good idea," BJ said. "Best not to leave your parents in the dark."

Lyndsey skipped to the hallway and paused. "You two behave now." She shook her finger at them both, and then disappeared.

BJ couldn't wait any longer. At the sound of Lyndsey's door shutting, she leaned toward Ransom and whispered, "From the look on your face when you got here, something's up. So, spill it."

He rose and went to the CD collection in the corner. He popped out a disc and placed it in the player.

BJ's pulse quickened with each second he ignored her.

After turning on the music, he returned to the table, grabbed BJ's hand, and pulled her up against him.

She swallowed back a gasp. He held her tight. His body was solid as twenty-five years ago. Being this close to him affected her in ways she hadn't felt in years. She became aware of his breathing, the tightness of his hold, every part of him. She couldn't be sure if her shaky knees had to do with whatever upset Ransom or being so close to him.

Who was she kidding? She knew why her heart pounded in her ears.

Ransom had yet to say anything, which only worried BJ more. "What's wrong?" She tried to focus on the music instead of his woodsy scented cologne.

He slowed his pace. "There's a group of them."

"Group of who?" Her mind had to work to focus on anything but his nearness. It'd been so long since she'd had a man hold her tight. And the fact it was Ransom, for some reason, only made it more enticing.

"Men involved with Mason. He'd find kids for them." He continued to sway her. "I can't be sure there isn't one watching Lyndsey right now."

BJ stopped. Her lunch bounced in her stomach. "You're saying any one of these creeps could still come after her?"

"Sh. I don't want Lyndsey to overhear." Ransom tightened his grip on BJ. "I know she's been part of all this, but some things a kid her age shouldn't know. At least not just yet."

He told BJ about the telephone call from his former boss and the group of men the FBI suspected of being part of a sex ring. "I imagine that's where Bernadette ended up." His features darkened.

Tears blurred BJ's vision. The whole idea of men using children for their sick sexual desires made her want to either punch someone, cry, or both. How could a child deal with such terror? BJ pressed her cheek against Ransom's shoulder while George Strait's song "A Fire I Can't Put Out" played through the speakers. Would this nightmare ever end? Ransom's strong arms gave her some comfort. At least she wasn't alone.

And what must he be going through? She clutched him tighter. How could he not be hunting down each and every one of these men right now? Instead, he chose to protect a member of her family. One of the few good men left.

"What are you two doing?" Lyndsey walked up behind BJ.

"It's called dancing." Ransom looked deep into BJ's eyes. "There's something I've wanted to do since I first saw you again." His voice was low and inviting.

He licked his bottom lip. A shiver raced through BJ. Her heart galloped in her chest. Anticipation rushed through her. What was she be thinking? She had to stop this before—

Ransom bent her back then raised her up. "That's the ticket."

"Well, that was sure disappointing." Lyndsey smirked and rested one knee on the sofa arm. "I expected more than a dip."

So had BJ. Her heart skipped a beat imagining Ransom's lips on hers.

"Maybe I'd try to take advantage of your aunt if you weren't chaperoning." He continued to spin BJ, a cocky grin on his face.

Even with all he must be going through right now, he knew how to make her feel better. She raised her chin up. "Don't I have anything to say about those advantages you might take?"

He dipped her again. "Only yes."

BJ blurted a laugh.

RANSOM PACED THE LIVING room, waiting for the photographs to come in. It'd been a couple of hours since he'd spoken with Frazier. Unfortunately, it could take days, but time was of the essence in this type of case.

"Still nothing?" BJ returned from the back bedroom

"No."

"You know all you're doing is wearing a path in my carpet."

"We could always dance some more." He took her in his arms again. How bad he'd yearned to kiss her earlier but with Lyndsey watching, he thought better of it.

Ransom's throat caught at how beautiful BJ was. His pulse increased. Her lips parted with shallow breaths. His heart thudded. He became aware of her body pressed against his. Ransom swallowed hard, fully aware of the rise and fall of her chest. The heat coursing through him could have caused a five-alarm fire. Hypnotized by her full lips, his gaze lingered on her mouth. A mouth he'd wanted to taste since he got there. He leaned toward her.

Seconds before their lips met, gravel spun in the driveway. He released her with a grunt then walked to the picture window. The DEA agents who'd visited Riley's office earlier got out of a dark blue sedan.

"I wonder what they want." BJ leaned around Ransom.

"To interrupt," he said.

"Interrupt what?" She spoke with a lilt in her voice.

He laughed out loud. "I guess locking the deadbolt wouldn't keep them out."

"They'd probably just knock until we let them in." After opening the door, BJ directed the men into the living room. "Ty Davenport, this is Ronald McNeely. We saw Rayleen last night at the gallery. I'm sorry you missed it."

The big man swallowed hard. Ransom stood six foot even. This guy had to have at least three inches on him. Not to mention about fifty more pounds, all muscle. His hair went to just below his collar. Ty's hand took hold of Ransom's, not tight enough to hurt, but enough to control. This was a man used to being in charge even if he didn't say it in words. However, the mere mention of his wife cast a sad shadow over his stubbled face.

"This is my partner, Ignacio Howard," Ty said.

Howard rocked back on his heels, hands in his pockets. He stared out the large picture window, his back to everyone in the room. The man didn't have near the height or the weight of his partner. In fact, Howard looked like he spent all day in an office pushing paper. His pressed blue suit was crisp, and the close-cropped haircut screamed military.

"We need to speak with Lyndsey Chapel," Howard said.

"About what?" BJ's posture straightened.

"We can always take her to the sheriff's station."

A gasp sounded behind BJ where Lyndsey had returned to the room.

Ransom stepped forward. "Go ahead. We'll meet you there with a lawyer."

Howard turned and matched Ransom's glare.

"And since she's a female," Ransom continued. "I have no intention of letting you take her alone. I'll insist you bring a woman to ride with her."

"As you might have heard, Mason was one of our informants." Ty interrupted the staring contest. "We need to see if Lyndsey knows anyone he might have been doing business with. Mason's supplier has a big shipment of drugs coming in from South America. We'd like to be there when it arrives."

"He never mentioned anyone." Lyndsey stared down at the carpet. "And I never asked."

Ty stepped toward her. "Did he ever answer the phone? Maybe spoke a name when you were together?"

"No," she whispered. "He used to tell me I deserved all his attention, so he turned his phone off."

"There is a guy who appears to work with him," Ransom said. "He wears gold teeth and drives a Cadillac. The sheriff should have more information on him."

"He's already mentioned the man." Howard kept his piercing green eyes on Lyndsey. "If it doesn't pan out, we'll be back."

"Or better yet," BJ said. "Call ahead, and we'll meet you at the sheriff's office with an attorney."

Ty patted BJ on the back on the way out. Once the door closed, both Ransom and BJ looked over at Lyndsey.

"I really don't know anyone." She collapsed onto the sofa. "I didn't even know he sold drugs." She shook her head. "I'm so stupid."

"No, you're not." BJ rushed to her side and pulled her into a hug. "You fell for some guy's lines. It happens to all of us."

From the gaze she directed his way, Ransom knew BJ was recalling their past.

BJ HOOKED THE STRAP of the helmet below her chin and steered the yellow Can-Am Spyder from the garage. Never one for a motorcycle, it only took one ride on Riley's for her to get the itch. And now she'd fallen in love with this three-wheeled beauty. Lyndsey bounced from foot to foot at the end of the drive. The purple helmet made her head appear twice as big on her narrow shoulders.

Once at the end of the drive, Lyndsey hopped on behind BJ, and they took off. The teen's grip tightened around BJ's waist. After traveling down the main street for a couple of miles, BJ turned down a side road toward the lake. They stopped at the edge, and she glimpsed over her shoulder to her passenger.

"How are you doing?" BJ yelled over the engine.

"Wonderful." The girl had a large smile. "It's pretty out here."

"Yes, it is," BJ said.

The velvet sky sank into the lake water, reflecting orange in the ripples. She filled her lungs with fresh air, the smoke from the earlier fire gone. Only a slight remnant of burnt wood remained. "I almost bought that cabin over there instead of the house I'm in now." She pointed to a white building at her right. A faded For Sale sign sat out front.

"Why didn't you?"

"Too fancy." She referred to the wrought iron railings and aluminum siding. "It was also larger than what I needed."

"No one's bought it yet?"

"With the economy tight like it is, a cabin isn't in everyone's price range." She patted Lyndsey's leg. "Ready to head back?"

"Yeah. I think Ransom wants a ride next," Lyndsey sang.

BJ needed to find a way out of Ransom being on the back behind her. During their dance, she'd anticipated that kiss a bit more than she should have with everything going on right now. No matter how hard she tried to talk herself out of it, she'd started to care for the man all over again.

Within minutes, they pulled into the driveway, and Lyndsey climbed off. "Your turn," she said to Ransom.

"As much as I like your idea," he said. "I'm not about to leave you here alone."

"Oh. I forgot." Lyndsey's smile disappeared. She glanced up and down the road.

BJ had forgotten also.

"Of course, if your aunt would permit me." He tilted his head sideways.

"I'd consider it, but without the proper license, I can't." BJ shrugged. "Too bad."

"Well, it just so happens." He tugged out his wallet from his back pocket and showed her the Motorcycle Endorsement on his Florida driver's license.

She rolled her eyes and tossed him the keys. "Wreck my trike, don't come back," she ordered.

"Yes, ma'am."

BJ stood with Lyndsey in the middle of the street. The view of Ransom on the motorcycle stole her breath. After all, what wasn't there to like about a man on a bike?

An hour later, the motorcycle was back in the garage, and BJ busied herself in the kitchen, putting dishes away and wiping off counters. She even had another glass of tea. Doing everything she could to keep from looking at the man standing within a few feet of her. Dancing with him, feeling the warmth of his nearness, worse, wanting the kiss he'd teased.

"Lyndsey's going to be all right." He leaned against the door jamb. "She's a good kid."

"Yes, she is." BJ stared out the back window. "I hate the DEA wanting to talk with her."

"If we get lucky, they'll find the guy with the gold teeth. I have a feeling he knows a lot more about Mason's operation than anyone."

She nodded. Her heart kept in rhythm with each of his footsteps coming up behind her.

"I'm sorry for hurting you all those years ago." His voice was soft and soothing. "You're wrong, you know."

"About what?"

"You wouldn't have cheated. I knew that the first day I met you."

"I wish I could be so sure." She stared at the magnolia tree out back. The blossoms were gone, but the leaves still deep green.

"You can be. Your conviction is what intrigued me about you. As time passed, I grew to hate your husband more and more for having something I wanted." He combed his fingers through her hair. "A strong, beautiful woman. No other has ever measured up. It's why I fell in love with you then. Why I've never stopped loving you."

The lump in BJ's throat kept her from saying anything. It would be so easy to fall into his arms. So many years of being alone, and the yearning to feel like a woman again made her heart ache for his words to be true. But no matter what she felt, her main focus had to be on keeping Lyndsey safe.

She turned to face him. BJ needed to find the words to stop this. Before she could speak, his hand caressed her cheek. His lips touched hers. First soft, then with more passion. Within seconds her hands played with his hair at his collar. He pulled her against him. The bristle of his whiskers over her chin only increased her longing for more. The warmth from his hold escalated to where she didn't at first hear the telephone ringing. She could barely breathe when he released her.

"Excuse me." She picked up the handheld connected to the wall in her dining room. "Hello." Her voice trembled over the line.

"BJ?" Calley said, "Are you all right?"

"Yes." She gave a quick cough. "I'm fine. Just a frog in my throat."

"Rrrribbit." Ransom poked her in the ribs with his index finger.

A blush burned BJ's cheeks. She smacked Ransom on the arm then thrust her shoulder out blocking him.

"I was wondering if I could borrow Lyndsey tomorrow night." Calley continued, apparently not hearing Ransom. "Sheryl and I have work at the gallery and could use her help."

BJ sat in one of the high back chairs in the dining room. "I think that'd be a good idea. Helping you might get all this business off her mind. It would also give Lyndsey someone she trusts to talk with. Though she hasn't said it, I believe she's having a hard time with Mason dying."

"I thought she might be upset. At least I can say I know a bit of what she's going through," Calley said. "We might be late, so I'll just have her spend the night."

BJ hesitated.

"Don't worry. Riley plans to be around to do the heavy lifting."

BJ's apprehension vanished. "I'm sure she'll be delighted." After a few pleasantries, BJ disconnected the call. Ransom had moved to the sofa, his ankle crossed over his knee.

"Is everything all right?" he asked.

"Yeah. Calley wants Lyndsey to stay with her tomorrow night. She's got some work she needs to do."

"Hard with a small one, I imagine."

"I guess I'd better check with Lyndsey before volunteering her for anything." BJ headed to the hallway.

Ransom reached out and grabbed her arm as she passed. "And with her gone, you and I will go out to dinner. Get to know each other again." He kissed the back of her hand.

BJ studied his expression. Sincerity, kindness, respect. Could he really be sorry for the past? They say you can't go back, but sometimes letting go of the pain made it easier to move forward.

18

Ransom pulled to the curb in front of Carmines Flower Shop in Ringgold, Georgia. A grin remained on his face he could not erase, not that he wanted to. It'd been a while since he felt this good.

In less than one hour he'd be picking up BJ for their date. The plan was for them to drop Lyndsey at Calley's and then head out to dinner. He hopped out of the rental car and headed inside. A multitude of aromas hit him. Every color flower was available. A tulip in a vase to his left was white with pink tips. How'd they get it like that?

The place was a lot larger than he'd realized from outside. It was at least two rooms at the front, and one in the back. He'd just rounded the corner of the first room when he caught sight of Melanie Newman looking over a vast array of bouquets.

Before he could speak to Ms. Newman, a young girl came up on his right. "Is there anything I can help you with?"

He gave the girl his order but kept his eye on Melanie. Her paleness concerned him. "Melanie."

She turned and looked up at him. After a moment, she smiled. "Mr. McNeely." Softness came over her features, and her beauty shined through. "What brings you into Carmines today?"

"I have a date with someone you know." He raised his eyebrows and smiled.

She gave a quick laugh. "Good for you. So how are you holding up?"

"Much better. Thank you. And yourself?"

"Taking it one day at a time." She bent and smelled a yellow rose. "I just pray my Jimmy had the spirit in him before he died."

Ransom had never thought of that with regard to Bernadette, yet something inside told him she waited in Heaven. He took Melanie's hand in his. "I have little doubt he's with Jesus. Maybe your son's even up there watching over my Bernadette."

Her lip trembled into a smile. "That is such a wonderful thought. Thank you for that." She touched his jaw. A tear rolled from her left eye. "Thank you."

The clerk from earlier tapped him on the shoulder. "Mr. McNeely, here are your arrangements."

"Red roses." Melanie leaned over to him and whispered, "You do know what they symbolize, don't you?"

"Oh yeah." Heat raced from his neck to his cheeks.

"You don't believe in wasting any time, do you?"

"I've already wasted enough. It's time to start living again." He kissed Melanie's wet cheek. "I suggest the same for you."

She smiled and nodded. "BJ's a very lucky woman."

After saying goodbye, Ransom walked out of the shop. The more he thought about it, the more he actually felt better since he'd spoken with Melanie the day before.

Ransom started the car then paused. He folded his hands and lowered his head. "God, please help me through this. I've tried to do it on my own, but now I'm giving it up to you. And please, forgive my anger toward you. I just needed someone to blame other than myself. You were my easiest target. Even if you're not willing to help me, please help Melanie Newman. She needs to feel you there beside her right now. Amen."

Would God forgive him for all the terrible things he'd said to Him? As Melanie said yesterday, it might just be that Ransom needed to forgive himself for not saving Bernadette. He scrubbed a hand down his face.

"Time to stop this and move forward." He nodded up at the blue sky. And one town over was a woman who might be able to help him do just that.

BJ STARED AT THE MIRROR and traded her small, hooped earrings for the pearls. The wedding ring caught her eye. Her heart rate slowed. Was she doing the right thing, going out with Ransom?

She stared at Perry's photograph on the dresser. "I'll always love you." BJ stared down at the ring set and nodded. "I think it's time." She slid the rings off her finger and placed them in the jewelry box.

"What's taking you so long?" Lyndsey bounced into the room. "He'll be here any minute."

BJ's heart pounded so hard she was sure Lyndsey could hear it. Ransom would be along to pick them both up momentarily. She paced between the kitchen and dining room area. What could she have been thinking? Better be careful asking questions she might not want the answers to. At fifteen minutes to seven, a four-door Nissan Avenger with dark tinted windows pulled into the driveway.

"Who's that?" Lyndsey stared out the window. She'd grown as cautious as BJ in these last couple of weeks.

"I don't know." BJ jerked back when Ransom popped out of the driver's side.

"Wow."

Though young, the girl knew how to call it. Ransom sure looked "wow" in the black slacks and buttoned-down dark purple shirt. In his arms he carried two bouquets of flowers. BJ wasn't anywhere ready for this with her simple sundress.

"Maybe I should change." BJ spoke under her breath.

"You look wonderful." Lyndsey patted her arm. "I can't believe it. You have a date." She giggled and rushed to let Ransom in. "What's up with the car?"

"If I didn't rent something, you'd end up sitting on the floor," he said.

"Why?" Lyndsey furrowed her brow.

"The van only has seats up front," he explained. "These are for you." He handed Lyndsey a half-dozen pink carnations.

"What are these for?"

"I figured I should thank you for allowing me to go out with your aunt."

"Wow! I never got flowers before." She sniffed them.

BJ smiled. The man sure knew how to get to a girl.

Ransom paused and stared at BJ. "You look beautiful." He kissed her cheek before handing her the bouquet. "These are for you."

She inhaled the floral aroma. "Red roses?" BJ looked at him with her face buried in the blooms.

Ransom shrugged.

She and Lyndsey carried their arrangements to the kitchen and placed them on the countertop. They were lovely. Smelled good, too. "I'll cut the stems back and put them in a vase when I get home." BJ released a breath. No more excuses. "I guess we'd better get this girl over to the gallery," she said. "Calley seemed pretty desperate."

"Our reservation is at eight." Ransom bent his elbow toward BJ. "That should give us plenty of time to drop her off and visit with the Owens a moment."

"We don't have to go to Chattanooga just for food," BJ said.

"Fred's isn't exactly my idea of a place to impress a date." He chuckled. "Besides, Chattanooga is just up the highway."

"Come on, you two. I need to get going." Lyndsey ran outside.

BJ rushed forward.

Ransom held tight to her arm, slowing her momentum. "She's all right. I already checked the area. Same with the gallery." On the front steps he leaned over and whispered in her ear. "Tonight, you relax and enjoy yourself."

How was BJ supposed to do that when she had a million butterflies fluttering in her stomach?

RANSOM'S HEART HITCHED a notch when he first saw BJ. Talk about beautiful. She really went all out for tonight. The blue dress tapered in at her waist and flared at her knees. And she no longer wore the wedding ring on her left hand. He hoped that was a good sign.

Lyndsey had already hopped in by the time they got to the Nissan. Ransom opened the door for BJ and waited until she sat. He couldn't help noticing her sleek legs and pink-painted toenails in white sandals.

He sprinted to the other side, not wanting to lose any time with her. Once inside the sedan, her perfume carried to him. A different aroma than the one she'd worn before. This scent reminded him of Italy. Freesia and irises. Also, a hint of citrus. He allowed his senses to take it all in, including her warm, soft hand in his while he drove.

Five minutes later they entered the gallery. Riley stood in the center of the room. Calley and the baby were at the back counter. A smirk held on Riley's face.

"Not a word, young man." BJ rolled her eyes.

Ransom took a quick walk throughout the gallery and questioned Riley about his home security. The sheriff didn't appear offended with all the questions. Once the tour was complete, Ransom input the Owens' home address into his phone.

"Sheryl's on her way," Calley said. "You two have fun now." She waved at Ransom and BJ before disappearing in the back with Lyndsey and RJ.

"Are you sure you want her to stay?" BJ asked Riley. "We can always come get her after."

"You need a break. Enjoy yourself." He shot a mischievous grin to Ransom. "Just not too much."

BJ smacked her nephew on the arm, causing him to flinch.

Ransom led BJ back to the vehicle. "On to Chattanooga."

The drive out of Lincolnville became quiet without the teenager in the backseat. Once on the highway, BJ finally spoke. "So, what made you retire?" Her voice was low and provocative. "Seems you're still quite good at your job."

"Getting too old to be traveling from place to place. All the new technology is more suited to the younger set. Besides, might be time I settled down."

She laughed. "At your age?"

"My soul has been bothered since learning about Darcy, my daughter. She was already in college when I found out about her. In time, I wanted to get to know my child."

"Her mom hadn't told you she was pregnant?" The shock was evident in BJ's voice.

"No." He flicked on his blinker to exit the highway. "In fact, I found out by mistake. Her mother and I both worked for the government and ended up at a conference together. Darcy happened to be with her. One look and I knew."

"Wow. How did Darcy feel about her mother never telling you?"

"She doesn't know. Her mother died of cancer a few months later. It would only have hurt Darcy more to know." He hesitated. "With the way I was back then, more children could be lurking. I've checked around but haven't found any so far. But I don't lie to myself about the type of person I was. And not a day goes by my daughter doesn't remind me with that angry look in her eye."

"And what type of man are you now?"

"Now, I'm looking for the right woman to spend the rest of my life with." He gave her hand a squeeze, and she smiled.

At Rider's Steakhouse, Ransom pulled into the circular drive. He bounced out, tossed the keys to the valet, and then led BJ inside. The pictures on the internet didn't do justice to the décor. The host led them to a table with napkins folded like sailboats. Two long, white, tapered candles stood lit in the middle of the table, surrounded by multi-colored flowers. White chandeliers brightened the deep brown paneling.

They spent the evening chatting about their families and old times. Thankfully, there was no talk of the pain he'd caused in the past. The cook had seared the steaks to a perfect medium rare. Once they finished with their dinner, they ordered coffee.

"Okay, so I'm going to ask you the one question I was afraid to ask you years ago." BJ played with the stem of her water glass.

"You? Afraid?" She definitely had Ransom intrigued.

"Everyone's afraid of something."

"So, ask away."

She leaned forward, looked at the other patrons, and then whispered, "Where did you get your nickname?" Her eyes sparkled with her grin.

Ransom laughed. "It's not really that impressive." He took hold of her hand and played with her fingers. "I was about eleven and my cousin was four if I recall. She had trouble pronouncing words as I've heard most four-years-olds do. We'd just moved to Atlanta and were having a family reunion. One of my aunts apparently said I was handsome, and my little cousin overheard."

"Already the ladies' man."

His cheeks heated. "Anyway, my cousin came over to tell us what her mother had said. The word handsome came out *randsom*. The other cousins teased me all weekend. I started a new school the next week, and one of the boys introduced me to his friends as Ransom. It stuck," he said. "And when the teenage girls found out where it came from, they thought it was sweet, so…" He shrugged.

BJ released her hand from his grasp and placed her chin on her knuckles. "So, basically your real nickname is Handsome?"

He groaned "I never considered that."

"You're just lucky it suits you." She reached over the table and patted the back of his hand.

This woman knew how to get to him every time. He loved her teasing ways and wonderful sense of humor.

The waiter interrupted their talk by bringing the bill over. Once Ransom paid, they strolled to the car, his hand on her back. Stars sparkled like glitter in the clear, black sky. Ransom couldn't have asked God for a more perfect evening.

The drive back to Lincolnville came with laughter and more talk about family. Once at the house, they strolled to the front porch. BJ opened the door, turned on the light inside, and input the code for the alarm.

"Would you like to come in for coffee?" The light behind BJ haloed around her head.

"I would, but I really need to check out the area by Riley's." He hated ruining their date this way, but he needed to regain his focus. "I know he's capable of watching over Lyndsey, but two sets of eyes are always better than one." He held both her hands in his. "Besides, you could probably use some sleep. I imagine you haven't had much these last couple of weeks."

As if on cue, she let loose a yawn. "I guess you're right." She laughed.

He touched her cheek then moved his hand to the back of her neck and leaned toward her. He fondled her lips with his own, next exploring her mouth. A moan escaped from deep in her throat. His mouth strayed to the lobe of her ear. Desire raced through him, searing his entire being with a weighted sigh. When he finally released her, his breathing was ragged.

ONCE IN THE HOUSE, BJ pushed the curtain aside and watched Ransom's taillights fade in the distance. As much as she hated to admit it, he was right about being concerned for Lyndsey's safety. And sleep sounded like a wonderful idea. Not as good as that kiss he'd given her. She touched her hand to her lips.

She recalled a warm ripple raced through her as he leaned toward her. His intense breathing filled her with a fierce longing to taste his mouth. When his lips traveled to her ear, she had no choice but to take in a large intake of air. Their bodies seemed to mesh so well together.

Her pulse still pumped in her ears. If it didn't slow, she'd surely have a heart attack. How could she have allowed this to happen? Her body tingled from his touch. And she wanted more still.

"Meow."

Stubby stole her attention. Oh, well. No matter how this ride ended, BJ planned to enjoy it to the end.

She recalled Ransom's face saddening with the mere mention of Darcy's name at dinner, and his daughter's anger toward him. *Please God, help them both find each other through Bernadette's tragic death.*

"Mew." Stubby glared up from her position at BJ's feet.

"What are you looking at?" She grabbed the tabby and cuddled him in her arms. BJ carried Stubby to the kitchen where she filled the cat's water bowl. Then she cut the stems from the bouquets Ransom had brought earlier and placed them in two separate vases. "Well, I guess I'll let you out, then once you're done gallivanting throughout the neighborhood, we can get to bed."

"Mew."

BJ picked him up again and hugged the stray to her neck, caressing his soft fur. His purr bounced off the walls of the quiet kitchen. BJ lowered him to the porch. Lightning flashed off to the left, and a breeze blew in from the east. She stood for a moment, taking in the smell of impending rain. Afterward, she went to her room and changed into a pair of shorts and a T-shirt. Clicking through the television stations, she found the old Cary Grant movie *Bringing Up Baby*.

"Perfect." She reclined on the sofa to watch.

An hour later, BJ woke to scratching at the back door. She hadn't realized how tired she was. The movie had finished and another black and white had started with actors she didn't recognize.

"Mrrrr," Stubby hollered.

"I'm coming. I'm coming." BJ turned on the kitchen light and unhooked the deadbolt to let Stubby back in. "Since when did I become your servant?"

She barely got the knob twisted when her body flew backward. She landed hard on the cool tile floor. Before she could get up on all fours, someone grabbed her arm and tossed her onto her back. She shook her head to get her bearings. BJ looked up at a pistol held by a man with gold teeth.

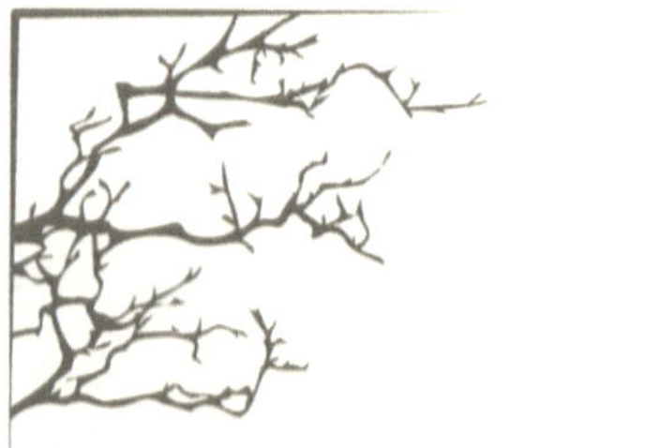

19

Ransom bounced his leg to the beat of the music on the local country music station. The wind blew through his hair from the open car window. The aroma from a gas barbeque grill hung in the air. Streetlights shadowed the silhouette of manicured lawns and hedges.

When George Strait's *Check Yes or No* came on, he couldn't help but smile recalling his dance with BJ earlier that day. Different song, same great singer. The wonderful feeling inside wouldn't quit, no matter his thoughts. Between Bernadette's death and trying to find her killer, he'd kept himself closed off far too long.

He'd been impressed with Lincolnville thus far. Overall, it was quiet, and the people seemed nice. This small town might make a good place to settle. It'd been a while since he'd seen all four seasons. Miami only had two, warm and hot.

This would make a fine place to rest his head. Especially if he could convince a certain woman his intentions were solid this time around.

He had spent the last hour or so keeping watch around Riley's. They appeared to still be up, but he didn't want any questions about his date with BJ. That was his secret to keep for now. After a quick couple laps around the neighborhood, both in the car and on foot, he decided there was no reason for concern. But just in case, he headed back to BJ's to check on her place.

Rounding the corner of Front Street, his heart stopped cold. A blue Cadillac sat on the side street. Ransom slowed. The scratches and a dent on the front panel told him who owned the vehicle.

He stopped in the middle of the street, took his phone out of his jacket pocket, and dialed BJ's cell number. It rang three times then went to voicemail. He then called the landline but got no response there either. BJ wouldn't keep out of communication with Lyndsey away from home.

He looked at the black sky. "Just in case." Ransom pressed his foot down on the accelerator. With his cell still in his hand, he dialed emergency, hoping to get the local sheriff's station.

"Nine-one-one," a woman answered. "What's your emergency?" She had a strong southern drawl.

"Is this the Lincolnville Sheriff's Department?"

"Yes, sir."

Thank you, God. "This is Ronald McNeely. I spotted the Cadillac that ran me off the road. It's on Front Street." He took the corner back onto Desmond on two wheels. "You need to contact Riley Owens to make sure everything's okay at his house. Also send a cruiser to BJ Owens's home." He tossed the cell phone onto the passenger seat.

If it turned out to be nothing, he hoped BJ would forgive him. If not... His blood ran cold.

Seconds became hours while all types of possibilities dashed through his mind. "Please God, I can't fail this time."

Ransom released a stuck breath when BJ's house came into view. The inside lights were still on. There didn't appear to be any movement inside, but it was hard to be sure with the shades drawn. He screeched the sedan to a halt in the driveway. He ran up to the front porch. An inch opening between the panels of curtains allowed him to view inside.

Gold-tooth. Where was BJ?

Ransom's heart leapt into his throat. He raced back to his car and took out his .38.

THANKFULLY SHE WAS no longer on the floor. BJ's stomach stood in knots from the intruder in her home. She'd never been so scared. At any moment, she was sure she'd throw up. *Please, God, don't let it end like this.*

"Did you understand what I said, lady?" The man shoved her against the countertop. His hands gripped her by the hair. "I don't want to hurt you, but this gun says I will."

Her skin crawled from his nearness. She scanned the counter for anything she could use as a weapon. With the knife set on the opposite side of the kitchen, a microwave, toaster, and spatula were the only things close by. Not much unless she planned to cook him to death.

"I asked you a question." He jerked her head back.

Fear inched through every part of her being. She had to stay calm to get this maniac out of her house. *Please, God.*

"Tell me what you're gonna say to your boyfriend." His breath reeked of alcohol.

"As far as you're concerned," her voice shook, "everything's even, and he's to lay off with the cops."

"That's right." He released his grip on her. "He stays away from me, and I have no need to come back. He refuses to listen, and..." The intruder let loose a deep laugh and slid a hand down BJ's arm.

Her body flinched at this touch.

His gold teeth reflected in the microwave. He took a step back.

In one swift movement, BJ grabbed the toaster, spun, and smashed it against the man's head. His gun bounced from the counter to the tile floor. A shot went off. Stubby streaked out of the living room toward the back. The trespasser stared at her with a glazed look on his face. She smacked him again, and he crumpled to the ground.

"Don't ever come in my house again," BJ screamed. She dropped the appliance and fled out the back door where she collided with Ransom.

"BJ?"

Both stopped and stared at each other.

"Are you all right?" He pulled her into his arms.

BJ clutched his shirt. His strong arms enveloped her. Tightness gathered in her throat. She swallowed back tears. She was stronger than this. BJ pushed herself away from him and gave what she knew was a weak smile.

"BJ?"

"I'm fine. Better than he is." She used her thumb to point inside. Her knees folded. Ransom placed a pistol she hadn't realized he was holding in his waistband then guided her to a nearby patio chair.

He looked at the heap on the floor. "When that gun went off, I about kicked in your front door, but the officer suggested otherwise."

Deputy Green rushed up. "Ms. Owens, is everything all right."

The man inside groaned.

"I think he'll need to see a doctor." She got up and led them into the kitchen. "Then you can arrest him for breaking in and making me ruin a good toaster."

"We'll need you to come down to sign a formal complaint." Green clicked his handcuffs around the stranger's wrists.

More shouts and car doors slammed outside. BJ recognized one of the voices as Riley's. Within seconds, he walked in, followed by Lyndsey. Their mouths hung open when they saw Deputy Green jerk the guy from the floor. A trickle of blood came from a gash on his forehead.

"Are you all right?" Riley crossed the kitchen threshold and hugged BJ.

Lyndsey did the same.

"I'll be all right," BJ assured them.

"I understand he's the person who ran you off the road." Riley turned his attention to Ransom.

"Sure is." Ransom nodded. "He's also someone the DEA can use to get their attention off Lyndsey."

As if they had overheard, Ty and Agent Howard walked through the open back door.

"We'll take him from here," Howard said.

Deputy Green gave a quick glance to Riley who nodded.

"I ain't talking to no cops." The gold-toothed man shoved his chin into the air.

"Don't have to. Just listen." Howard guided his prisoner out the back.

Riley took a step toward Ty. "You'd better keep that animal under wraps. No matter what deal you make with him, he comes back to my town, I'll put him in jail and not bother with constitutional rights."

Ty nodded. He turned to BJ. "Are you okay?"

"Would everyone stop asking me that? I'm fine." She continued to hold on to Lyndsey. "Now what are you doing here, young lady? I thought you were helping Calley."

"We were watching a movie when they called Uncle Riley. I had to make sure you weren't hurt." She clung tighter to BJ's torso.

"She insisted," Riley added.

"As you can see, I'll live. Now get back to your film." She used her hand to shoo them away.

Lyndsey tightened her grip around her aunt. "I want to stay here with you." Her concern warmed BJ's heart, but she hated the fear in the girl's eyes. There was no way she'd send the teen away. Not with everything that'd happened in the last couple of days.

"I suppose we can pick up your bag tomorrow." She combed her fingers through Lyndsey's hair.

"Once they're done processing things here," Riley said, "I'll have an officer park in the driveway."

"That won't be necessary." Ransom folded his arms over his chest. "I plan to stay inside from here on in."

"Excuse me." BJ twirled and faced him. "What makes you think I need a babysitter?"

"You can argue all you want, but I have no plans to leave." His jaw held tight. "This guy went after you because of me. No one else will get a chance."

"Maybe you didn't notice, but I can take care of myself." Her hands were planted firmly on her hips.

"Not without sleep. And you need to know you can rest without worrying about not only yourself but Lyndsey as well. So, unless you have another toaster around..." He lifted his left shoulder in a shrug.

She finally resigned with a sigh. "On the sofa then."

"At the dining room table. I'll sleep when you're awake so we can make sure no one else tries to get in here."

RANSOM STARED AT THE computer screen. His mind couldn't focus. That gunshot earlier jolted him good. If anything had happened to BJ, he'd never have forgiven himself. The aroma of Gold-tooth's hair gel still permeated the air. A constant reminder of how close BJ came to getting hurt.

He closed the lid on his computer and stared at the dark backyard.

"Meow." Stubby rubbed himself against Ransom's legs. A loud purr emanated from the feline.

"Sorry, bud. Beef jerky's in the van." He reached down and patted the cat on the head. Stubby licked Ransom's fingers with his sandpaper tongue.

"Mew." Stubby hopped up on the chair next to Ransom. "Mrrw."

"You're a stubborn thing, aren't you?" Ransom got up and searched through cupboards until he found kitty treats. He tossed one to Stubby who jumped down and ran away.

Ransom returned to his spot in the dining room. He folded his hands on the table and whispered, "God, thank you for protecting BJ.

I don't know what I'd have done if anything happened to her." He stared up at the ceiling. "Help me see if there's something I'm missing. If someone's out there still after Lyndsey, show me a way to discover who it is."

He lowered his head into his palms. "And God, please find a way for Darcy to forgive me if I can't find Bernadette's killer. I know I was never a father to her, but thankfully you took on my duties, which I appreciate. But now it's my turn. Show me how to end her pain, Lord." A tear rolled down his cheek. "Let her know I'd do anything to bring Bernadette back. Anything." He sat for a while, waiting for an answer. He recalled a Bible verse a friend had shared with him when Bernadette first disappeared. Hebrews 4:16. He couldn't remember the exact wording so he opened the laptop and typed in the verse. It read, *Let us then approach God's throne of grace with confidence, so that we may receive mercy and find grace to help us in our time of need.* Ransom smiled. Always listening when we need Him most. "Thank you for never letting me go, though my angry words should have driven You away."

Ransom's e-mail dinged, and a box popped up in the lower right corner. Frazier. Ransom gave a nod to the ceiling. "Amen."

He pulled up the pictures and scanned through them. Mason showed up in several. The smug jerk didn't seem to care if anyone saw him walking into those buildings. His chin held high and a grin on his face showed his arrogance. That was the problem when a perp had the government protecting his backside. No worries.

Nothing in the pictures indicated where they'd been taken. Could any of these buildings have held Bernadette? Ransom mentally shook the thought out.

"Focus." If he didn't, BJ or Lyndsey could find themselves in danger again.

Ransom continued glancing through the thumbnail pictures. He stopped on a familiar face. Joe Mercer. Yeah, Mason and a rapist in the same small town. Definitely too much of a coincidence. These pictures would find their way to Riley Owens's office later. Ransom clicked on the next frame. His heart stopped. Memories rushed in of the phone call Mason had placed in Jacksonville to the buyer with the accent. He couldn't be sure what type with the static that had come over the line. But what if...

He lowered his head into his hands and recalled his thoughts when he first bumped into BJ. He glanced at the picture again. His mouth went dry. Yes, she'd definitely been a distraction he couldn't afford.

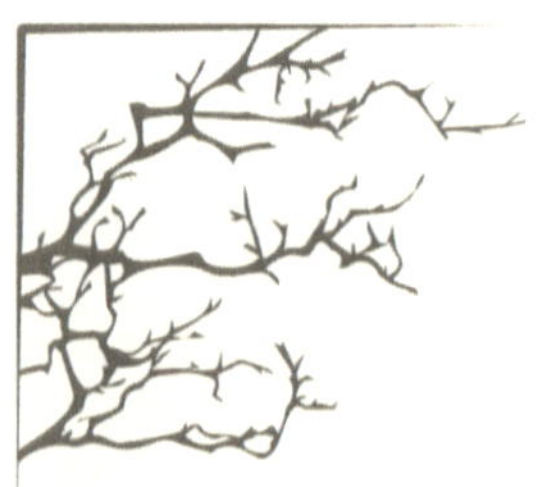

20

BJ rolled over and glanced at the clock. Eight sixteen. She couldn't recall the last time she'd slept so late. Surprising with everything that happened the night before. Ransom had been right. Knowing he was there to protect them helped her peace of mind. She pulled herself out of bed and hesitated. Her shoulder hurt from the door hitting her the night before. A hot shower might help with that.

Once dried off and dressed, she wandered to the kitchen. Her arm was still sore but better. Ransom shut his laptop as she neared. Stubble dusted his cheeks and dark rims decorated his eyes. He'd been up at least twenty-four hours. More if you counted the restless sleep in the van.

"I suggest you get some rest after I fix you some breakfast," she said. "Unless you've eaten already?"

"Not yet."

"Eggs and bacon?"

"Perfect."

"You can take my bedroom once you're finished," she said. "I'm done in there for a while."

"I need to run the rental car back and get the van from the hotel. Maybe once I get back." He had yet to look at her, instead his eyes focused on the laptop.

"What's going on? Did you get some news?"

"Sit." He patted the table.

She slid into the chair. "What is it?"

"I received the photos of the men who are from this club where Mason supplied the kids. One of them is Joe Mercer."

BJ gasped. "I knew that man was no good." She bolted from her seat and rushed to the phone. "Riley needs to know."

"He already does. I sent him the info last night." Ransom got up and walked over to her. "He's getting a warrant to search the creep's stuff, then he's bringing him in." Ransom took her hand in his. "He said I could listen in."

"You'd better." BJ squeezed her lip between her forefinger and thumb. "Maybe Lyndsey and I should head over to Calley's later."

"Apparently her sister is on the way." Ransom returned to his seat. "What do you know about their mother?"

"She's a foolish woman. Why?"

"She refuses to believe her brother would do anything like this and is accusing Riley of trying to frame him." He paused. "I hope she doesn't warn him."

"She will." BJ walked into the kitchen and pulled out a pan from the cupboard. "You know, it might be wise for Riley to have someone else there when he goes after Joe. I'd hate for him to get caught up in something because of a jerk like Mercer."

"That's what we thought. So, Ty Davenport's agreed to meet us. It's not the DEA's jurisdiction, so the feds will take over later today."

"And Ignacio?" She grinned, using Howard's first name.

"Apparently our gold-toothed friend is singing like a bird," Ransom said.

"That should get Lyndsey out of their sights." BJ pulled out a carton of eggs from the refrigerator.

"Whose sights?" Lyndsey's sleepy voice came from the hallway.

"The DEA is apparently getting info from the guy who broke in last night," Ransom explained. "Should keep you off their radar."

"Good." She dropped down in a chair at the dining room table. "So, what's for breakfast?"

"How about some scrambled eggs?" BJ said.

Lyndsey let loose with a yawn.

"Why don't you take a quick shower and get dressed? By the time you're finished, the food should be ready."

Lyndsey dragged herself to the back room.

Ransom tiptoed up behind BJ. "There's more." He glimpsed over his shoulder to the hall and spoke low. "I found out something else."

"What's that?" A slice of bacon sizzled then spit grease at BJ's wrist, stinging her.

He leaned close to her ear. "It involves Elaina, Lyndsey's friend."

RANSOM HATED THE LOOK of anxiety on BJ's face, but he had to tell her the rest. He listened for the shower.

"Here." He stepped over and opened his laptop. "This is one of the men apparently involved in the group."

A hand went to BJ's throat. "Bernard?"

"Yeah." Ransom jaw tensed.

BJ tossed the spatula in the sink. "We have to get Elaina out of there."

"Riley's looking into it. For all we know, she really is his granddaughter. If so, she might not be part of this group of traffickers. All they have is a photo of him talking with Mason. Could be he was buying drugs from the guy."

"But still."

"We're planning to speak with him after the interview with Mercer. He might give us more information on Bernard to use against him."

"What if he is one of *them*? Elaina could be in danger." BJ grabbed a nearby dishtowel and wiped the counter.

"The sad part is if she is part of this group, she's already gone through hell. Nothing much will change between now and this afternoon." He hesitated before going on. "And Riley can't just rush in and take her away, based on a picture."

The bathroom door opened, followed by the closing of the bedroom door. After a couple deep breaths, BJ nodded. "But I want to be there when Elaina's brought in. She needs to see a friend."

The smell of soap drifted to the dining room. Ransom glanced over his shoulder and then said low, "You'll also have to tell Lyndsey."

"This is a nightmare." BJ threw the dishtowel on the counter.

Footsteps padded in their direction. BJ turned to flip the bacon.

"Breakfast ready?" Lyndsey plopped down on the dining room chair. A drop of water ran down her arm from her wet hair. "Smells good."

"Just have to cook the toast, and we're all set." BJ glanced around the counter. Then she must have realized her dented toaster was confiscated the night before because she shook her head. "Maybe we'll have fruit instead."

Ransom would have done anything to keep BJ from knowing, but everything would eventually come out. Earlier, he'd sent Frazier information on the two men he recognized. The FBI would be in Lincolnville by the end of the day. Poor Elaina wouldn't get much of a break for the next week or so with all the questioning she'd have to go through.

"So, what's up for today?" Lyndsey shoved her wet hair over her shoulder.

"How about we go to Chattanooga and do some of that shopping we talked about?" BJ placed steaming plates in front of Lyndsey and Ransom. She then returned to the kitchen for her own.

"Sounds good. Can Elaina come?"

BJ looked at Ransom who gave a quick nod, agreeing. It'd be a good way to get Elaina out of harm's way.

"Good idea," BJ said. "We'll make a day of it. Even eat lunch there. Maybe dinner, depending on the time." She shoved a forkful of eggs into her mouth.

What a wonderful woman. Little doubt when the dust hit the fan, BJ would be there to help Elaina get through any trauma she had endured.

BJ TRIED HER BEST TO calm down, but she couldn't stop pacing in her bedroom. At least she and the girls would be out of town when the authorities came by to get Bernard. Once done shopping, she'd call Ransom to decide whether to bring the child to the sheriff's station or back here.

Lyndsey and Elaina had been texting back and forth for the past hour. They appeared too distracted to know what was going on.

BJ bounced down on the bed. "God, how do people hurt others like this?" She shook her head. "Please don't let Elaina be a victim. And if she is, let her know you've been with her all along." BJ couldn't understand why God didn't do away with these types of people. Far as she cared, anyone who hurt a child wasn't fit to live. *I know God. Ours is not to judge, but it's hard not to hate people like this.*

Her cell rang on the nightstand. Ransom's number popped up on caller I.D.

"Hello." Her voice sounded weary even to herself.

"We've got the warrant and are on our way to the hotel where Mercer last used his credit card. You might want to stay close in case Calley needs you. Her sister got caught up in traffic."

"Okay. We'll wait to hear from you." She walked to Lyndsey's bedroom and knocked.

"Come in."

BJ glanced upward. *Give me strength.* She turned the knob and entered. Freshly sprayed perfume rushed into her. "We need to wait about an hour before we can leave."

"What's wrong?"

"You remember hearing me tell Ransom about Joe Mercer?" BJ sat on the bed next to Lyndsey.

"Calley's uncle?"

"He was also a friend of Mason's. Riley's on his way to pick Mercer up now. If something goes wrong, Calley may need us."

"Okay." She stared down at her cell phone. "I guess it wouldn't be right to bring Elaina with us."

"I'm afraid not. But Allison is on her way. Once she arrives, we'll pick Elaina up and take off." She brushed back Lyndsey's hair from her cheek. "Okay?"

"Sounds good." Even though she smiled, disappointment lingered on her face. "Keep me informed so I can tell Elaina what's going on."

BJ returned to her room, leaving Lyndsey tapping away on her cell. BJ sat in the chair next to the window. *Please God, hold Calley and RJ in your protective arms. And don't let me be too late getting Elaina out of town.*

Fifteen more minutes of wringing her hands went by before the phone rang again.

"Any news?" She could hardly contain herself.

"Yeah, none of it good."

"What do you mean?"

"Mercer's checked out of the hotel." Ransom let out a weighted sigh. Another voice came over the line. "Okay," Ransom said. He then returned to BJ. "Riley's going to have Matthew run by to check on Calley. This way you can pick up Elaina because they want Bernard in custody before noon."

"We're on our way." She hung up without saying good-bye. After running a brush through her hair, she went to Lyndsey's bedroom door and knocked. No one answered.

"Lyndsey." BJ tucked her head in, but Lyndsey wasn't there. BJ couldn't find the teen in the house either. BJ walked outside. "Lyndsey". No response. After a quick rush through the nearby woods and around the house, BJ returned inside to double-check. Her pulse ratcheted up a notch with each step. On Lyndsey's nightstand, BJ found a note.

Aunt BJ, I'm all right. I have to help Elaina get away from her grandfather. No more time to wait. I'll explain later.

Panic exploded through her. What if Bernard found out?

RANSOM STARED OUT THE windshield of the cruiser while Riley and Ty Davenport spoke with the manager of the hotel Mercer had been staying in. The sheriff's mouth was tense and worry lines creased his forehead. He marched back, his cell phone to his ear.

"I know Matthew can handle it but don't take chances. Love you, too." Concern layered his features as he ended his call. No doubt, he wanted to be home protecting his family himself. Once inside the air-conditioned automobile, he swiped a sheen of sweat from his forehead.

"Where to now?" Ransom needed to get the sheriff's attention back on the job. "Bernard?"

"Still waiting to hear if there's anything on Bernard from England. We've got nothing to hold him on here. I'd hate to go too fast."

"With Mercer missing, why don't we just ask Elaina if she's been abused by these guys?"

Riley looked over at him and nodded.

"Isn't your home on the way?" Ransom buckled his seatbelt.

"Yeah."

"Might be a good idea to stop by and check."

A sense of relief crossed into Riley's face. Ransom had given the sheriff the excuse he needed. Before pulling out of the parking lot, Ransom's cell rang. BJ.

"Hello," he said. The sound of rustling came over the line. Could she have dialed him by mistake? "BJ?"

"Lyndsey's gone." BJ's voice sounded like it was out of air.

"What do you mean, gone?"

"She left a note saying she had to get Elaina away from her grandfather."

Ransom relayed the information to Riley.

"I think we'd better get over there quick," the sheriff suggested.

Ransom agreed. His heart lodged in his throat as Riley sped out of the hotel parking lot. *Please God, don't let Bernard get hold of Lyndsey.*

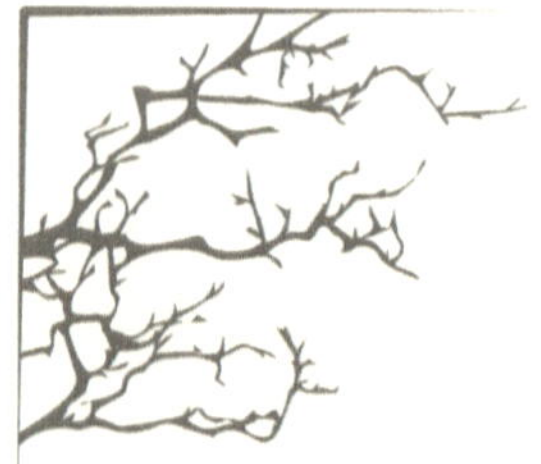

21

Ransom's pulse rate slowed once BJ called twenty minutes later to say she'd made it to the sheriff's station. From the note left behind, it appeared Lyndsey took off on her own. How could teenagers think they were so indestructible? *Please God, watch over that girl.*

Ty Davenport stayed at the hotel, waiting on the feds to arrive with a search warrant for Mercer's room. If Mercer showed, Ty promised to bring him into the station, though Ransom wasn't sure how much he trusted the DEA agent.

Ransom stared out the passenger window at the lakefront property. Beautiful scenery with the blue-green lake. A nice backdrop to the pine trees. Too bad he had little time to enjoy the view.

Riley pulled the sheriff's cruiser into the driveway of the large gray house. The trunk of Bernard's BMW sat open, and suitcases lay inside. Ransom jumped out before Riley had a chance to put the car into park. Bernard strolled through the garage, another bag in his hand.

"Ronald?" Bernard's face layered in sweat. "What can I do for you?"

"Going somewhere?" Ransom asked.

"I'm needed in England. My brother had a stroke." Bernard walked between the two vehicles. He glanced over at Riley. "What brings you and the sheriff by?" He reeked of perspiration.

"We're looking for Elaina." Riley remained standing near the cruiser's open car door. "We have some questions for her."

"About what?" Bernard tossed the bag into the vehicle.

"It's imperative I speak with her." Riley stepped forward. "*Before* you leave town."

166

"Unfortunately, it's too late. I drove her to Atlanta last night to stay with an uncle while I'm away."

"Which one?" Ransom's fists tightened. "Joe Mercer?"

Bernard gave them a quizzical look. "Who?"

"You'll have to come with us." Riley placed his hand near his gun belt. "We have some questions for you also."

"I need to catch my plane," he said. "You have no right to hold me."

"Until we find your granddaughter and Lyndsey Chapel, you're staying right here." The sheriff stood with his feet apart and his hand still resting on his waist.

"Lyndsey?" Bernard's eyes widened. "What's happened to Lyndsey?"

"You can either go quietly, or..." Riley unclipped his handcuffs.

"I don't know what's going on, but I have rights. I'm a citizen of Great Britain."

"I imagine merry old England doesn't care anymore for perverts than we Americans do." Ransom hadn't moved from the spot where he'd been standing.

"What? I'm not..."

"Then you'd have no problem proving to us Elaina is truly your granddaughter." Ransom unzipped a suitcase in the trunk and thumbed through it. Mostly silk shirts. Disappointment flourished. He didn't know what he'd hoped to find, but this wasn't it.

"You have no right to go through my things. You're not even an officer of the law." Bernard bounded around Riley and slammed the trunk, barely missing Ransom's fingers.

Ransom grabbed him by the collar. "Show us the documents to prove you have custody of Elaina."

"I don't have to show you anything."

"That's right." Riley stepped between the two, releasing Ransom's hold on the man. "But you have to show me."

"And how do I prove I'm related to someone? This is preposterous." Bernard eyes volleyed between Ransom and the sheriff. His face flustered to a deep red. "How do you prove you're related to your wife or child when you go on vacation, Sheriff? Do you carry documentation?"

Ransom hated that this man had all the answers.

"Then we'll just wait right here until I get confirmation from my people telling me Elaina really is your grandchild." Riley leaned back on the hood of his car. "If you're determined to make that plane, tell me Elaina's whereabouts. I'll have someone in Atlanta ask her my questions."

The more Ransom got to know the sheriff, the more he liked him. It took all Ransom's power not to grin.

Within seconds, Bernard's head drooped down. "We had an argument, and she left on my bike this morning."

Ransom's head raised in surprise. "And you planned to hop a plane and leave Elaina here alone?"

Bernard's eyes again darted between the two. "She's twenty-two years old. I can't force her to do what I'd like."

Shock entered Ransom. He thought Elaina was closer to seventeen or eighteen. Of course, Bernard could be lying.

"I tried to get her to go to a drug treatment center in Atlanta," Bernard continued, "I made it clear if she refused, I was through with her and her *friends*." He sighed and pulled his keys from his pocket. "Now if you don't mind, I have a plane to catch."

Ransom stepped forward, not about to let Bernard leave.

"Unfortunately, we can't take your word for it," Riley said. "You need to come with me."

BJ HELD HER HANDS BENEATH her arms to keep them from shaking. What must Elaina have gone through? It was all anyone in the sheriff's station could talk about. Mason and the trafficking of children. Her breath hitched, imagining the nightmare this child's life must have been.

A car door slammed out front. Riley opened the back door for Bernard to get out of the cruiser.

"You didn't have to bring me in to get your questions answered." Bernard stopped short when he saw BJ.

Ransom rushed over to her. "He claims he doesn't know where Lyndsey or Elaina is."

"Do you believe him?"

Ransom shrugged. "Can't be sure. Says Elaina took off this morning."

"How can you not know where she is?" BJ marched up to Bernard. "Everywhere she went, you were there. You kept a tight rein on that girl."

"She's of age. I can't force her to do things anymore."

"Lyndsey left to help Elaina." BJ's heart had lodged in her throat since finding Lyndsey's note.

"Help her do what? The only thing Elaina's interested in right now is drugs." His eyes cast down. "I wish I could tell you more."

"You have to know." BJ placed her hands on her hips. "You're supposed to be her grandfather."

"I am her grandfather. I've done everything I could to save that child."

"Save her from what?"

"Herself."

"And you want us to believe Elaina isn't some girl you kidnapped and used for your own pleasure?"

"What are you talking about?" Bernard's shoulders squared. "I never used anyone." He looked at the people standing around staring. "This is ridiculous. I'm a minister."

"Ministers have been known to go after kids," Ransom said.

"But not me, Mr. McNeely. I left my church to help my granddaughter. Nothing more sinister about it than that."

"Then why didn't you join us for church when I asked?" BJ titled her head sideways. "I know you were home."

"My breakfast meeting got cancelled, and I'm not much for these new contemporary services." He straightened his shoulders. "Give me a traditional church service anytime."

Ransom's breathing increased. "But your picture is in one of the F.B.I. photos taken of Cliff Mason."

"Picture? FBI?" Bernard's face paled. He turned to Riley. "Can we talk somewhere private?"

"And I suggest you tell my nephew everything." BJ got right up in Bernard's face. "The people of this town aren't too keen on men who use children."

"I. Do. Not. Use. Children." His jaw held tight. "Sheriff?"

"This way." Riley caught Ransom's eye. "You coming?"

Ransom hesitated.

"Go." BJ patted his arm. "In fact, it might be wise to get Riley to ask him about Bernadette."

"Good idea," Ransom said.

BJ kept her eyes on them as they walked through the door to the interview rooms. *Please God, let him tell us where Lyndsey is before it's too late.*

RANSOM'S HEART WARMED at BJ's insisting he find out about Bernadette. How could she think about anything but Lyndsey right now? Maybe he should stay to give her some support. He hesitated inside the doorway leading to the interrogation room and turned back to her. She waved him on. What a wonderful woman.

Within minutes, Ransom watched through a two-way mirror at Riley inside the next room with Bernard.

"Okay." Riley scribbled something on a notebook. "What do you need to tell me?"

Bernard remained silent, his bottom lip over his top.

"Maybe we can start here." Riley pulled out a picture. "The feds took this photo outside one of the sex parties they believe Mason was involved in."

"It's Elaina." Bernard voice lowered. "She's not right. Hasn't been since she got into drugs."

"What kind of drugs?"

"Whatever Cliff Mason provided her." Bernard twisted his hands on the interrogation room table. "Never saw such a waste for a human being."

Ransom raised his eyebrows. Could this man be responsible for Mason's murder?

"Go on." Riley leaned back in the chair.

"She met Mason quite a few years back. Got into cocaine and selling herself." Bernard let out a weighted breath. "Her parents were never much good. Terrible thing for a father to say about his son, but it's true. Both cared way more for their needs than taking care of their child." He placed his elbows on the table and for the first time looked at the photo. "I went there looking for my granddaughter."

"You're saying Elaina was at this party?"

Bernard shrugged. "I didn't know. It was Mason I followed. Elaina traipsed after him like a love-struck pup. There wasn't anything she wouldn't do for him."

"How'd you two end up here?"

"She'd been arrested in Atlanta and got put in a rehab center. I picked her up. She seemed to be getting better. Said she'd driven past here, thought it was nice. I figured it'd be good for her to be somewhere she might enjoy. But when I saw Mason in that park, I..." His lips made a straight line.

"What do you know about Mason's murder?" Riley asked.

"Nothing. I was pretty mad about him being in town, but I didn't kill him. Elaina claimed he must have followed her."

"Did you believe her?" Riley's voice remained monotone, like a stranger taking notes for a questionnaire.

"I don't know. He was a worse drug for Elaina than cocaine. But I told her we were heading to England. Getting her away from him for good."

"What was her reaction?"

"She seemed happy to be going. She was pretty upset when they came across Mason's body. I wanted to leave immediately, but Elaina felt it would look funny if we left right after he was killed." Bernard hesitated. "Especially if you discovered she knew him."

Riley's eyes widened. "You believed she was responsible?"

Bernard's body folded. "I'm not sure what I thought."

"But you considered it." Riley raised his eyebrows.

Bernard nodded.

"So, what happened this morning?" Riley continued.

"I caught Elaina yesterday with needles. I knew she was using again. Told her if she didn't go to rehab, I was washing my hands of her. If she wanted help, this time she'd have to call me, not the other way around."

"And she took off?" Riley sighed like he'd heard this story before.

Bernard leaned back. "If she's with Lyndsey Chapel, I have no idea where they could be."

Ransom paced the small space. Could Elaina have killed Mason to keep him from getting to her? If so, she might be running from a murder conviction and leading Lyndsey right into the arms of trouble.

BJ STOOD AT THE WINDOW in Riley's office, watching a squirrel carry a large acorn between its teeth. *God, the way we hurt our young, some days I wonder if you didn't give the animals more sense.* How could anyone find anything sexually stimulating about a child?

Could Bernard be telling the truth when he claimed he knew nothing of Lyndsey's whereabouts? Her note said she needed to help Elaina. Help her do what? A check of her watch told BJ she'd been waiting over thirty minutes.

Where would Lyndsey and Elaina go to be safe? They should have come to the house. BJ would have protected her. Maybe they were afraid the authorities would send Elaina back to Bernard. But if she was over eighteen, she could live where she wanted.

After much thought, BJ decided a bicycle wouldn't get the girls too far. But they were intelligent enough to find a place where they'd have privacy. BJ squeezed her lip between her thumb and forefinger.

Someplace people wouldn't think to look. BJ stopped short. She couldn't be sure how well Elaina knew Lincolnville, but only one place came to mind that Lyndsey would know of. BJ walked to the main area. Sylvi stood in the corner by a fax machine spitting out paper.

"Where is everyone?" BJ asked.

"They got called out to the Dunlap residence. Them boys started drinking last night and are still going at it."

With the size of those men, it'd take all the available deputies to get a handle on them. BJ had no time to wait.

She returned to Riley's office and found a notepad on his desk. After scribbling a quick note as to where she was going, she headed to the front door. Even if the lead proved false, at least she'd be doing something.

"Tell Riley I'll be back." She waved to Sylvi.

"Where are you going?"

"I have an idea where the girls might be hiding. If so, I'll bring them back with me."

"Maybe you should wait"

"It might prove to be nothing. I'd hate to waste the time and resources of an officer if I'm wrong."

Ten minutes later, BJ parked the Jeep on the side of the road leading to the cabin. If the girls were there, she didn't want to scare them off. Once through a clearing, she spotted a blue bicycle leaning against the side. *Thank you, God.*

Thunder rumbled overhead. BJ looked up at the sky which had darkened in the last half-hour. Rain sprinkled down on her. Maybe she should have parked the Jeep closer. Oh well, she didn't melt. She'd almost bet neither of the girls would either.

A car door slammed nearby jolting her. A man in a dark blue shirt and blue jeans ran up to the cabin. BJ hid behind a bush and watched him. He stopped on the front porch and glanced around. BJ's breath caught in her throat when Joe Mercer turned and faced her hiding place.

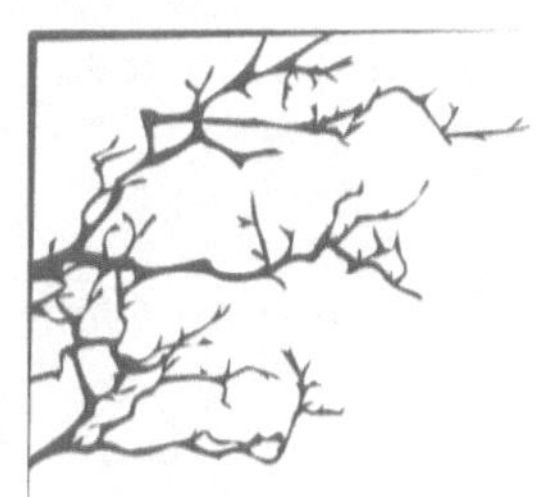

22

It'd been over forty-five minutes since Ransom entered the small observation room. His mind raced, playing over scenarios of where Lyndsey could be. If Elaina killed Mason, she'd be terrified of jail, not realizing people in this town would be willing to help her. They'd see Mason as nothing more than a drug dealer and pimp. Ransom had a hard time himself even seeing the man as human.

Bernard sat on the other side of the mirror, his hair askew from having run his hands through several times. Riley, who'd disappeared moments earlier, entered the door to Ransom's right.

"How do you read it?" Riley asked.

"I believe him." Ransom turned to face the sheriff. "It'd be too easy to prove his story."

"I already did." Riley held up a folder. "Elaina was busted for prostitution in Atlanta, and they found a vial of coke on her. She got six months in a treatment center."

"Another victim of Mason's." Ransom returned his stare to Bernard. Ransom had seen that same tiredness in the mirror.

"She had motive for killing Mason," Riley said.

"If he wanted her back working for him. Except..."

"Except what?" Riley asked.

"Why kill the guy if he gave her drugs?"

"She could have taken them off him once he was dead." Riley flipped through the file.

"If so, why light the car on fire?" Ransom leaned with one hand on the cool cement wall. "And where'd she get the knitting needle?"

"Could have been anywhere. Melanie lost three of them that I know of." Riley's eyes narrowed.

"What?"

"Elaina was arrested in Tampa also. About the time your granddaughter died."

"You think she knows who murdered Bernadette?"

"If she was involved in Mason's sex group, I'd almost bet on it." Riley closed the file and looked at Bernard. "Be a good reason to run. Killer might be looking for her."

"Great. And Lyndsey's with her." Ransom ran a hand over his jaw. He had to find her before something happened. He'd not let BJ go through the pain he had. "What do you plan to do with Bernard?"

"He actually has a brother in England who had a mild stroke," Riley said. "I got the airlines to switch his ticket to an open one; this way he can leave when he wants. I don't believe he had anything to do with this."

"But maybe Elaina will try to contact him." Ransom's cell vibrated in his pocket. He glanced at the screen. A text message from BJ.

Before he could read it, Sylvi rushed into the room. "Riley, BJ called. She's at Donald Fisher's place on the lake. I think she's in trouble."

Ransom pulled up BJ's message.

Lyndsey at Fisher cabin. Mercer here. Going in. Hurry.

BJ SNUCK AROUND BUSHES and worked her way to the cabin. The rain had increased from sprinkles to downright pellets. Lightning flashed in the sky. She was going to be drenched by the time she got inside.

It'd be easy for someone to spot her coming from the front, so BJ crept around the back. Waist high azaleas hid her tiptoeing to the back porch. She paused every few feet to look and listen. At the bottom of the porch steps, she darted from her hiding place to the door.

She stared at the wooden entry frame. Claw marks near the lock marred the nice white wood. Her hand shook, taking hold of the knob. A chill had set in. Not sure if it was from the weather or her situation. BJ twisted the handle. Unlocked. She paused.

Maybe she should wait for Ransom. No. With Mercer in there, Lyndsey and Elaina were definitely in trouble. *Please God, get us through this.*

She pushed the door open a sliver, then more. A creak shattered the quiet. Her heart raced. Did anyone hear? BJ paused and then darted into the dim kitchen.

The door slammed shut behind her. She about jumped out of her wet tennis shoes.

Once inside, she recalled from her walk through, the layout of the building. Two bedrooms, a bathroom, and a kitchen made up the main floor. A basement lay beneath her. They could be anywhere in that house.

No air circulated, making the place stuffy. She inched along the wall, conscious of the squeaking of her shoes on the ceramic tile floor. With no sun shining through, it made the corridor dark. Murmurs drifted through the open door to the basement. BJ paused at the entrance leading down.

"Maybe you'd like to join us."

BJ spun at the man's voice. Joe Mercer smiled like a Cheshire cat.

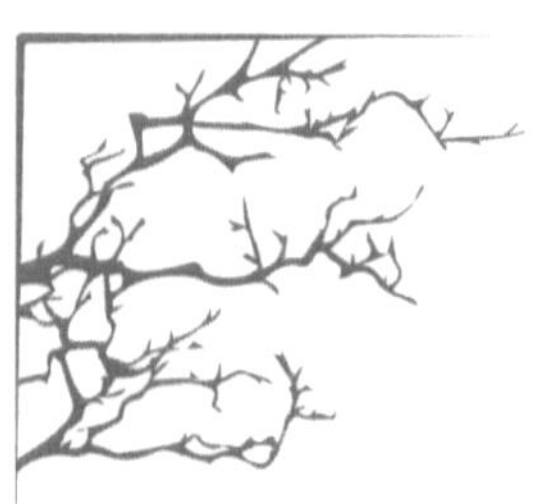

23

"We have to get over there." Ransom was half-way out the door when Riley caught up to him.

"If we don't take it slow, we could be risking their lives." Riley's expression tightened. He took a deep swallow then turned back to his staff. "Sylvi, get me the layout of that cabin."

Ransom didn't want to wait. He'd take his chances. Two deputies pulled up outside.

"Okay, let's go." Riley came up behind him. "You coming with me or walking?"

Ransom bit back a comment and followed Riley. Ransom had no idea where this cabin was, so the officers were his best bet of getting there in time. But once they got there, he'd do what needed to be done. With or without the sheriff's help.

A PUTRID ODOR IN THE basement told BJ water had caused something to mildew. As if that didn't make her skin crawl enough, now she watched Mercer with his hand caressing Lyndsey's arm. Piece of garbage.

"She's what I've wanted ever since my sister showed me Calley's wedding photos." He ran his fingers through Lyndsey's hair. She recoiled at his touch. "And I always get what I want."

BJ's jaw tightened. Someone should take Calley's mother out and beat her.

"Let go of me." Lyndsey's voice quivered. She raised her elbow to shake off his hold, but Mercer's grip tightened.

"We had us a deal," Elaina said. "Where's my money?"

"You'll get it soon enough." A sick grin sat on Mercer's face.

"I want it now," Elaina spit.

BJ hoped that by remaining silent she wouldn't make the situation worse. The longer they talked, the more time for help to arrive.

"You sure are a pretty thing." Mercer's tone dripped sugar. He touched Lyndsey's cheek. "The others will pay me a lot for you."

"Others?" Lyndsey choked. Her eyes volleyed between the three adults, finally landing on Elaina. "What's this about?"

"You never told her?" Mercer laughed. "Your good friend here sold you to the highest bidder."

BJ's stomach knotted. Riley's words resonated in her mind about Mason having a female accomplice working with him. BJ's nails dug into her palms. She stepped forward. *Patience*, a voice whispered in the back of her mind. It was right. Besides, what was she going to do? It wasn't like she had much of a chance against the both of them. She scanned the room for any weapon to use. A rake and a shovel sat against the wall but were too far to grab without anyone noticing.

"Give me my fifty grand. Now," Elaina shouted.

"Elaina?" Lyndsey's eyes widened. "You were supposed to be my friend."

"Don't look so shocked, little girl." Mercer snickered. "Elaina here was one of the best recruiters we had. There wasn't anything she wouldn't do for Mason."

"You knew Cliff?" Lyndsey's high-pitched tone sounded as shocked as BJ felt.

"Knew him. They were very close." Mercer finally let loose of Lyndsey who scooted against the far wall. She glimpsed at BJ who tried to give her a reassuring nod, unsure if it worked.

"Cliff was my fiancé," Elaina said.

Mercer grunted.

"What?" Elaina's face twisted with anger. "We *were* engaged."

"Mason wasn't going to marry you." He shook his head. "Not after what you did. Maybe that's why you killed him."

"I didn't kill him. How can you..." Elaina sputtered. She jerked out a Beretta sub-compact pistol from beneath her shirt.

"Hey, hold on there." Mercer raised both his hands.

A loud bang of thunder overhead caused the lights to flicker. BJ wasn't sure what caused her to jump more, the loud boom or the gun in Elaina's shaking hand.

"You had more to lose with Mason being alive than I did." Elaina pointed the pistol at Mercer.

"I just burnt the car." Mercer shrugged.

"Only 'cause you were afraid something in it might incriminate you," Elaina snorted. She swiped her arm over her nose. "Give me the cash or you'll never get a chance to enjoy the lil' virgin girl here."

A heavy weight sat on BJ's chest, making it hard to breathe. How could she have been so wrong about this girl?

"I mean it." Elaina's nostrils flared.

"You won't shoot me." Mercer pressed his hands against his chest. "Not when there's a chance to get your money."

"Don't bet on it." Elaina barked out the words. "You've got five seconds or me and the kid are out of here."

"I don't think so." BJ's breathing intensified, looking at this evil woman who bought and sold children. "You're not taking Lyndsey anywhere."

"If you want your money," Mercer used his head to point at BJ, "she's a wrinkle you need to deal with."

Elaina turned the gun on BJ. How could she not have noticed before? Elaina's frailness, the dark circles under her eyes, her pale skin. It never dawned on her drugs were the reason. Elaina's hand shook, making BJ even more uneasy about the gun the woman held. *Please, God, protect us all from Elaina's weapon.*

Elaina's eyes half-shut and her brow furrowed. It was not a look of courage or evil. Instead doubt and hatred hung over her. BJ almost bet that dislike in her eye was more for herself than anyone else.

"No. Don't." Lyndsey walked up and touched Elaina's arm. "I'll do whatever you want. Just don't hurt her. Please."

"It's okay, Lyndsey." BJ was surprised her voice sounded as calm as it did. "Elaina's not a killer."

The thunder almost drowned out Mercer's laugh. "You apparently don't know who you're talking about."

"Shut up." Spittle formed in the corner of Elaina's mouth.

"Ask the girl she killed in Tampa."

Lyndsey gasped. "You killed Bernadette Lewis?" Her eyes widened in terror. She released her hold on Elaina's arm and scooted back to the corner.

BJ had to find a way to get her out of here.

"Mason liked her." Mercer rocked back on his heels. "Was going to put her in movies instead of Elaina here. Ticked her off, so she dealt with the girl."

"She was a whore. He loved *me*." Elaina bounced the barrel of the Beretta off her chest and then pointed it at Lyndsey causing her to crouch down and raise her hands for protection. "You never meant anything to him either."

"Give me a break," Mercer sneered. "You're nothing but a used-up piece of meat."

"Shut up." She screamed expletives at him.

He laughed harder.

"I said shut up." Her finger trembled on the trigger as she turned it toward Mercer's midsection.

Mercer's laughter ceased. His adam's apple bounced and his eyes widened.

As much as Mercer's life didn't mean much to her at that moment, BJ had to end this. *God, let your words come through me.*

"Elaina." She kept her voice intentionally low. "Now is the time to stop this. Before it goes too far." Her mouth was dry as a glass of sand.

"Too far?" Elaine's feeble voice squeaked. "Didn't you just hear? I'm a killer. Now no one will ever care about me."

"What about your parents?"

"They never loved me unless it meant using me for their own needs." A tear rolled down her cheek. "Selling me just to feed their habits."

BJ gulped back tears. This poor child. Mason must not have had any trouble getting hold of the girl. She'd probably hoped she'd found someone to love her. BJ stepped forward.

"Stop right there." Elaina jerked the weapon toward BJ.

Mercer let out a loud breath. His jaw quivered. He moved to within inches of the bottom step of the staircase.

Elaina seemed oblivious to his movements, her attention instead focused on BJ.

"You have people who care about you," BJ said. "Just look around. No matter what's happened here, I still care about you. I'm sure Lyndsey does, too."

Elaina's eyes narrowed in confusion.

The lights flickered, causing darkness to mix with light.

"And God's never stopped loving you."

"God can't love the likes of me. Murder's a sin."

"Everyone sins. No one is perfect. You just need to ask Him for forgiveness." BJ said. "And there is someone else who loves you very much. Your grandfather. He wouldn't have given up his career in England to come take care of you if he didn't love you."

"He tried to control my life." She shifted sideways, away from BJ, taking a step toward the wall. "Always telling me what to do. Not letting me see Cliff."

"Only because he loved you and knew Cliff wasn't good for you." BJ paused, then added, "Deep inside, you knew it, too."

Elaina's eyes went downcast. A tear dripped onto the floor. The lights sputtered again. She glanced up at the ceiling as if trying to will them to stay on.

"Hasn't your grandfather tried his best to get you well?" BJ said.

Elaina shook her head. Pain came out in the way of tears. "I can't. I'm not worth it." After a second or two, she ran a trembling hand through her hair. Her sleeve inched up, revealing a bruised arm full of needle marks. "I gotta get something to help me think." The tears faded as fast as they came. She turned a glare on Mercer. "Where's the money?"

"Looks like the deal's off." He glanced between Lyndsey and BJ. "After all, if I don't get what I want, neither do you. Get rid of the old lady."

BJ's jaw tightened. Elaina glared at Mercer and then BJ.

"Finish her off," Mercer growled. "Now."

Elaina placed her trembling palms over her ears. The gun aimed toward the ceiling.

BJ rushed at Elaina, taking them both to the ground. The gun crashed to the floor. She and Elaina struggled, each stretching for the weapon. Just as BJ's fingers touched the grip, Mercer picked it up.

"Enough wasting of my time." He pointed the weapon at BJ. "Consider yourself lucky I'm not a killer. Besides, I've got other things on my mind. Like teaching my new pet here a few tricks." He stepped toward Lyndsey.

BJ bounced up from the floor. "Leave her alone." Her fists curled. "I contacted the police before I came in here. I suggest you get away while you still can."

The lights blinked, causing them all to look at the overhead fixture in the center of the room.

Mercer paused. "I don't believe you."

"It's true. Check my phone." She tugged her cell out of her back pocket. Great no bars. Must be a dead zone.

"Doesn't matter. We'll be gone before they get here." He took hold of Lyndsey above her elbow.

BJ shoved him away.

"You are a real pain, you know that, old lady." He slammed the gun into the side of her head.

"No," Lyndsey screamed.

White spots danced in front of BJ's eyes, and her legs gave out on her. She fought back the bitter taste of bile rising in her throat. Her knees buckled.

"Let's go." Mercer grabbed hold of Lyndsey and shoved her to the staircase. "I'm betting you taste real good."

"Where's my money?" Elaina shrieked. "You owe me."

"So, sue me." Mercer laughed.

Elaina tore up the stairs after him. He turned and punched her in the face. Her arms flailed for a moment, then she tumbled down and landed in a heap on the floor.

Mercer pushed Lyndsey through the door.

BJ shook her head to get her bearings. It took all her strength to pull herself up those steps. When she reached the top, she discovered the door locked. She glanced down at Elaina who had yet to move. BJ headed down and checked the girl's pulse. Weak.

Panic raced through BJ. Her head pounded louder than the thunder, but she had to get to Lyndsey, or they might lose her forever.

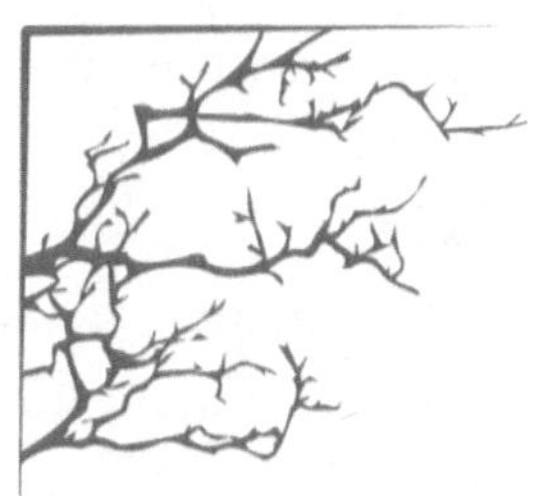

24

Ransom's breathing increased with each bounce of Riley's finger on the steering wheel. Two other officers followed behind them in another vehicle. Time stood still on the drive to the Fisher cabin.

God, please keep them safe. He'd said the same prayer for the hundredth time since getting in the car. Hopefully, he'd make it in time. Dark clouds blanketed the sky, causing a dimness that Ransom felt deep in his soul.

Riley tore off the main street and cut back onto a two-lane road. The tires skidded across gravel, tossing rocks to the side. Within seconds he steered the cruiser to a dirt road. BJ's car came into view. Riley braked.

Ransom's heart ratcheted up a notch. *God, please keep them safe.* He followed the officers to BJ's Jeep. They did a quick glance in the vehicle and found BJ's purse, her gun still inside.

Every second dragged for Ransom.

"We'll walk from here," Riley said. "The building's on the other side of the woods. When we get into the clearing," Riley continued, "you two stay low and head to the back. We'll take the lake side."

The deputies nodded.

"And don't take any chances. Mercer could have been joined by a friend or two. And they all might be armed."

They took off at a jog, going about a quarter of a mile before they came across Mercer's car. Ransom's heart ripped from his chest with each step. *God, please keep them safe.*

A drop of rain bounced off his cheek. While it currently sprinkled, Ransom knew it was just a matter of time until the big storm hit. He

185

prayed it would only be the weather that poured down on him, not more tragedy.

His urge to protect BJ grew with each beat of his heart.

Once they broke through the trees, a white house came into view. The place was bigger than what Ransom would consider a cabin. A blue bike leaned against the building. The deputies ran off to the right.

God, please keep them safe.

He followed Riley up the front porch. The sheriff leaned over and glanced in a large window. He clicked on his two-way radio. Static crinkled over the line.

"Looks clear from here. Proceed with caution." Riley whispered so low Ransom could barely hear him. "We're going in." He opened the screen and tried the knob. Locked.

Ransom stood to the side, his leg bouncing. *God, please keep them safe.* Why could he think of nothing else to pray?

Riley pressed the button on his radio again. "The door's locked. Check your end."

While they waited to hear from the deputies, Ransom walked to the window and looked in. Two people were heading their way. From the shadowed silhouettes, he could tell one was male. The other, smaller, led the way.

"Someone's coming," he whispered to Riley.

The sheriff hopped off the porch to the side of the building all the while whispering into his radio. Ransom stood out of sight of the window, beside the door.

The door swung open, and Ransom was greeted with Lyndsey's terrified eyes. Joe Mercer stood behind her. Ransom jerked the girl away. The door slammed shut in Ransom's face.

"I've got two hostages in here," Mercer shouted. "If anyone comes in, I'll kill them both."

Ransom tried the knob, but it didn't budge. He glanced around for something to use. Nothing.

"We have to get BJ out." Lyndsey fisted Ransom's sleeve. "She's hurt bad."

Ransom's heart pounded violently inside his chest. No way could he live through the death of someone else he loved so much.

BJ'S SWEAT PERMEATED the area. She walked to the far wall of the basement. Her head exploded with each step. A window. With dirt covering it, she couldn't see through. She tried to force it open, but it wouldn't budge. She went back and checked on Elaina. Her eyes finally opened.

"How are you doing?" BJ asked.

"I can't feel my legs." Tears welled in the girl's eyes. "I'm sorry."

"We'll have time for that later. Right now, we have to save Lyndsey."

Voices sounded overhead. Then the door upstairs slammed shut. Footsteps pounded. *Please God, let it be Ransom.*

BJ walked back to the window and tried to force it again. Nothing. The lights flickered. The lock scraped on the door heading into the basement. BJ stared up the staircase. Her heartbeat so loud, it sounded like a rock concert in her mind. The door creaked open. Mercer stood at the top of the stairs and glared down at Elaina.

"This is all your fault," he grumbled. "You'll pay real well for this. I've been looking for someone to try out my new game on."

Terror cast into Elaina's eyes.

"It won't take much for me to make a deal in exchange for a killer." Mercer took a step down. Loud and deliberate. He turned and closed the door. "But before I go, you and I will have some fun. I'll need some memories while I'm locked away." He took another step.

Anger raged in BJ. She inched her way along the wall. A box blocked her way. She got down on all fours and crawled around it until she was under the staircase. Her breathing stopped. Through the slats in the steps, BJ spotted the gun in Mercer's hand.

"Oh yeah. We'll have a lot of fun," he snickered. "Maybe I'll have you and the old lady entertain me until I decide to give up." He stood three steps from the top. "Lots of interesting toys down here."

His voice sent chills over BJ. She glanced around the floor for anything to fight with. A crowbar. She bent and gripped it to her chest. She caught Elaina's eye and gave her a nod. It did little to ease the fear that hung over the girl.

"Where's the old lady?" He glanced around. "Come out and play."

BJ tightened her hold on the weapon. She'd show him old lady.

Elaina looked straight at BJ, then off to the side. She shook her head. "I think she found a way out." She paused, and then added. "I can't feel my legs."

"In time, that might be a godsend."

Boom. His footsteps loud and deliberate over BJ's head. "Shall we find some toys to play with?"

BJ's heart sat in her throat. Her hands spun the crowbar around in a circle. It slipped in her sweaty palms. She caught it before it hit the cement floor.

"Please." A tear slid from Elaina's right eye.

BJ couldn't tell if Elaina's plea was toward her or Mercer.

"Trust me. You'll be asking for mercy by the time I'm done with you." He looked around the room. "Lots of interesting tools that the rest of the group would never allow me to use. But then there's no one here to stop me, is there?"

Elaina whimpered.

BJ fought to keep from throwing up. Mercer stood on the fifth step down. Two more to go. She rested the crowbar through the stair in front of her. *Patience* again echoed through her mind.

"Let's play."

The lights went out, making the room pitch black. There was no sound but breathing from the two on the staircase. BJ's hands trembled, waiting, and listening.

Boom. He stomped just above BJ's head. Then another. She sucked in a deep breath. He lifted his foot, and BJ prayed she'd get it right.

The explosion from the gun echoed off the walls.

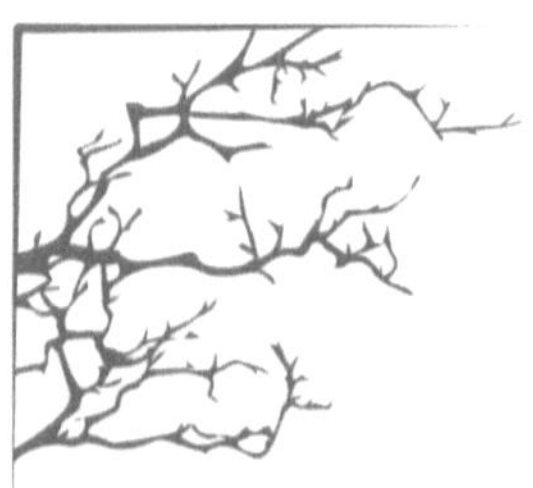

25

Ransom's heart bounced into his throat at the sound of the gunshot. A quick glance at Riley's furrowed brow said BJ's nephew was concerned also.

"You stay here." Ransom handed Lyndsey off to Riley.

"But I want..."

"Don't argue." Riley then whispered something into his radio.

Ransom wasn't going to stay. He kicked the door by the lock. It gave easily.

"BJ," Ransom yelled. "BJ."

"Down here," she hollered through a closed door to their left.

Ransom's shoulders released the tension that had set in since he'd left the sheriff's station. He raced to the door at the end of the hallway. Half-way down the basement stairs, the stench of gun powder drifted into him. Joe Mercer's limp body lay slumped against the wall. Blood stained his shirt. Ransom bent beside him and felt his pulse. Riley came up behind, his gun trained on Mercer. No need. The man wouldn't be hurting anyone anymore.

Elaina sat staring at his dead body.

"What happened?" Riley asked.

"Mercer shot himself falling down the stairs." BJ rushed into Ransom's arms. "Where's Lyndsey?"

"She's outside." Ransom touched her cut forehead.

BJ's facial muscles relaxed. "Elaina was part of that sex group. She planned to..." She squeezed her eyes shut and folded against Ransom.

"I think the rest of the story can wait until you see a doctor." He lifted BJ into his arms and carried her up the steps.

190

Once outside, Lyndsey rushed up to them.

"You can put me down now." BJ dangled her feet in the air.

"What if I don't want to?" Ransom grinned.

BJ shook her head and slid from his arms. She pulled Lyndsey into a hug. "Are you all right?"

"I guess." Lyndsey's voice was weak. Tears fell from her eyes. She raised her hands and covered her face, sobs racking her body.

"There, there. You're safe now." BJ led Lyndsey to the bottom step of the porch where they sat down. "It's all over."

"I was so stupid." Lyndsey's voice came out in hiccups. "I should have called you, but she said her grandfather was hurting her, and if I told, she'd kill herself."

"You did what any good friend would do." BJ's voice was soothing.

Ransom knelt beside them both.

"But she was going to..." Lyndsey's words came out in sputters. "She killed ..." Sob. "Bernadette."

Ransom dropped onto his backside. "Elaina?"

BJ nodded. "Apparently she thought Mason was attracted to Bernadette, so she did away with her competition."

After a few deep breaths, he returned to one knee beside Lyndsey and placed a hand on her back. "Thank you for discovering the truth."

"I'm sorry." Tears dripped onto her bare legs.

"Everything's okay." He combed her hair from her wet face. "In fact, if you hadn't pulled this stunt, we probably wouldn't have ever found out."

BJ touched her fingers to his cheek.

"Did she stab Mason, too?" he asked.

"No," BJ said. "At least she claimed she didn't."

Something in his gut told him as much. Frazier's words about the weapon being one of convenience wouldn't leave Ransom's mind. He had a good idea who'd killed the creep. But first things first.

He rose. "Excuse me. I need to call my daughter."

BJ grabbed hold of his hand. Ransom squeezed it back and gave her a forced smile before he trudged off to the side of the cabin. He stared at the sky.

"Thank you, God for giving me answers." He pulled out his cell and tried to dial, but tears blurred the numbers.

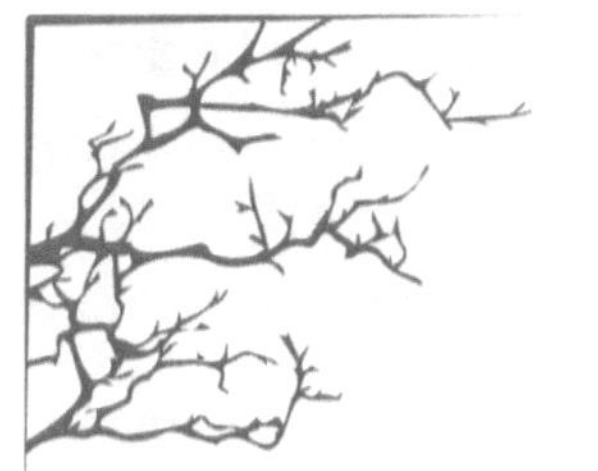

<h1 style="text-align:center">26</h1>

Two days had passed since Elaina's arrest, and Ransom still felt numb. He'd held on to anger for so long, he had no idea how to feel anything different.

Darcy's husband waited on a plane to fly out of Brazil. He should be the one here, comforting Darcy. Instead, she found herself stuck in this courtroom with someone she despised. Her jaw had been rigid since Ransom met her at the airport. And when they discovered the sheriff's office had transferred Elaina to the main station in Catoosa County, her mood only darkened. Somehow, she'd hoped to be able to speak with the person who killed her child.

What would Darcy say to Elaina if she could sit down with her?

"Why's it taking so long?" Darcy crossed and uncrossed her legs. "This is ridiculous. How could they even consider bond?"

Ransom couldn't find the words to comfort his daughter. In the small courtroom, people whispered to each other. The main door opened, and BJ stepped over the threshold. A large bruise decorated the left side of her face, but she was still the most beautiful woman he'd ever seen.

After looking over the crowd, BJ settled her gaze on him. She marched over. He stood and pulled her into him. He needed to feel her strength and comfort now more than any other time in his life. His throat constricted as he held her in his arms.

"How's Lyndsey?" His voice shook.

"Doing better. She's off shopping with her mother. They didn't want her around this." BJ touched Ransom's cheek. She grabbed hold of his hand and reached past him to his daughter. "I'm BJ Owens. You

193

must be Darcy. Your father's told me so much about you." She shoved past him and placed a hand on Darcy's shoulder. "How are you holding up?"

Ransom released his hold on BJ's hand. His child needed her more than he did.

"Okay, I guess." Tears welled in Darcy's eyes.

BJ plopped down beside her. She placed her arm over Darcy's shoulder. "This can't be easy for you either. Just remember there are a lot of folks in this town who might not know you, but care all the same."

Darcy cocked her head to one side. "Thank you. I appreciate it."

"Well, if there's anything you need, you let me know." BJ patted Darcy's back. "I understand you're staying at Anna's Boarding House instead of the hotel with your father."

"I wanted to be here in town in case something happened."

"I assume Anna's taking good care of you."

"Yes. She's been real nice." Darcy brushed at her cheek.

"And she made you eat?"

Darcy blurted a laugh. "The largest blueberry muffin I've ever seen in my life." Tension released with her smile.

The entry opened for the officials to bring prisoners into court. Ransom took hold of Darcy's hand. Her smile disappeared when a deputy rolled Elaina to the defense table in a wheelchair. The fall down the stairs had severed her spinal cord leaving her paralyzed from the waist down. Ransom thought it was an appropriate reminder of what she'd done to all those kids.

The orange jumpsuit appeared three sizes too big, and Elaina's stringy hair hid her face. Were her trembling hands from nerves or the desire for drugs?

Ransom's heart sank. He'd been prepared to hate Bernadette's killer, but he could only feel sad at how two young women who'd been connected to Mason turned out. One dead, the other probably in jail for the rest of her life.

Bernard fidgeted in the row behind the defense table. He kept his focus up front. Elaina glanced over her shoulder at him, then she looked their way. Her shoulders slumped, and her bottom lip trembled.

Darcy gasped. "She's not even—what, twenty?"

"Twenty-two." Ransom looked at the girl responsible for killing his granddaughter.

Darcy grip tightened on Ransom's hand. "How could someone that young hate Bernadette so much?"

He wished he had an answer for her.

They remained silent while the judge denied Elaina bail. He scheduled an extradition hearing in the next week to determine whether to send her to Florida on murder charges.

Once they led Elaina back out, Bernard marched past them without saying a word. This couldn't be easy on him either, but at least he'd be able to see his grandchild.

"I just can't believe no one could stop this from happening." Darcy snatched her hand away from Ransom's. "No one discovered Mason was helping this group of guys get children?" Her palm smashed a tear against her cheek. "Someone should have been able to save my daughter."

Ransom wished he had the right words to comfort her. But what do you say when your own heart ached as bad? He fixed his eyes on the floor. If he'd only checked up on Mason, Bernadette would still be here. He ran his palm down his face.

"Are you all right?" BJ leaned over and touched Ransom's knee.

"Yeah. I just need some fresh air." He stood. "I'll be right back."

"How about we meet you over at the station?" BJ said. "I need to go over my statement with Riley again."

On his way out, several visitors shook his hand or patted him on the back. It did little to comfort him. Would there ever come a day when his daughter forgave him for not saving Bernadette? Pain sliced deep with each step he took.

BJ STARED AFTER RANSOM. Sadness had crawled over him at Darcy's words. He'd probably saved a few people in his day with the CIA, yet he couldn't protect the one person he loved the most.

"I keep saying the wrong things." Darcy shook her head. "He doesn't know how it feels."

"He hurts, too."

"I know." She picked a hair off the seat in front of her and let it float to the ground. "I mean..." She let loose a loud breath. "I'm the reason Bernadette left."

Two men stood in the row behind them but didn't leave. A press badge hung from the lapel of one of the men's jackets. They remained silent and glanced down at Darcy every few seconds, their attention unmistakable.

"Why don't we get some air also?" BJ rose and held her hand toward Darcy. "A nice walk might do you some good."

Darcy allowed BJ to lead her into the sunshine. BJ was amazed how much Ransom's daughter looked like him. Her smile and those blue eyes were a dead giveaway.

They strolled in silence for a block before Darcy finally spoke. "I'm so consumed with guilt and unanswered questions. So many what ifs. Wondering what I could have done different. Every time I bring it up, I see disappointment in his eyes."

"Whose eyes?"

"My dad's." She paused at a corner before checking for traffic and walking across. "They were so close. He and Bernadette. He'll never forgive me for what happened."

"You're so wrong." BJ stopped and turned Darcy by the elbow, so they faced each other. "It's himself he blames. Guilt has consumed him over this."

"Guilt? For what?"

"He's the big spy with all the fancy gadgets and friends who can find out anything. Yet when the time came to check up on some guy his granddaughter dated, he chose not to snoop." BJ combed a finger through Darcy's hair. "He thinks if he'd checked out this Mason, things would have been different."

"But he couldn't have known what would happen."

"No." BJ placed her hands on Darcy's cheeks. "And neither could you." She released her hold and directed them toward the station.

"You don't understand." Darcy slowed her pace. "I was so jealous of them. I wanted the connection they had."

"Your dad wants you to be happy. And there's nothing he wouldn't do to help you through this pain." They stopped and sat on a bench in front of the sheriff's station. "Your father is a good man. He loves you very much. And it's not too late for that connection."

"It's not like we have much in common."

"You have two very important things. You both loved and lost Bernadette."

Darcy nodded, looking at her hands. "I'm having trouble with the whole forgiving part. There's the girl who killed my daughter, then my father for not being there while I grew up, and finally, my mother for not telling him about me."

BJ reeled back. "You know?"

"My mom left me a letter to read after she died. It's worse when I get angry at her because she's gone." She frowned. "All this guilt and only one place to go. Inside."

"No more." BJ patted Darcy's shoulder. "From this moment on, you lay your guilt at the feet of Jesus. And refuse to take it back."

"I wish it were so easy."

"In time it will be. And if you need it, I know a very good minister you can speak to." BJ allowed Darcy to lean against her shoulder. "And talk with your father. I believe you both can help each other."

The slight breeze did little to ease the heat. Darcy brushed at her face. BJ tightened her grip on the woman. *God, please help her and Ransom through this pain.*

"So, are you and my dad seeing each other?" Darcy asked.

"Somewhat. I'm not real sure what our relationship is right now."

"Well, if he lets you go, he's a fool."

BJ smiled. This woman had very good insight.

RANSOM AMBLED DOWN a lane trying to clear his mind. He had to stop this. Darcy needed him. He'd find time later for wallowing in his loss. Police crime scene tape flittered to his right. He recalled Riley mentioning they'd discovered Mason's body in some woods off a path. This must be it.

The creep died too quick for what he'd done to all these kids. Hopefully eternity showed Mason the pain of true suffering. Ransom stopped short. "Sorry, God, but I really hate Mason right now. He started this whole nightmare rolling."

Through a clearing was a burial yard. Melanie Newman leaned forward on a bench in front of a grave marker. Ransom stopped and stared up at the sky. *You could have given me some time.*

Mercer hadn't stabbed Mason. It would've been more premeditated. And Elaina had no reason, not if she truly loved him. Besides, the person responsible hadn't planned to kill Mason. Unless the killer happened across the knitting needle used to carry it out. Too much of a coincidence. No, Ransom assumed the killing had been a split-second decision. BJ's prints still being on the weapon pretty much proved it. Pure luck Mercer removed the car from the scene muddying up the water.

Ransom walked over to where Melanie sat, her attention focused on a stone which read James Newman, IV, beloved son. Running the dates in his head, Ransom realized their son hadn't even been thirty when he died.

"I understand Calley's uncle was involved in this whole mess." Melanie spoke without looking at Ransom. "Something about kidnapping children."

"Appears so." Ransom glanced off to the area where Mason had died.

"I'm glad Lyndsey's all right. She seems like a nice girl." Melanie finally looked at him. She stared for a moment. "You know. Don't you?"

He nodded, unsure what she saw in him that told her.

"How did you figure it out?" she asked.

"The fingerprints." A lump rose in his throat. "They should have been smudged if someone else had used the needle, even with gloves."

"I didn't mean to," Melanie whispered.

"No doubt." He sat next to her.

"Funny. Nobody ever came out and asked me." She smiled. "Riley just wanted to know about the missing needles. Nothing else." She exhaled a loud breath. "I'm a Christian woman. If he'd asked, I'd have confessed."

Telling her an omission of the truth was probably a sin also would only make them both feel worse. "What happened?"

She refocused on the marker. "Jimmy didn't have a chance to turn out good before someone took him."

Ransom knew that pain. What would Bernadette have become, if given the chance?

Melanie patted his leg. "But you know those feelings yourself."

She returned her gaze to the grave. "I got up early and came here. My boy's birthday." Melanie brushed at her eye. "I'm not sure what Mr.

Mason was doing in those woods, but he sauntered up with a smug look in his face."

"Did he hurt you?" Ransom's breathing intensified.

"No, but he said some dreadful things about my son, though I'm sure they never met."

Ransom waited for her to go on.

"I got up to leave, but he grabbed hold of my arm. I told him he was a waste to his mother. He slapped me and shoved me to the ground. My bag dropped, spilling everything out. That's when I saw it." Her voice trembled. "All I could think about were all those families destroyed by the drugs he sold. Before I knew it the needle was in my hand." Her bottom lip wobbled. "He stumbled off, and I stood there not knowing what to do. I don't recall a whole lot after."

A few minutes later, Melanie stood. "Would you kindly escort me to the sheriff's office?"

Ransom rose and cocked his elbow. Her silky hand slid over his skin. "On the way," he said, "we'll call your husband to meet us with an attorney."

"Like I said, I'm a Christian. I stabbed a man. I won't deny it." She patted Ransom's hand. "There's no point in wasting money on a lawyer."

"But I think there is." Ransom purposely slowed his pace. "Mason threatened you the night before. That morning, he assaulted you. Hard telling what he had in mind. Sounds like you might have a good argument for self-defense." Ransom nodded. "Yeah, I believe an attorney is a real good idea."

"You're very persuasive."

A short time later, they paused outside the sheriff's station. "Just do me one favor," Ransom said. "Don't talk to an officer until you've spoken to an attorney. Promise."

"I promise." Inside she strolled up to the counter.

"Hello, Mrs. Newman," Sylvi said without getting up. "What can I do for you?"

"I'd like to speak to the sheriff, please." She paused. "Once my husband gets here. It's about the young man found in the woods."

"Okay." Sylvi hesitated. "Have a seat over there, and we'll wait for Mr. Newman."

Melanie turned and faced Ransom. "If I give you the number, would you kindly call James for me?"

"Yes, I will." He patted her shoulder. "It's going to be all right. You'll have a lot of people on your side."

"Ransom, Melanie." BJ stood behind them while Darcy watched from BJ's left. "Is everything all right?"

Melanie turned to BJ. "Would you sit with me while your beau here makes a phone call?"

Ransom cleared his throat and then dialed the number she'd given him. After hanging up with James, he explained to Darcy that Melanie killed Mason.

"I suppose throwing her a party isn't an option," his daughter said.

Ransom looked down at the floor. "Probably not."

"Can you walk me back to Anna's? I want to talk to you."

"About what?" His tone was harsh. The last thing he needed right now was his daughter telling him to get out of her life.

"What I'm going through. From what BJ tells me, she seems to think we have a lot in common in that department."

He glanced over at BJ. What a woman. Leave it to her to try to fix in an hour what he'd tried years to repair. Maybe in time he and Darcy could have some sort of relationship. And just maybe BJ could help him heal the ache he still carried inside. *Thank you, God, for bringing her back into my life.*

"Lead the way," he finally said.

Darcy nudged him with her elbow. "I also need to make sure you're doing right by that woman of yours."

Ransom nodded to BJ before leaving. Something inside told him Melanie would be all right under the watchful eye of BJ Owens until James arrived.

He smiled. His daughter didn't need to worry. He definitely planned to do right by her.

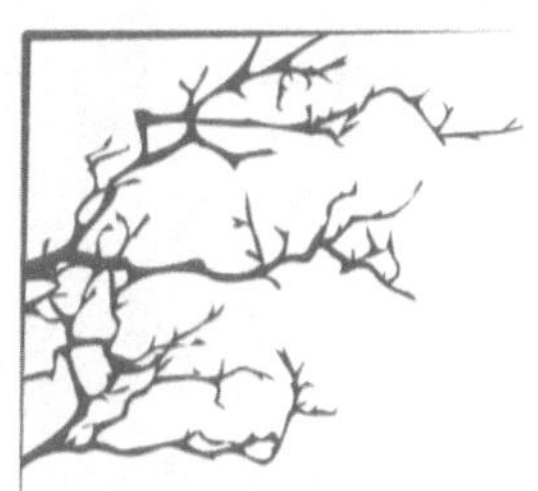

<h1 style="text-align:center">27</h1>

BJ stared out the window at Lyndsey, sitting on the deck with her parents. Miriam barely let Lyndsey out of her sight these last couple of days. Understandable with all they'd been through. Unfortunately, Lyndsey didn't seem to appreciate it as much as she should. She'd told BJ the night before she felt suffocated by her mother's attention.

Riley cleared his throat at the dining room table. "Are you okay?"

"Yeah. Just a bit worried about Lyndsey." BJ carried two mugs and sat in the chair across from Riley. "They wanted her to come home, but Lyndsey wants to stay. I suggested it might be a good idea for her to be here where she wouldn't be alone all day when they were at work. Give her too much time alone to contemplate what might have been. They agreed it'd be better if she were kept busy. We're planning to drive down to Jacksonville for the fourth." She sipped her coffee. "So, how's Melanie's case going?"

"Her attorney is claiming self-defense," he said. "Mason hitting her first might cinch it. Too bad it's up to the state attorney to decide. I'd let her go."

"She's in jail?" BJ couldn't hide her shock.

"No. The judge let her out on her own recognizance." Riley shook his head. "It never crossed my mind Melanie would be responsible. I knew she always left those needles lying around. Anyone could've come across them."

"That, my dear, is the problem with knowing someone too well." She took hold of his hand. "You don't want to believe they're capable of killing anyone."

203

"Good thing she didn't turn out to be a cold-blooded killer."

"Yeah, but she'd have made a good one."

He leaned to one side and cocked his eyebrows.

"She could have skewered half this town, and no one would've thought she was the culprit."

Riley chuckled. "Also, the feds found a list of names at Mercer's home. Eight kids have been saved."

"That's good." BJ nodded.

"I suppose Calley told you her mother thinks I set up her brother."

"Yes. I called Allison and invited her to come stay for a while. This can't be easy on her with everyone knowing her mother was complicit in the whole thing."

"Wouldn't be surprised if she took you up on the offer." Riley stared out the back window. "They're sending Elaina to Florida tomorrow. Apparently, her grandfather's gotten her a lawyer down there."

"I know. After getting the okay from Ransom, I recommended a fellow I know." BJ leaned back in the chair. "We both feel bad for her. After all, if she'd had decent parents and never met Mason, things might have turned out different for the girl."

"No one made her go off with Mason. She did that on her own."

"So did Bernadette and most of the others. Besides, Elaina was looking for someone to love her. Not that I can excuse her for getting the other kids involved, but I imagine most of that was to please Mason. I plan to visit her once they decide where to place her. Take her a Bible."

Riley shook his head. "Always trying to save the world."

"Nah. Just my little piece of it."

A car door slammed shut out front. They both looked toward the window. Ransom trotted up the sidewalk, a skip in his step. BJ's heart bounced against her ribs. He looked good in that blue T-shirt. She recalled how her body tingled at Ransom's touch.

"So, what's up with him?" Riley raised his chin in Ransom's direction.

"What do you mean?"

"You two serious?"

BJ shrugged. "Only thinking."

"About what?" Riley asked.

BJ leapt to her feet and went to the front door. Before she responded to Ransom's knock, she turned to Riley and said, "I'm thinking it might be nice be for Lincolnville to have its own spook."

THANK YOU FOR READING *One Last Breath*. Turn the page to read the first chapter of *Take Her Breath Away*, the next in the Lincolnville Series.

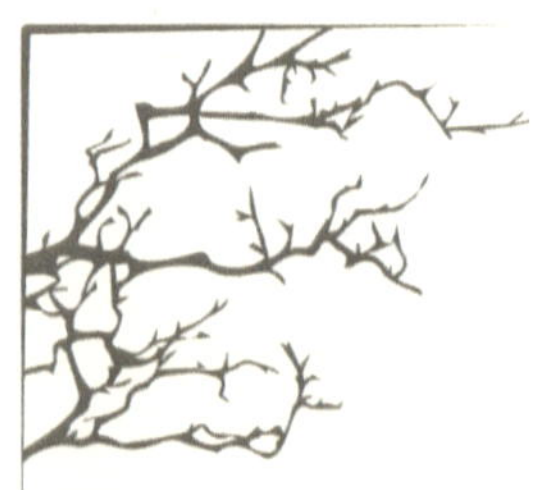

1

The rancid smell of garbage coated the Atlanta, Georgia air to the point Ty Davenport could almost taste the spoiled lettuce at his feet.

He was getting too old for this.

He stood between the dumpster and the older model Harley-Davidson; the Glock secured in the waistband of his jeans. Every nerve in his body told him this deal might blow up in his face. Lack of a Kevlar vest didn't help, but Hector Jones didn't deal with people who wore them for fear of coming up against a cop.

The black Lexus IS 250 pulled up. Three men inside. Hector got out of the backseat. His two comrades followed his lead, one got out from the driver's side, the other from the front passenger door. Under all their jackets, clearly, they had Kevlar vests.

What the... Ty's stomach knotted. Too late to change things now without looking suspicious.

The old, dilapidated buildings in the warehouse district gave no sense of security. Revitalization was occurring blocks away. Of course, no one worked construction on a Sunday.

His eyes darted in every direction. He scanned his surroundings. The best escape route would be out the alley on the bike. Potholes slowed most cars. Too bad the same couldn't be said of bullets.

He mentally shook the thought from his mind.

Instead, he turned his focus to the new guy, Michael Ware, stooped down at the corner of the building. His job was to make sure no one, like some poor homeless guy looking for a place to sleep, came along and screwed up the case.

206

Hector's two comrades waited next to the Lexus. All three scrawny drug dealers looked as though they were still in their early twenties. Nothing stood out about two of the three men to get them noticed in a crowd. But the driver had a scar down the length of his left cheek.

Who'd he tick off to get such a reminder?

No one brandished any weapons, but each man knew the others were armed. The nature of the drug world. Guns and death.

"So, you got the money?" Hector asked.

"You got the stuff?" Ty pushed back a couple strands of hair that had come loose from the camo bandana on his head. He looked at Michael, whose bald head nodded the go-ahead.

"I got it." Hector jerked his head in the direction of the car.

"Is it the good stuff?" Ty asked.

"Test it if you'd like." Hector pulled a small plastic bag of white powder from his pocket. "Just a sample of what's in the others."

Ty reached for a vial of an acid compound in his shirt pocket. He inserted a tiny spoon into the bag given to him. Then he scooped a sample of the powder and shook it into the solution. From the purple color, definitely an opiate.

"Well?" The drug dealer's smile showed perfect white movie-star teeth.

A flock of geese squawked overhead, heading home for the evening. They all looked up. Once the birds had passed, Ty reached over and flipped open one of the saddlebags on his bike. The bulky manila envelope got stuck for a second, so he had to force it out.

Hector turned to the scar-faced guy who pulled out a shopping bag from the back seat and walked over to them. The guy held the bag in a gloved hand, a sneer on his face. Ty took the package and handed over the envelope. Heroin for one hundred grand.

"Nice doing business with you." Hector walked back and slid into the backseat of his Lexus. "Let me know when —"

Bang. Pain exploded down Ty's leg. He hit the ground before the second shot got off.

From the sound, a rifle.

The Lexis spun a circle, spraying gravel and debris. Ty slid around the dumpster away from the gunshots. He looked over at Michael who held his position a few feet away behind the water barrier. He shook his head, and then glanced around, waiting.

Clink. A bullet bounced off the dumpster where Ty had been standing.

Who? What the…? Where was backup? Too many questions with no answers.

Sirens sounded. Loud voices followed footsteps. DEA agent Ignacio Howard stuck his head around the corner of the building. He looked in all directions. After a second, he rushed over. He pulled out a knife from his pocket and cut open Ty's jeans.

"This is going to hurt." Howard shoved his finger into the bullet wound in Ty's thigh.

Ty let out a sharp yell. His breathing quickened. His mind rushed to his wife and screwed up marriage. He grabbed hold of his partner's shirt. "Tell Rayleene I love her."

"Quit being such a drama queen. It's not a big hole."

Ty choked a laugh as pain burned through his entire body. A shadow cast over his shoulder. Michael had moved to the dumpster, gun at the ready.

How could a little bullet hurt so much? He lay back onto the warm pavement. "Hector?"

"Got him." Howard grinned.

Ty stared up at the sky that was beginning to dim. What dealer brought a high-powered rifle to a drug buy?

RAYLEENE DAVENPORT put the finishing touches on the picture of the Brown's daughter. Only three-months-old and already her personality had begun to show with those bright blue eyes and large toothless grin.

Tears blurred her vision. What would her child have looked like?

The door to her home office squeaked open behind her.

"What do you want for dinner?" Morai, her grandmother, stood in the doorway. The aroma of mentholated ointment followed her into the room.

Not one for a lot of makeup, her pale Irish complexion made her appear washed out.

Growing up, whenever Rayleene asked for makeup, her grandmother ranted on about how those painted on colors made a woman look like a tramp. Morai repeatedly quoted Bible verse 1 Peter 3:3, Do not let your adorning be external—the braiding of hair and the putting on of gold jewelry, or the clothing you wear. By the time Rayleene got to college, she had no idea how to apply makeup, so she claimed not to like it. Even today, she used very little.

Good thing she got her father's coloring. Never meeting him, she couldn't be sure, but since she tanned in the summer, she assumed his skin had to be darker than her grandmother's.

Since Ty had left a month ago, Morai arrived minutes before dinner, either here at the condo or the photography studio. Rayleene wished she hadn't given her grandmother the extra set of keys to be used in case one of them had locked themselves out. Morai saw fit to enter the condo whenever she wanted. Rayleene never asked for the keys back to avoid starting trouble.

"Are you all right?" Morai hadn't moved from the entry. No hand on her granddaughter's shoulder for a show of support. No soft tone in her voice for comfort.

"I'm fine," Rayleene said. Morai didn't care for anyone's tears, especially from the granddaughter she'd raised. "My eyes are tired. That's all."

Morai could never understand the loss of an unborn child. Hers had survived only to destroy her life in a world of drugs and alcohol.

"Dinner?" she asked again.

"I'm not really hungry." Rayleene saved the final slide and clicked off the computer screen. "What are you in the mood for?"

Her phone rang before Morai could answer. Rayleene held up a finger, indicating she'd be with her in a moment. She'd been tempted not to answer when Howard's name came up on caller I.D. Probably wanting to let her know more of Ty's wonderful qualities.

She didn't need someone to spout his traits. They'd been married long enough for her to know them. But he was also the only one who could tear her heart out the way he had. She glanced at Morai. Some choice. She finally slid her finger across the phone.

"Hello, Howard."

"Rayleene, Ty's been shot." A tremor of excitement came through the phone line.

Her stomach bounced into her throat. It'd only been a couple of weeks since he moved out but being apart did little to destroy the love she still had for him. "Is he going to be all right?"

"He's on his way to Atlanta Medical Center. I've called his brothers, but his parents are out of the country."

"On their anniversary trip to Europe." Rayleene barely realized she'd said the words. Her mind focused on the fact that Ty was being taken to Atlanta Medical Center, one of the city's best trauma facilities.

"I suggest you come in case documents need to be signed." Howard paused. "You're still his next of kin."

"All right." Her pulse raced. Next of kin. The words sounded ominous.

She sat staring at the phone once Howard hung up. No matter what happened between her and Ty, she never wanted this. All her old concerns climbed to the surface. The one thing she always worried about during her marriage. Ty getting hurt.

"What's wrong?"

She startled at her grandmother's voice. "Ty's been taken to the hospital." She gulped down the words. "He's been shot."

"So?" Morai folded her arms in front of her chest. "He's worth more dead than alive to you anyway."

"Morai!" Rayleene jumped up, sending the chair rolling backward. "How can you say that about Ty? About anyone?"

"Don't tell me you're going to rush to his bedside?" Disdain came over Morai's face.

"I have no choice. I'm his Health Care Surrogate and need to be there." Rayleene's voice lowered. "In case."

"He'll only hurt you again. Once a cheater always a cheater."

"He's nothing like Grandpa." She shoved past her grandmother, trying to ignore the ugly words. Ty's one-night stand had been something she had a hard time forgetting, much less forgiving. Morai's constant reminders didn't help. Walking out had done little to fix the situation. And now this.

Tears filled her eyes. She swung her purse strap over her shoulder and raced out the front door. With the back of her hand, she brushed back hot tears.

Calm down. She closed her eyes and inhaled a long, drawn breath.

Just what she needed, to get into an accident on top of everything else. People needed to be called, particularly Matthew Winters. Whether Ty was in bad shape or not, his best friend would want to know.

After inserting the key into the ignition of the SUV, she paused and looked up at the sky. "Please God, don't let him die."

THIS IS THE END OF Chapter 1 of *Take Her Breath Away*. To read more, order on your favorite book retailer.

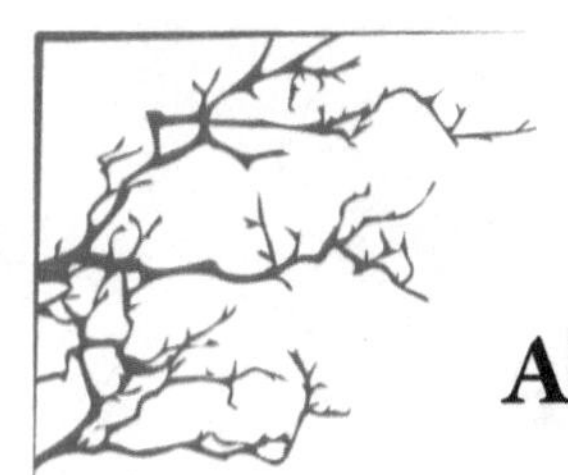

About the Author

Kathryn J. Bain's first release *Breathless* came out January 13, 2012. She has won several awards for her writing including First Place in the International Digital Awards (IDA), First Place in the Royal Palm Literary Awards, Second and Third Place in the Heart of Excellence Readers' Choice Contest, and more.

She became a bestselling author in 2020 when her book *The Chain You Forge* hit number one under Amazon's Holiday Fiction category and stayed there for four days.

She is the former President of Florida Sisters in Crime and Public Relations Director and Membership Director for Ancient City Romance Authors.

She has been a paralegal for over thirty years and works for an attorney who specializes in elder law.

Kathryn grew up in Coeur d'Alene, Idaho. In 1981, she moved to Boise, but it apparently wasn't far enough south, because two years later she headed Jacksonville, Florida and has lived in the sunshine ever since.

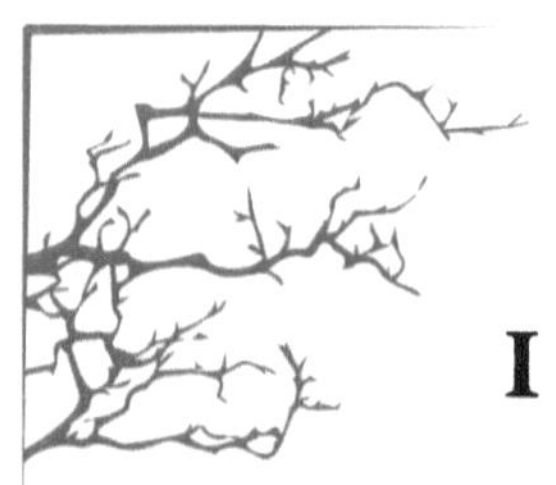

I Need Your Help

1. Write a review. It doesn't have to be elaborate, just something as simple as "I really liked this book."

2. Share my books with your friends and on social media. Word of mouth works better for book sales than any form of advertisement.

3. Post of picture of you reading one of my books and tag me on Facebook or Twitter. (Or your dog, cat, horse, etc.)

4. Join my newsletter for updates and events at https://landing.mailerlite.com/webforms/landing/g4n8h9

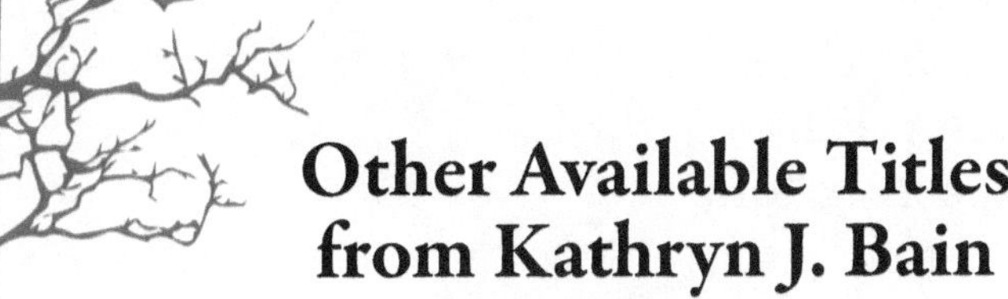

Other Available Titles
from Kathryn J. Bain

THE KT MORGAN SHORT SUSPENSE SERIES

A Touch of Suspense (Vol. 1-3 of the KT Morgan Short Suspense Series), pub. 2017

A Touch of Suspense (Vol 4-6 of the KT Morgan Short Suspense Series), pub. 2022

The Visitor, pub. 2014

Small Town Terror, pub. 2015

The Reunion, pub. 2016

Run Away, pub. 2019

The Game, pub. 2020

Sucker Punched, pub. 2021

OTHER FICTION BOOKS available

Fade to the Edge, 2019

The Chain You Forge, 2017

THE LINCOLNVILLE MYSTERY Series

Breathless, pub. 2012
Catch Your Breath, pub. 2012
One Last Breath, pub. 2014
Take Her Breath Away, 2016

MIDDLE-GRADE

Seven Sisters Road, co-written with Jessi Bain, pub. 2020

www.ingramcontent.com/pod-product-compliance
Lightning Source LLC
Chambersburg PA
CBHW020330160726
47992CB00004B/1777